Death of an Old Girl

"Isn't that a car coming up the drive?"

He went over to the window.

"Scotland Yard," he said a moment later. "Four of them."

"Four?"

"The detective-inspector, his sergeant and a couple of technicians, I imagine. For photography and finger-prints."

"This is the sort of thing that happens to other people, isn't it?"

He came across the room and sat down again.

"History suggests," he said, "that Meldon possesses a quite remarkable resilience."

She had just time to smile back at him when Koyce Kitson announced Chief Detective-Inspector Pollard of Scotland Yard.

One

'Festival, the Society's Annual Reunion, shall be held at Meldon on the Saturday after the end of the summer term. The Sixth Form shall be invited to attend.'
Extract from the Constitution of the Old Meldonian Society

'PATCHES OF MIST will clear rapidly, and the day will be fine and warm throughout the region. Further outlook : the fine spell is expected to continue, at least over the weekend,' a voice announced impressively. 'Just a quick run through of some of today's programmes,' it went on, becoming brisk and persuasive. 'Nine-ten, A Look Round the Larder. Nine-fif—'

Thank heaven for that, thought Helen Renshaw, flicking off her transistor, and switching on the electric kettle. She went over to the open window of her bedroom in the headmistress's flat, a sturdy figure in well-cut pyjamas. The sun was still low in the eastern sky suffused with gold, and down in the park the elongated shadows of trees lay in echelon on the grass. She was long-sighted, and just where the straight drive reached vanishing point between the pillars of the gates she could see Eccles, the head gardener, outside the Lodge, prospecting the morning in his shirt sleeves.

Returning to bed with her early morning tea, she reflected that everything, including the weather, seemed to be lined up for a successful day ... With the possible exception of Beatrice Baynes and her little clique, of course, who never missed an opportunity of engaging in a rearguard action, however futile ... Really, it was incredible how the years slipped by. This would be her twelfth Festival. Seven years, wasn't it, since Olga Feather, her outraged predecessor, had taken final umbrage and ceased to attend?

Helen closed her eyes, projected herself ten days into the future, and began to walk down to Zermatt from the Gorner Grat.

Jock Eccles finished a hearty breakfast of porridge and kippers and went out of the lodge, carrying a wooden board, about two feet by three. It bore in black lettering on a white ground the legend OUR VISITORS ARE ASKED TO PARK IN FRONT OF NEW HOUSE. He hung it with meticulous care on a nail in one of the pillars, stepping back to survey it before making a minute final adjustment.

'Did ye see yon Baynes wumman?' he asked his wife on returning to the kitchen.

'Aye,' she told him from the sink. 'Keekin' frae the stairheid windae noo.'

He gave a short, satisfied bark, and set out once more.

The sun was rapidly gaining power and his heavy boots sent up puffs of dust from the drive. Ahead of him rose the early Georgian façade of Old House, with its mellow rose-red brickwork, beautifully proportioned windows and fine portico. Jock glowered at the fresh white paint : yet another example of the Governors' spendthrift policy towards the buildings, while they grudged every penny spent on the grounds, cut down manpower and set a gormless Gardens Committee over him, to interfere with an experienced man's ideas ... About a hundred yards short of the School he took the righthand fork of the drive.

Considering the piecemeal character of the original house, Meldon had a surprisingly satisfactory unity. New House had been built on in the eighteen-nineties, to keep pace with the rapid increase in numbers. In contrast with the hideous yellow pitchpine inside, its exterior had been kept in harmony with Old House, as had that of New Wing, a further extension running out eastwards. On the opposite, or west side of the Quad, School Wing consisted entirely of classrooms, laboratories and other teaching accommodation. The latest addition, enclosing the Quad on the north side, was the new Assembly Hall, a well-designed functional building, with a stage and greenrooms. A further short drive led from the car park outside New House to the Sanatorium.

Jock Eccles went on through the car park, casting a resentful glance at the display of white and chromium visible through the windows of the kitchen on the ground floor of New House. Turning to the left through an archway, he entered the Quad close to the Hall, the doors of which were standing open. Bert Heyward, the resident caretaker, had already arranged the seating for the Annual General Meeting of the Old Meldonian Society. On the stage half-a-dozen chairs, a table and a carafe of water awaited the committee. At the sides were magnificent arrangements of gladioli in two enormous copper buckets. Jock stood in the doorway, eyeing them complacently. Suddenly his face darkened, and a crimson flush mounted slowly to the bald crown of his head, which was encircled by strands of ginger hair. Giving his boots a perfunctory rub on the mat, he advanced towards the stage and started counting the spikes.

'Thirrty-eight, an' I cut but thirrty,' he muttered angrily. 'You thievin' bitch of a hooskeeper . . .'

He stumped out angrily to go and inspect his ravaged flower-beds. Rounding School Wing in the direction of the gardens he encountered two Sixth Formers returning from an early morning swim. They were in irrepressible spirits and greeted him hilariously. He scowled at them, jabbing with his forefinger.

'I saw ye baith the nicht in yon carr parrkt b' the gates. Wi' yer brithers, nae doot.'

They uttered delighted shrieks.

'Our grandfathers, you mean, Jocky.'

'All signed-for-and-correct. Pre - Festival - exeat - with friends-approved-by-parents.'

'Shamless hussies, the pair o' ye,' he growled, and continued his way.

'Bet he'd've liked to be in on the party,' panted one to the other, as they cantered across the Quad.

'He's yours . . . hairy ginger chest and all,' replied the other, dodging an amicable kick.

The rattle of crockery and clash of cutlery floated out of the kitchen windows. Jean Forrest, the domestic bursar, a competent spectacled figure in a white overall, dissected cold chickens and ham with expertise, oblivious of the babble around her. A baker's van drew up outside and began to disgorge a consignment of dinner rolls.

'Check them before he goes, Mrs Heyward,' called Jean Forrest. 'Remember two years ago?'

An overpowering smell of cold viands hung in the air . . .

Members of the teaching staff began to arrive in their cars. They appropriated the shadiest pitches in the parking-ground, and vanished on their various concerns. Joyce Kitson, the School secretary, sorted and distributed the morning's mail. Just before nine o'clock Helen Renshaw came down from her flat and went into her office on the left of the front door, looking distinguished in a beautifully-tailored frock of sage-green wild silk, with a matching short coat and an antique necklace of garnets. A few minutes later the domestic bursar looked in on Joyce Kitson.

'Four more last-minute acceptances, I'm afraid,' said the latter. 'And no cancellations.'

'Let 'em all come,' replied Jean Forrest robustly. 'I can take anything on a fine Festival.'

'When are you hoping to get away?'

'Friday, with luck, if all the women turn up to clean next week. What about you?'

'Friday, too, I hope. Most of the teaching staff'll be off tomorrow. Nice to have real school holidays!'

'Not to mention Burnham Scale.'

They exchanged commiserating glances . . .

'All the other letters can wait till Monday morning,' said Helen Renshaw. 'Sign the ones we've done p.p., Joyce. I shall be out to lunch and tea tomorrow, by the way. Margaret West wants to get off quickly after breakfast. And do take a day off yourself. It's been a gruelling end of term.'

'I'll try. I'm rather at the can't-stop stage.' Joyce Kitson turned her head towards the door and listened. 'I think that *is* Margaret West. Shall I see?'

'Yes, do. And if it is, perhaps you could get coffee sent in right away, while we run through the agenda.'

Helen Renshaw eyed the President of the Old Meldonian Society with satisfaction : intelligent, mature and easy to look at, she thought. Margaret West had been what she called a Late Feather, at Meldon herself late enough in Olga Feather's over-long period of office to realise that the school had been hopelessly static and out-of-date. She had supported Helen's drastic reforms from the start, rallying her own con- temporaries and even the more enlightened members of ear- lier generations. Now the wife of a successful barrister, her own two daughters were in the School.

'It all seems pretty plain sailing,' she said, looking up from the agenda. 'Unless there's anything in your review of the year likely to spark off the Old Brigade, H.M.?'

'Nothing deliberate, at any rate,' Helen replied, 'but I'm certainly going to mention the art department's successes, especially Miss Cartmell's travelling scholarship, and that might do it. She's Beatrice Baynes's *bête noire* at the moment.'

'Why? What's the poor girl done?'

'Nothing, beyond being a modern young woman and a highly successful teacher on present-day lines. Don't miss the exhibition of work in the studio, by the way.'

'I won't. She's certainly done something to Sarah and Kate.

9

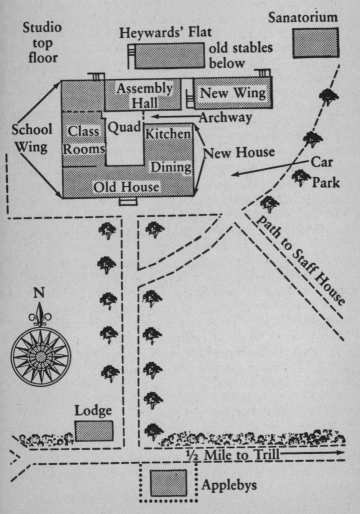

But I can quite see the new régime's a bit startling after Miss Leeke's. We used to call her the Drip, poor dear. In my day, you know, we were still drawing watering-cans and rakes, and admiring The Monarch of the Glen.'

'De mortuis,' said Helen, 'but it was a deliverance. I could never have winkled her out : she'd been here man and boy for thirty-five years, and was only fifty-six. She and Beatrice were great buddies, of course. They sketched together, and Beatrice haunted the studio.'

'You were lucky to get anyone as good as the Cartmell girl at such short notice. Just a week before the autumn term started, wasn't it, two years ago?'

'Yes. It was entirely thanks to the Chairman. He'd met Clive Torrance, who runs the Domani Gallery. Ann Cartmell had just been at a summer school he was involved in, and he knew she was out of a job. She'd come to grief in her first school : a touch secondary modern, quite the wrong place for her. She's the sensitive, idealistic type, a bit immature in some ways. Incidentally, Clive Torrance has gone on taking a keen interest in the art here, and I suspect Ann of having a secret passion for him.'

'Let's hope he won't marry her, anyway, as she's so good at her job. It's something to have a chairman like Sir Piers, isn't it?'

'I don't believe I could have survived my first few years with anyone else.'

'Have you ever regretted taking us on, H.M.?'

'The Old Brigade brought me pretty close to walking out once or twice, early on. Beatrice Baynes is the only real nuisance now, though. It's still a thorn in the flesh having her just across the road. She snoops continually, and her endless letters of complaint get beyond a joke at times.'

'Complaints about the girls, I suppose? Noise, and mufti for the Sixth, and so on?'

'Not only the girls. She's so vindictive about the young

staff. And everything that happens goes over to Applebys by way of Madge Thornton, of course.'

'She's B.B.'s godchild, isn't she?'

'Yes. Not a bad sort, really, but the dreariest teacher of music, and completely under B.B.'s thumb. She's just back from her mother's funeral, poor woman. I told her she needn't reappear this term, but she seemed to want to.'

'B.B. should have seen a psychiatrist years ago,' said Margaret West emphatically. 'Ought we to start moving over to the A.G.M.? There seems to be a pretty good noise outside.'

An amorphous crowd drifted slowly across the Quad towards the Hall. Small groups formed and re-formed round Helen Renshaw, the staff and the O.M.S. committee. A few solitary figures looked about anxiously for contemporaries. Young things of recent vintage, with up-to-the-minute outfits and hair-dos, reunited noisily with each other and with the Sixth. Recently-joined members of staff with no O.M. contacts clung together, ill at ease and faintly resentful. The seats in the Hall filled up slowly, people constantly getting up to greet new arrivals, and changing their places. Finally Margaret West rapped on the platform table and opened the meeting by reading a greetings telegram from Olga Feather.

'My thoughts are with you today, and with Meldon's great traditions' it said equivocally.

Polite applause, protracted by a group in the front row, followed the reading of this missive, and Margaret West called on the secretary to read the minutes of the last meeting.

Helen Renshaw, seated on her left, allowed her attention to wander. A good cross-section of the generations, she thought . . . extraordinary how the Baynes set in front managed to convey disapproval by the way they sat . . . and their *hats* — simply not true! By an association of ideas she looked about for Ann Cartmell, and was pleased to see her sitting between two of last year's leavers . . . Margaret was managing very well, keeping people to the point without sergeant-majoring

. . . She tried to fix with her eye a group of very young O.Ms who were showing signs of incipient hilarity . . .

Shortly after twelve the routine business came to its end.

'And now,' said the President, 'we come to the really interesting part of our A.G.M. : Miss Renshaw's review of the past year in Meldon.'

Helen was a good speaker, fluent, coherent and amusing. An uneventful, but very satisfactory year, she told them. She paid tribute to those who had left, congratulated individual O.Ms on their achievements . . . The Governors were considering an extension of New Wing, owing to the rising demand for places . . . The audience laughed heartily at her account of the disorganisation caused by the 'flu epidemic of the spring term, and applauded an impressive list of academic successes.

'And I want to mention here an outstanding academic success by a member of the staff,' she said. 'As many of you already know, Miss Cartmell, our art specialist, has been awarded a scholarship to the Anglo-American Summer School for Art Teachers, which is being held in New England during the holidays, and she is flying out next Thursday to take it up. We are very grateful,' she went on, when the burst of clapping had died down, 'to Miss Cartmell, for all her enthusiasm and hard work in the art department, and I am sure you will be interested in the exhibition of work in the studio. It includes paintings which we are entering—not without some modest hopes—for the Commonwealth Schools Art Competition this autumn. Still on the subject of art,' she went on, 'I want to tell you that we have opened a fund to buy really good reproductions of a wide range of pictures for all parts of the School. The present girls have been very enterprising in raising money, and there have been some generous gifts from parents. If any O.M. would care to contribute, we should of course be most grateful.'

Aware of the slight drawing-together of the group in the front row, she passed on smoothly to achievements in the

13

athletic sphere, and finally sat down amid loud applause.

'I think this fund is a great scheme.' The speaker, a young woman in her late twenties, had been one of Helen's first head-girls. 'I've always thought our pictures pretty sub-standard, to say the least of it. The ones already bought for the library are in a different street. I'd like to propose, Madam Chairman, that the Society makes a generous dona-tion to the fund.'

'I'd like to second that,' said several voices at once.

As the secretary scribbled hastily, Beatrice Baynes rose to her feet, and stood half-turned towards the body of the Hall, a beringed hand gripping the back of her chair. She was ex-pensively and unbecomingly dressed in a navy-blue edge-to-edge coat, and a matching toque with a Queen Mary feather which contrived to underline her small stature. Her natu-rally red face, innocent of all cosmetics, was deeply flushed with heat and anger. She darted militant glances first at the meeting and then at the platform.

'I wish to say, Madam Chairman, that some of us object strongly to the Society's funds being used to buy pictures in the choice of which we are apparently to have no say what-ever.'

There was an uncomfortable pause.

'You mean, Miss Baynes,' asked Margaret West courte-ously, 'that you would prefer the Society to buy pictures of its own choosing for the School?'

'Who's going to choose them?' demanded a ragged chorus.

'A properly-constituted sub-committee, elected for the purpose,' snapped Beatrice Baynes, on her feet once more.

'At this moment,' Margaret West said, 'there is a proposi-tion before the meeting that a donation'—'a generous dona-tion,' interpolated a voice—'thank you, Daphne Moorhead, a generous donation be made by the Society to the fund for buying pictures for the School. Do you wish to move an amendment, Miss Baynes?'

'Certainly I do. I propose that a sub-committee is set up to buy suitable pictures, up to an agreed sum.'

'Thank you, Miss Baynes. Does the amendment find a seconder? Thank you, Mrs Elkinshaw. Those in favour? . . . Those against? . . . The amendment is defeated by a large majority. I now put the original proposition to the meeting, that a generous donation is made by the Society to the fund. Those in favour? . . . Those against? . . . Carried by a large majority. One moment, please. We now have to decide the amount of our donation. May I have—'

Beatrice Baynes interrupted brusquely.

'Before any such decision is made, I absolutely *insist* on registering a protest on behalf of senior members of the Society about the deplorable modern trend in Meldon's art. It is an absolute negation of the life work of Miss Leeke. I have seen these so-called paintings which are to represent our school at this competition. All of them are crude and grotesque, and one of them actually represents an unclothed figure—'

'Male or female?' enquired a ringing young voice.

In the outraged and delighted silence which followed, Margaret West seized her opportunity.

'I'm afraid I must rule you out of order, Miss Baynes. Now, may we have a proposition from the meeting, please?'

Not without noise and flippancy, a donation of twenty-five pounds was agreed upon.

'Is there any other business?'

None was raised. Struggling to keep the relief out of her voice, the President declared the meeting adjourned.

'I suggest a drink before lunch,' Helen Renshaw said to the committee.

Two

'Quiet on the stairs, please.'
Notice in School Wing

TO MOST OLD Meldonians the unorganised afternoon was the best part of Festival. After lunch there was a general dispersal. A fair number of people made for the hard courts, to watch the annual tennis-match in the intervals of chatting to friends. The fine weather had encouraged the young to bring bikinis and swimsuits, and their suntanned bodies in gay, exiguous garments sprawled decoratively on the concrete surrounds of the swimming bath. Everywhere small groups sat and talked, or wandered about visiting old haunts, noting the minutest changes with unfailing accuracy.

In the background Jean Forrest and her staff moved between kitchen and dining-room with the precision of automata, as they cleared up lunch and prepared to launch a buffet tea.

Ann Cartmell had gone straight up to the studio. It was a large room on the top floor of School Wing, at the far end, with a big north light, below which a door gave on to a fire-escape. To convert the room into an exhibition gallery its normal equipment had been stacked away. Easels and drawing-boards were propped under the windows, and stools, chairs, puppet-theatre, paper press and laden tables jostled each other round the walls. Screens on which drawings and paintings were mounted were grouped about the floor, and a centre table carried specimens of pottery, leatherwork and other crafts practised at Meldon.

Ann looked round critically, and went on to the little platform at the top of the fire-escape to await visitors. She leant her arms on the iron railing and looked across the games pitches to the hills. She was aware of a medley of thoughts and emotions. The attack on her work that morning had shaken her, in spite of its almost ludicrous source and heavy defeat. It had brought back nightmare memories of hopeless failures and hostile classes . . . but then there had been the praise from Rennie for everyone to hear . . . Thrilling, even if slightly daunting, was the prospect of next Thursday at London Airport, and what lay beyond . . . He'd said he might be able to run down and say good-bye . . . Mummy and Daddy would be there of course. She really couldn't try to choke them off, they'd be so hurt. Still . . . every lineament of Clive Torrance's face was visible to her, blotting out the summer landscape.

Footsteps and voices roused her sharply, and she turned and re-entered the studio, a little taut at the prospect of possibly critical strangers. She felt suddenly clumsy and defensive as a group of people came in. Then she recognised the O.M.S.'s President. Margaret West smiled and held out her hand.

'Miss Cartmell? I've managed to escape for a few minutes. I was absolutely determined to get up here after all I'd heard from Sarah and Kate. Do show me everything.'

Immediately warmed, Ann lost her self-consciousness.

'How nice of you to come,' she said. 'There are two things of Kate's in the exhibition. She and Sarah are awfully nice to teach.'

The publicity which the art department had received at the Annual General Meeting brought a constant flow of curious visitors during the afternoon. To her surprise Ann soon found that she was enjoying herself. They were all so unexpectedly friendly, interested about her scholarship, and some really quite intelligent about modern methods of teaching art. Her pale, sensitive face became attractively flushed, and when absorbed in a discussion she made the characteristic gesture of rumpling her short dark hair.

'Yet, these are all by Form I,—eleven-plus,' she told an enquirer. 'No, none of the children are particularly gifted. It's just that most children have a natural sense of form and significance, and if you don't fuss them too much about technique at the early stage, they often express ideas astonishingly well. Look at this one,—A Windy Day. Can't you just feel that tree tugging at its roots?'

'Well, Miss Cartmell, I think they're very lucky to be taught by someone like you. D'you remember trying to copy those ghastly urns outside Old House, Molly? I gave up drawing by persuading my people to let me learn the clarinet, and that I'd need extra time for practising.'

'Nobody bothered to find out if *I* had a natural sense of form . . .'

'Hul-lo, Miss Cartmell! How's things? Do show us the nude that sent off the Bayne this morning . . . why, it's only a sunbather's back! What a sell! Fab, though, isn't it, Micky? Is it one of Jane Winton's? I thought so. Lumme, that girl can paint! Surely that'll win something?'

'Is there anything of my young cousin's, Miss Cartmell? Mary Foxworth? I'm Annette Moresby. Before your time, of course.'

'When do you let them start oils?'

Absorbed in answering questions Ann did not notice the Sixth Form girl at her side until she touched her arm.

'Sorry to interrupt, Miss Cartmell, but there's a 'phone call for you. Mrs Kitson says take it in the inner office—it'll be quieter.'

'Oh! Thanks, Diana. I'm so sorry, Mrs Annersley. I shan't be long.'

Slightly startled, she ran downstairs. Home? Something come unstuck about Thursday?

'Did Mrs Kitson say who it was?' she asked, catching up the girl who had brought the message.

'A personal call from London, I think she said.'

Surely ticket agencies were shut on Saturday afternoons? Ann ran into Old House, dodging groups of people standing about in the entrance hall, and arrived breathless in Joyce Kitson's office.

'Take it in there,' said the secretary, indicating a glass partition. 'Endless interruptions here.'

Ann dived in and took up the receiver, her hand trembling a little.

'Ann Cartmell here . . . Yes, I'm here to take a call.'

There was a click and a short pause. Then a man's voice came through. Her heart gave a single painful leap.

'Oh!' she gasped. 'It's you . . . oh, but that will be marvellous. Are you quite sure you can spare the time? . . . About eight? I may not be out of Festival supper until just after, but will you go straight up? You know the way . . . Yes, they're all on show, and we've got to choose three . . . Yes, I'll tell her . . . of course she'll understand . . . Oh, it's super! . . . yes, I will . . . on the table. It's most frightfully good of you to come in . . . Good-bye, Mr Torrance.'

She stood for a moment trying to control her excitement, and then, feeling an urge for immediate action, thrust open the unlatched door and dashed into the main office, almost knocking down an elderly Old Meldonian in black who was standing by Joyce Kitson's empty desk with Beatrice Baynes . . . Snooping, I bet, thought Ann, making a perfunctory apology and hurrying out. To hell with the old hag, anyway . . . He'c coming tonight . . . in only a few hours from now . . .

The buffet tea was always an informal, protracted affair, and on this occasion it seemed endless to Ann Cartmell as she hovered impatiently for a chance to speak to Helen Renshaw. At last there was a brief lull in the slow stream of departing O.M.s, and she bore down on the headmistress.

'Oh Miss Renshaw,' she said speaking rather hurriedly, 'Mr Torrance rang up just now. He's passing near here about eight this evening, and offered to come in and tell me what he thinks about the final choice of paintings for the competition. I'd be awfully glad of his opinion. He said he didn't want to bother you on such a busy day, so I said it would be all right for him to come. I hope it is?' she ended, on an anxious note.

'Of course,' Helen Renshaw answered, observing Ann's flushed cheeks and excited eyes with interest. 'It's good of him to take so much trouble over us. I shall be sorry not to see him myself, but Mrs West is staying overnight in the flat, so I'm rather tied this evening. In any case it's an art department matter which I'm sure you'll cope with very nicely. Give him my thanks, naturally. The entry form's signed, by the way. It's in Mrs Kitson's office.'

'Oh, thank you, Miss Renshaw. I'll file in the names and do up the parcel before I go.'

'When are you getting away?'

'Early tomorrow. I want the time at home for packing and everything.'

'Well, as we both seem to be in for a busy evening, shall we say good-bye now? And the very best of luck for America. I'm delighted that you're having this chance.'

'Thank you so much . . . and for everything. It's been a marvellous year — I've loved it. Good-bye . . .'

Back in the Staff House, half a mile away on the outskirts of Trill, Ann soaked in a hot bath after a strenuous hour of getting the studio back to normal. It looked pretty good now, she thought, and as though she were right on top of her job. Suddenly afraid that she had lost count of time, she sprang up, scattering water in all directions and grabbing her bathtowel. She used talcum powder liberally and hurried back to her room. No, it was all right, she had heaps of time. Her hair was awful—if only she'd had it done instead of waiting till Wednesday . . . Attending to her make-up with unusual care, she decided to wear a very simple frock with a striking abstract pattern in different shades of blue. Anyway, it's not commonplace, she thought, looking at herself in the glass, and collecting a coat and handbag. As she came out into the landing, the sound of a nearby door opening sent her running downstairs and out to her car. Someone else could give Madge Thornton a lift. She just couldn't face trying to make sympathetic conversation when she wanted to sing and shout out loud . . .

The gathering at supper was comparatively small, as invitations were restricted to long-distance O.Ms and the elderly and infirm who wanted to stay for the night. The staff, however, were expected to be present and help entertain the visitors. Ann controlled her nervous impatience with difficulty. She had chosen a seat with a good view of the Quad, and as the hands of the clock crept slowly towards five minutes to eight she began to feel almost sick with anticipation. He could arrive at any minute now . . . She refused a meringue with her fruit salad, and because involved in a tiresome conversation about American food. It momentarily distracted her attention, and when her eyes returned to the window she realised with horror that she had almost missed Clive Torrance's arrival. With a sharply indrawn breath she saw him disappear through the door at the foot of the stairs leading up to the studio, and gave an agonised glance in the direction of the high table.

Precisely at this moment Helen Renshaw rose to her feet.

'Benedicto benedicatur,' she said in her clear, controlled voice, as the scraping of chairs died away.

Without apology Ann slipped out of the nearest french door. Running across the Quad and up the stairs, she paused outside the swing doors of the studio to take breath, pushed them open and went in.

Clive Torrance was standing in front of one of the screens, his left hand in his trouser pocket and his right arm crooked behind his back, a characteristic attitude which made Ann's heart turn over. He swung round, smiling, as she came in.

'Good girl,' he said. 'You've escaped from the pussies then?'

'Yes,' she answered, coming towards him and feeling hopelessly tongue-tied. 'It—it is good of you to come.'

He cocked an eyebrow at her.

'That frock suits you. It brings out the rather unusual blue of your eyes.'

'I didn't know it was unusual.'

'Didn't you? And you an artist? It suggests variations on the theme of blue. I hate those hard, clear blue eyes, especially in women. That's not an English design, is it?'

'No. It's Italian. This is one of the frocks I've got for America. I don't want to disgrace you when I'm staying with your friends.'

'I shouldn't have sent you to them if I thought there was any chance of that, my dear girl, either personally or professionally. By the way, I heard from Ryder Vanderplank this morning, confirming that everything's lined up for meeting you at the airport and taking you on a lightning tour of New York. Have you heard, too?'

'Yes, I had an awfully nice letter from Mrs Vanderplank. I do think it's good of them to do all this for me—at least, it's for you really, of course.'

Clive Torrance laughed, his eyes still on her.

'It'll be for you all right when you've been with them half-an-hour. Even if you indulge in a bad bout of self-depreciation they'll put it down to British reserve, and think it's cute!'

Ann looked at him in dismay.

'Am I really as bad as all that?'

He sat down on the edge of the table, and took out a cigarette case.

'May I? You don't ever, do you?' He flicked a lighter. 'Your reaction to life is still almost entirely defensive. Outside your painting and teaching, that is. Take me, for instance, that potentially dangerous thing, a virile male. For two years now you've cunningly cast me as a protective father-figure. A prominent role, admittedly, but inhibiting. Granted I'm twenty years older than you are, but not quite in the sere and yellow, I hope.'

Completely taken aback, on the brink of tears and yet aware of rising excitement, Ann slowly subsided on to the table, several feet away from him.

'Well?' he said, cocking an eyebrow again. 'Producer at the bar, are you guilty, or not guilty?'

'About the father-figure?' she said, hardly looking at him. 'I suppose so. I never even thought . . .'

He got up and came and stood in front of her, putting his hands on her shoulders. Still at a loss, Ann gazed up into the face which she had so often visualised in her day-dreams . . . the dark, dominant eyes under the thick brows, the well-shaped nose and the deep cleft between chin and lower lip . . . With a sudden movement he slipped his hands under her arms and lifted her to her feet.

'It isn't a father-figure you want, my dear, whether you know it or not . . .'

As he kissed her full on her lips, gently at first and then more passionately, Ann's initial shock passed quickly into ecstatic response. She pressed closely to him, thrilling to every practised movement of his hands, until the sound of a door slamming somewhere in the building made him release her swiftly, swinging her round and depositing her in front of one of the paintings. As their eyes met she experienced the pleasure of conspiratorial amusement.

'A girls' school is quite the wrong milieu, isn't it?' he said. 'Now, when you come back . . .'

Ann nodded, still unsure of paradise. Clive Torrance looked at his watch and exclaimed.

'My God,' he said, 'I'm late already. We simply must concentrate on these things . . . This one definitely, I think. Very good flesh tones. How old is this girl? Sixteen? She's promising—ought to go on. Now this one has got plenty of vitality, but the composition's top-heavy, don't you think?'

They moved from painting to painting, in the satisfying

23

harmony of a common enthusiasm. Clive Torrance's comments were penetrating, often bearing out her own opinions, sometimes congratulatory to herself.

'Now this one's the pick of the bunch so far. What's it called? Midsummer Stream? She's got a real hint of the shimmer in Manet's Summer. There's a very good reproduction in this month's *Artifex* : I've got it here. Look.' He extracted the periodical from his brief-case, flicked over the pages and showed it to her.

'Yes. That implied quivering in the air.'

'Exactly. Well, let's put Midsummer Stream in, anyway. Now for this last lot.'

Finally, the three paintings he had chosen lay on the table.

'Listen, I can take them up to town for you,' he said, after a last scrutiny, 'and save you all the trouble of packing them for the post. Can you just put something round them quickly?'

'Yes, of course. That'll be marvellous. I'm hopeless at doing up parcels.'

She rummaged in a drawer for brown paper and sheets of cardboard.

'I'll have to collect the entrance form in the office, though, and just enter the names and ages. Are you sure you can wait?'

'Quite. I'm so late already, a few minutes won't make much difference. Is this the oil colour-box? I hope Brocatti & Simpson's packed it properly?'

'Oh, yes, beautifully. Isn't it simply super? It's the most wonderful present I've ever had.'

'Glad you like it,' he said, examining the contents critically. 'You deserved a present—you're the first protégée of mine to get one of these awards, you know. Ready? Splendid. Put that damn parcel down and kiss me good-bye properly. I shan't dare embrace you in front of your parents on Thursday . . .'

They went down the stairs together and out into the Quad, still discussing the paintings, Ann concentrating with difficulty, her whole being in tumult.

'Have you got your copy of *Artifex*?' she exclaimed suddenly.

'Hell! I forgot to pick up! No, of course it wasn't your fault. I'll dash back for it while you run on ahead and fill in the form. Meet you in the office.'

Ann dashed into Old House, her heart singing, her whole world transformed. Joyce Kitson, still at her desk and surrounded by papers, looked up in surprise.

'Can I have the entrance form for the art competition? Miss Renshaw said you'd got it. Mr Torrance is here and he's going to take the entries up to London. He's in a frightful hurry.'

'That'll save a lot of bother,' Joyce Kitson said, searching in a drawer. 'Here you are.'

Ann bent over a corner of the desk, copying the three names from the rough list she had made in the studio.

'There, that's done,' she said, and began to struggle with the parcel. 'Oh, thanks awfully . . . that sticky brown tape stuff's much quicker than string . . . I'd better write something on the outside, I suppose . . . Just ready, Mr Torrance.'

'Good evening,' came Clive Torrance's voice from the door . . . that same voice which had murmured unimaginable things just now . . . 'So sorry to rush you like this, but I'm disgracefully late for my week-end date. That's fine . . . I must dash . . . Good-bye.'

He bowed slightly to Joyce Kitson, and took the parcel from Ann. They hurried out to his car, which was standing by the front door.

'I didn't see your parking notice,' he said, swinging into the driving seat and slamming the door. 'Till Thursday, then.' He pressed the self-starter.

'Till Thursday,' she answered, conscious of a slight feeling of disappointment as he shot off. She watched the car until it paused at the gates, turned right, and vanished.

Returning to the entrance hall, she stood irresolutely until her eye fell on the grandfather clock . . . nearly twenty to nine

. . . she must hurry . . . Bert Heyward would be wanting to lock up School Wing . . . As she came out into the Quad two girls materialised.

'Can we help you clear up the studio?' asked Rachel Rivers.

'Thanks,' said Ann. 'It's nearly all done, as a matter of fact, but I'm trying to get away quickly to pack.'

As they went across the grass together she sensed their interest and curiosity. Damn the children, she thought, they never miss a thing . . .

'Have the competition pictures been chosen, Miss Cartmell?' asked Nicola Stainsby.

'Chosen and sent off, Nicky. Mr Torrance came and helped settle it this evening. I expect you saw him.'

'We did see you with a male escort,' Nicola replied demurely. 'He's awfully good-looking, isn't he?'

'He was our pin-up Saturday evening lecturer of the year,' Rachel informed Ann.

'I must tell him. He'll be honoured. Now look here, these screens must be stowed away, and I haven't cleared out the rough paper drawer yet. Could you get on to that while I collect my own stuff?'

'O.K., Miss Cartmell.'

Ann retrieved her painting satchel from a corner, and rearranged its contents to make room for the oil colour-box. She wondered if canvases and sketching-blocks would be expensive in the States, and decided to take two of the latter. She gathered up a soiled painting smock to be laundered at home.

'Finished?' she asked.

'Just about,' said Rachel Rivers, shutting the drawer and helping to stuff débris into the waste-paper basket. 'Can we carry that down for you?'

'Aren't you feeling madly thrilled about going to America?' asked Nicky, as they descended.

'I can still hardly believe I'm really going,' said Ann. 'Perhaps it's because I haven't started packing seriously yet.'

'Nine o'clock,' remarked Rachel as the clock over the Hall

began to strike. 'Nicky, my old pal, do you realise that in twelve hours' time the happiest days of our lives will be over?'

'Gertcher!' replied her friend.

Rather touched by the girls' unexpectedly warm farewells, Ann drove out of the parking-ground and instantly forgot them, her thoughts flying to her new and almost unbelievable happiness. Turning into the main drive she saw the tall, ungainly figure of Madge Thornton, and felt a pang of remorse at having fled from her earlier in the evening. It must have been pretty grim to come back from your mother's funeral and have to muscle in to end of term and Festival . . .

'Like a lift back?' she called.

Madge Thornton's large, weatherbeaten face peered in at the window.

'Oh, thank you so much, Ann, but I'm calling in at—er—Applebys, first. So nice of you to offer, all the same.'

Ann realised that Madge was embarrassed at having to refer, even indirectly, to Beatrice Baynes.

'Right,' she said, letting in the clutch. 'I hope someone else will come along later. Good-bye.'

In the driving mirror she could see Madge resuming her progress. Everyone knew how that bloody old woman bullied her . . . Pity she was so dreary . . . Perhaps that was why . . .

Halting at the gates, she turned left into the road. As she swung round and passed Applebys, a young man in a green shirt emerged from the porch. She wondered vaguely who he was.

Three

'Meldon is situated within easy motoring distance of London.'
The School Prospectus

A SMALL TRADESMAN'S van drew up with a shudder just short of a crossroads some three miles from Meldon.

'Yours, chum,' said the driver, with a wave of his hand to the left. 'Sorry I can't land you no nearer, but I'm late to-night. Matter o' three miles. Might be a farm car along if you're lucky.'

'This is fine. Thanks a lot for the lift,' replied George Baynes, leaping out and extracting a rucksack.

'O.K. by me. Cheerio!'

The van disappeared round a corner. George glanced at the signpost as he shouldered his rucksack : Trill, 3m. That, if his sense of direction was functioning properly, meant about two and a half miles to Applebys. His watch said 8.20. With any luck he'd make it by nine. Surely the old girl wouldn't go to bed before then on such a smashing evening? A frown furrowed his brow as he strode purposefully along, a slight figure a little under average height, with a thatch of brown hair and a rather narrow face. He had a faintly Puckish air, enhanced by amused, impertinent eyes and markedly protuberant ears.

It had been one hell of a day, he reflected. He'd overslept after last night's party, turned up late at the Kensington estate agency where he held a junior post, and got a raspberry from that old stick Blenkinsop. Being single-handed on a Saturday morning rota meant coping with about six people's work, and he'd made a bish over some keys and upset a client. Too broke for more than a sandwich at lunchtime, he'd stayed hanging round the radio only to learn that he'd backed two losers, one an absolute cert that he'd relied on to put right the couple of quid he'd just *had* to borrow from the petty cash. Then, returning to his euphemistically-styled service-flatlet, he'd found a stinker from the landlord about his arrears of rent, and a threat of action. That had clinched it : there was nothing for it but a shot at touching Aunt Beatrice. Hell, he'd only be asking for an advance on his birthday cheque, due next month. She'd never failed to cough that up so far. What difference could it possibly make to her, anyway? She was rolling, and instead of making him a decent allowance, doled out a mere couple of hundred twice a year, with a lot of guff about making his own way, and hints that she could leave her money where she liked . . . All the same, there was something likeable about the old trout. Once or twice he'd managed to wheedle her into getting him out of a hole, and she always liked having him at Applebys. Not that he could stick the atmosphere for long, but a comfortable bed and four good meals a day was quite a thing to have lined up for emergencies, and one could usually manage to slip into Trill for a quick one at the Plough. Important to keep on the right side of her, too . . . But he didn't really believe that she'd ever cut him out of her will unless he tripped up badly : too much sense of family.

George Baynes was, in fact, the great-nephew, not the nephew of Beatrice : the grandson of her elder brother Clarence, of whom she had held the poorest opinion from the nursery. Clarence, agreeable and lazy, had lounged amiably through life on a substantial inheritance from his father, meeting progressive inflation by drawing on capital. His only child, Edward, and his daughter-in-law, George's parents, had both been killed in the London blitz, and from that time on George had been brought up by his grandfather, who had flatly refused to hand him over to Beatrice. Furious letters had gone backwards and forwards, bandying expressions such as 'pernicious debilitating idleness', and 'stifling Victorian spinsterhood', but George remained with Clarence. When the latter died in 1951, his assets were found to be little more than his debts, and George, after a brief, exhilarating spell of riotous living, had been obliged to find a job. At twenty-five he had already failed to hold down two, having inherited to the full his grandfather's aversion to sustained effort, as well as his considerable personal charm. But a streak of shrewdness, perhaps harking back to his great-great-grandfather who had amassed the Baynes fortune, had so far kept him out of any serious entanglements, either financial or feminine.

Presently the road forked, and a second signpost indicated Trill, 1¼ m. It was a warm evening, and George stopped for a moment to mop his face with a handkerchief, and ease the straps of the rucksack on his shoulders. He swung round hopefully at the sound of an approaching car, but it took the other fork. He swore, and began to plod on again. He'd had rotten luck with lifts all the way . . . A bloody nuisance that Aunt B. had been out when he rang up to say he was coming. If she'd gone away he'd be completely sunk. Unlikely, though. Too keen on the garden. Why women who could afford to pay someone to do the donkey work spent their time sweating over flowerbeds . . .

The landscape became vaguely familiar. George glanced at his watch again, and judged that he was making good time. Aunt B. would be livid if he turned up after she'd gone to bed—or even near her bedtime. Not a hope of touching her if he stepped off on the wrong foot like that. She flew into stinking tempers if anything put her out, though to be fair, these didn't usually last long . . . Absolutely fantastic to go to bed so early, and then get up at some ungodly hour and expect everybody else to do the same . . .

Striding on, George breasted a hill. To his relief he saw the buildings of Meldon below, and the next moment picked out

Applebys. He exchanged good-nights with a yokel pushing a bicycle, and hurrying down a long slope came out at last into the road which ran along the valley. Five minutes later he arrived at the School gates. He read the notice about parking, and deduced that a do of some kind must be in progress. With dismay he remembered that they had some kind of reunion at the end of the summer term. He'd heard Aunt B., who was crackers about her old school, natter about it, and how the whole set-up was going down the drain because of the new Head . . . Blast! She'd come back tired, and be furious at finding him there without any warning . . . Crossing the road, he went in at the garden gate at Applebys and tried the front-door. It was locked. He rang the front-door bell just on chance, and listened. There was no reply, not even the unwelcome sound of a bedroom window being flung up . . . She might just conceivably be in the garden, he thought. As he came out of the porch to investigate, a small car driven by a girl came out of the School gates and went off towards Trill.

There was no sign of life in the garden, which lay on the far side of the house. George peered through the windows of the empty drawing-room and dinner-room, debating his next move. Before he could come to a decision, the click of the gate sent him to ground behind a handy clump of rhododendrons . . . He simply must have time to think . . . it might be possible to see what sort of a mood the old girl was in . . .

After a brief pause, he was astonished to hear the front-door bell ring. Who on earth would be calling at Applebys at this hour? In the still evening air he could hear the faint grating of the scraper under somebody's feet. Then footsteps sounded on the path leading round to the garden. He moved back to better cover, and watched through a convenient gap in the branches. The next moment Madge Thornton appeared, and stood irresolutely, looking up at his great-aunt's bedroom window.

Annoyance and mystification contended in George's mind. He disliked Madge, finding her an appalling bore, but even more as a potential rival in the matter of his expectations. Her frequent appearances at Applebys during his own visits and what he considered her kowtowing to her godmother had aroused his misgivings. However, he had a shrewd appreciation of Beatrice's mentality, and sensed that Madge's doormat propensity irritated her even more than his own casualness and spendthrift habits. All the same, he had decided to watch his step : some people carried the godmother racket to absurd lengths.

Madge's appearance at this particular moment could hardly have been more unwelcome. His mind moved quickly as he watched her peering in at the ground floor windows as he himself had just done . . . She was stepping back again now, and looking upwards . . . Where the heck *was* Aunt B.? Surely, if she was over at the School at some Old Girls' binge, Madge would know? It must mean that she'd gone out to supper with some of her buddies.

'Aunt Beatrice!' Madge suddenly called up at the bedroom window.

Quite a pleasant contralto . . . of course, she taught music . . .

There was no reply. After hesitating for a few moments longer, Madge turned away and slowly retraced her steps. George listened for the sound of the gate shutting, and then ventured out and sat down on a garden seat.

He suddenly realised how hungry and thirsty he was; he hadn't had a decent meal all day. Oddly enough, Aunt B. liked feeding hungry males. Visited by a sudden idea he went round to the kitchen window, and found it open at the top. Taking off his dusty shoes, he pushed up the window sash and swung in easily over the sill.

Inspection of the larder and refrigerator revealed a veal and ham pie, and ample supplies of bread, butter and cheese. Should he fall to at the kitchen table or carry the grub into the dining-room? Which brand of cheek would go down best with Aunt B. when she came in and found him? He wondered if there was any sherry about . . . Anything stronger would be under lock and key. Peeping into the drawing-room, he spotted four used glasses and a decanter on a silver tray. That was it . . . she'd had some old pals in for a drink after the show at Meldon, and they'd gone out to supper together afterwards, at the White Horse at Linbridge, probably. Picking up the decanter he went on into the dining-room. The heavy mahogany table shone like glass, reflecting the roses in the centre. His feet sank into the deep, if unattractive Turkey carpet. He sniffed the air, suddenly hankering after affluence and comfort, and strolled over to the window. A neat slip of paper lay on top of the bureau, under a china jug. Idle curiosity made him pick it up. It was a shopping-list, in Beatrice's clear, old-fashioned handwriting . . . Bank . . . Grenville (curtain lining material) . . . Foster's (pay bill) . . .

Bank . . . George stood motionless, the paper in his hand. Then, with an abrupt movement he tried the second drawer in the bureau, and found it was, as usual, locked. He hesitated again, and then quickly tipped the contents of the little jug into his hand. They included the key which he had so often seen his great-aunt drop into the jug after locking the drawer. It was the matter of a moment to open it and look inside. There was her cheque-book in a leather case, and beside it a great wad of notes secured by a rubber band. He picked them up and flicked with his thumb. Fifty quid at least . . .

Thoughts went racing through his mind as he stood with his ears straining for sounds of Beatrice's return. She might turn up at any minute now . . . Damn it all, she wouldn't miss the money . . . She'd probably be leaving it all to him one of these days, anyway. In a flash he revised his plans. Much better not to confront her at all, as things had turned out. If he took some food as well it would look just like a break-in. He'd sleep rough—it was a warm night—and cut down to Whitesands in the morning, mix in with the holiday crowd, and hitch-hike back to Town. Pay that old so-and-so the rent, and slip that couple of quid back into the petty cash first thing on Monday morning.

They'd never get on to him, but hadn't he better do something about finger-prints all the same? Pulling out his handkerchief, he wiped the jug, key, bureau and decanter, and returned the latter to the drawing-room. Acting on a sudden impulse he snatched up a Louis Seize snuff-box from a small table and dropped it into his pocket : just the sort of thing a casual breaker-in would do. In the kitchen he hastily made up a newspaper parcel of food, and added a bottle of milk. Leaving by the window again, he wiped the sill, scuffed the gravel for possible footprints, and having retrieved his rucksack made for the summer-house at the bottom of the garden.

It was half-past nine. Was it safer to make his get-away now, or should he wait until it was really dark, risking Aunt B.s return and a hullaballo breaking out? . . . Even now, in this half-light, he might cut through the school grounds to the Whitesands road without being noticed . . .

Four

'It is regretted that hospitality to Old Meldonians who are staying overnight cannot be extended beyond breakfast on Sunday morning.'

Official Invitation to Festival

IT WAS DAYLIGHT on Sunday morning before Madge Thornton fell at last into a heavy sleep from which she awoke unrefreshed, and startled to find that it was nearly nine o'clock. Dressing hastily she went downstairs to the dining-room of the staff house. This was empty except for two of her senior colleagues who looked up and greeted her sympathetically.

'I was on the point of coming up to suggest bringing you some breakfast,' Mary Brenyard, Meldon's classics mistress, told her. 'Come and join us instead.'

'I really don't think I want any,' said Madge, feeling sickened by the used crockery and cold ham in the serving hatch.

'I'm sure you can manage a cup of coffee, anyway.' Mary Brenyard switched on an electric kettle and slipped a slice of bread into the toaster. 'Nice and peaceful, isn't it? All the young things have gone off already—imagine it, after yesterday, and being up half the night packing, too! Still, they were quite reasonably quiet about it.'

Madge murmured something non-committal and sat down at the table. The coffee cleared her head a little, and presently she began to join in the rather desultory conversation of the other two. The sudden opening of the hatch made her start. The head of Mrs Milman, the housekeeper, appeared.

'Will you be in to lunch, Miss Thornton?

35

Madge hesitated.

'Well, it doesn't matter if you're not sure. It's a cold meal, I'm afraid. I thought you might be going to Miss Baynes.'

'I don't quite know yet, Mrs Milman. I'm so sorry. I'll let you know after church.'

'Don't trouble. The food will be there if you want it and if you don't, it comes in.'

Mrs Milman gathered up the crockery and vanished with a clatter.

'I couldn't find Miss Baynes last night,' Madge said, breaking in on a remark by Mary Brenyard. 'It was so strange . . . the house was all shut up.'

The others exchanged a quick glance.

'She had gone out to dinner with one of her old friends, I expect,' Ruth Layton said easily. 'Mrs Elkinshaw, you know, or Mrs Steadman, perhaps. They were both at Festival.'

'Perhaps she had,' replied Madge tonelessly. 'I felt a bit worried.'

'I'm sure you needn't have. Anyway, you're almost certain to see her in church. I'm afraid we're both having a godless morning and getting on with our packing.'

Madge walked the short distance to the parish church alone, and chose a seat from which she could keep the south door under observation. The faithful trickled in and took their places. The ringers brought their last change to its conclusion, and the five-minute bell took over. The organist embarked on a voluntary, and late-comers scurried into pews. An upsurge of the congregation greeted the appearance of the choir . . . Until the end of the Venite Madge continued to glance round uneasily.

During the last hymn she hurried out, dropping her prayer-book and drawing some curious stares. Regardless of the heat, for the fine weather was continuing unabated, she set off along the half-mile of road to Applebys as fast as she could. Her breath soon began to come in gasps, and she could feel her heart pounding, but she did not slacken pace until she saw Applebys, a couple of hundred yards ahead. Arriving at the gate at last, she paused as if to brace herself, and then went purposefully up the path to the front-door.

The sight of the *Sunday Times* in the letter-box, and a bottle of milk on the step brought her to an abrupt halt. After an indecisive moment or two she put her finger on the bell-push, and pressed tentatively at first, and then hard, for a full twenty seconds. Nothing happened. Almost running round to the garden she peered once more through the ground-floor windows, and finally discovered that the kitchen window was open at the top. Pushing up the bottom sash, she listened intently. Except for the rhythmic ticking of the hall clock audible through the open door, complete silence reigned within : the lifeless silence of an empty house. She called, and it seemed as though the echoes of her voice would never die away. She made a sudden movement of withdrawal, hitting her head painfully on the window, and almost crying, she hurried in the direction of the Meldon gates. Half-walking and half running, she covered the interminable length of the drive, and stumbling into Old House and up the stairs hammered on the door of Helen Renshaw's flat.

Helen Renshaw, on the point of going out to lunch, looked in amazement at the flushed, perspiring figure, with hat askew and shoes white with dust.

'Why, Miss Thornton!' she exclaimed, 'is something wrong?'

Madge nodded, tried to speak, and failed.

'Just come in here and tell me about it.' Helen took her by the arm and guided her to a chair in the cool sitting-room.

'Now, what has happened?' she said.

'It's—it's Miss Baynes. I've just been to Applebys.'

'Is she ill or hurt? Is a doctor wanted?'

'I don't know . . . She—she isn't there.'

'Isn't there?' echoed Helen. 'But Miss Thornton, why should she be? She's almost certainly out with some of her old friends who were here yesteday.'

'She can't be . . . she wasn't there last night either. And the

milk hasn't been taken in . . . We must tell the police quickly
. . . Oh, please ring them up.'

'But how do you know that Miss Baynes wasn't at
Applebys last night?'

With some difficulty Helen established the facts of Madge's
call at the house on the previous evening. Attempts to reason
with her achieved nothing : becoming increasingly incoherent
she reiterated that the police should be rung up. Helen tried
another tack.

'Look, Miss Thornton,' she said. 'Let's just think about all
this from Miss Baynes' point of view. I really can't ring up the
police, you know. She would think it the most impertinent
interference in her private affairs, and quite understandably.
After all, it's quite natural that she should stay out with her
friends later than nine o'clock, and make an early start on a
lovely summer morning, isn't it? She may even have decided
to spend the night at a hotel with Mrs Elkinshaw, who lives
in Yorkshire and doesn't come this way very often. You've
had a very sad and trying time this week, and it has upset you,
and made things get out of proportion. But if you will take
my advice, you'll leave Miss Baynes to her friends over this
week-end. She doesn't like interference, does she?'

This shot went home. Madge nodded, reminiscently and
unhappily.

'I'm going to drive you back to the staff house in a few
minutes,' Helen went on. 'Then after lunch, have a good rest
on your bed, and you'll feel much more yourself by tea-time.
Will you go down and sit in my car? I'm not quite ready.'

Madge got up still distressed, but calmer.

'Thank you, Miss Renshaw. You're so kind. I'm sorry I—I
made a fuss. I—'

'Don't worry about it any more,' said Helen, escorting her
to the door.

After Madge had gone, she stood in the middle of the room
frowning. It really was heartless of Beatrice Baynes to go off
like this without a word to Madge. The least she could have

done in the circumstances would have been to invite her to spend the day at Applebys.

Going over to the telephone she lifted the receiver and dialled the number of the School Sanatorium.

'Sister? It's Miss Renshaw speaking. I'm most reluctant to worry you, but I'm really bothered about Miss Thornton . . . You noticed it too, did you? . . . Well, in view of everything, a drive after tea and then supper with you would be just what she wants, I should think, poor woman . . . I'm more grateful than I can say : it would be difficult to cancel my own engagements, and she's badly in need of a little human kindness . . . You're a real Christian. Good-bye.'

It was as she went downstairs that she suddenly wondered why Beatrice Baynes had not gone to the funeral herself. Madge was her godchild, as she frequently emphasised, so there must have been some link with the family.

After some hours of the soothing, yet bracing company of Sister Littlejohn, and a bedtime sedative, Madge Thornton slept well on Sunday night. When she woke, she lay in bed for a time thinking. When she had had her breakfast she would go straight to Applebys. Aunt Beatrice never went out before ten.

Beyond this her plans were vague. She couldn't stay on at the staff house, of course : Mrs Milman was going on holiday at the end of the week. If there was no invitation to stay at Applebys, she'd better go home and decide what to do about the house and the furniture. It was all hers now. The lawyer had been very kind . . . perhaps he would help her, if Aunt Beatrice didn't.

It was a cooler day, with more wind and cloud than of late. Madge took the footpath through some fields and Meldon Park, branching off across the grass towards the Lodge. Her lips moved soundlessly from time to time as she framed sentences to say to Aunt Beatrice. She was so abstracted that at the gate of Applebys she almost collided with Mrs Hinks,

39

the daily woman, who had cycled along the road from Trill.

'Morning, Miss,' said the latter, a brisk person in her forties. I'm sure you must be real glad term's—'

She broke off abruptly at the sight of two full milk bottles and a copy of *The Times* outside the front-door.

'Bless my soul,' she exclaimed. 'And there's the Sunday paper too. I hope Miss Baynes ain't poorly.'

Closely followed by Madge who was babbling incoherently, she hurried round to the back-door on the west side of the house. It was locked.

'Kitchen window open, too,' she said. 'I can't made it out. What's that you're saying, Miss?'

Madge's narrative became increasingly disjointed.

'Miss Baynes never said nothing to me about goin' away,' asserted Mrs Hinks. 'Nor yet to stop the milk. Good thing I've got a key. We'll go inside and see if she's left a note.'

The hall was stuffy, with the scent from a bowl of overblown roses hanging in the air. Mrs Hinks hurried into the kitchen.

'Why, look there,' she said, pointing to a trail of old newspapers scattered over the floor. 'That's never Miss Baynes, leavin' the place like that. Proper queer, I call it. Reckon we'd better go over the 'ouse, Miss. There's no note, 'ere.'

After a hasty glance into the other ground-floor rooms, she led the way upstairs. The door of Beatrice's bedroom was propped open by a chair. The bed showed no signs of having been slept in, and the room was perfectly tidy, except for a pair of expensive-looking black shoes lying in front of a chair.

'She can't have gone away,' Madge burst out. 'There's her brushes and comb, and all her washing things.' She pointed to the fitted basin in the corner. 'I know something dreadful's happened—I knew it all the time, and they wouldn't listen. Oh, Mrs Hinks, what are we going to do?' She began to sob.

'Now, Miss, we've got to act sensible,' said Mrs Hinks

stoutly. 'Gettin' 'ysterical won't 'elp nobody. Sit down a bit while I takes a look round.'

Pushing the unresisting Madge into a chair, she quickly searched the other bedrooms, looking in cupboards and under beds. Then she went downstairs again and investigated the sitting-rooms.

'Miss Thornton,' she called excitedly a few moments later. 'Summat's bin took from the droin-room.'

Madge stumbled to join her, choking back her tears.

'See, Miss? The silver snuff-box off this table. Very valuable, Miss Baynes said. There's been a break-in, if you asks me.'

'But where's Aunt Beatrice?'

Something in the pitch of Madge's voice made Mrs Hinks decide to seek for reinforcements.

'I reckon as we'd better go across to the School, Miss. There's Miss Renshaw will say what's to be done. I don't want to take no liberties.'

'I said the police ought to be told. I said so yesterday morning . . .'

'That's right, Miss,' agreed Mrs Hinks pacifically, as they hurried up the drive . . . Proper gave me the willies, she did, she told her husband afterwards. Like a sleepwalker she was, you might say.

The secretary's office was empty. Mrs Hinks, unfamiliar with the front regions of Old House, gazed round helplessly, and was heading for the kitchen when Jean Forrest came out of the library.

'Oh, Miss,' Mrs Hinks exclaimed thankfully, 'Applebys 'as been broke into, and we can't find Miss Baynes nowhere.'

Helen Renshaw, interrupted in a session with Joyce Kitson, listened to Mrs Hinks with a slight sense of uneasiness, increased by the fact that Madge remained perfectly silent, staring straight in front of her. She made a quick appraisal of the situation and turned to Joyce Kitson.

'I want you to ring up the White Horse at Linbridge, and ask if Mrs Elkinshaw is staying there, and if Miss Baynes has been in. If not, try Mrs Steadman at Whitesands ... It may be,' she went on, addressing the other two, 'that Miss Baynes has moved the snuff-box herself for some reason. I don't want to call in the police until we've done all we can to contact her.'

'Yes, Miss,' replied Mrs Hinks, somewhat overawed by her surroundings. She unobtrusively patted her perm, and wished she were wearing something better than her working cotton frock.

In the ensuing silence Helen took up a pencil to give the appearance of working. It really was beginning to look rather an odd situation ... Ought she, perhaps, to have taken some steps yesterday ... ?

After an interval Joyce Kitson came back.

'Mrs Elkinshaw has been staying with Mrs Steadman,' she reported, 'and left for London by the morning train yesterday. They both went back to Applebys after Festival, and had sherry with Miss Baynes. Miss Watman was there too, and all three left together about seven. Mrs Steadman says Miss Baynes said nothing about going away, and she hasn't heard from her since.'

Helen put down her pencil.

'In that case,' she said calmly, 'I think we had better report this possible burglary to Constable Freeth at Trill. Will you see if you can get him for me, Joyce? And perhaps Miss Thornton and Miss Hinks could wait in your office? He may want to come up here before going to Applebys.'

Over the telephone this was the course of action she suggested. Constable Freeth agreed with alacrity, a burglary and a mysterious disappearance promising an interesting variation in his normal routine. In less than a quarter of an hour he had propped his bicycle against the portico of Old House, and was being shown into Helen Renshaw's presence.

He listened attentively to her brief summary of the situation.

'I think, madam, I'd better first have a word with the ladies that came over here from Miss Baynes's, and then go and take a look myself. If there are what you might call suspicious circumstances, like signs of breaking and entering, I'll be contacting the Inspector over at Linbridge. As to Miss Baynes herself, well, I don't rightly know just yet. Maybe something'll turn up to show it's all quite straightforward-like. Perhaps you'll call these two ladies in?'

Helen pressed a bell-push on her desk, noting with amusement a reluctance to become embroiled with Beatrice Baynes which was equal to her own.

'By the way,' she said, 'Miss Thornton is very distressed at the moment. Her mother died last week, and she is a godchild of Miss Baynes.'

'I'll bear it in mind, madam.'

It was obvious that while Madge still seemed to be in a kind of stupor, Mrs Hinks had reached the stage of pleasurable self importance. She gave Constable Freeth a brief nod, indicating that she realised they were meeting on official terms, and sat expectantly, her hands folded in her lap. In answer to his questions she gave a clear, if slightly discursive account of her arrival and subsequent actions at Applebys.

'I understand, madam,' he said to Madge, 'that you met Mrs Hinks at the gate, and entered the house with her?'

Madge turned her head slowly and stared at him, as if trying to get him into focus.

'I knew she wasn't there on Saturday night,' she said thickly. 'Then, on Sunday morning I asked her'—she made a gesture towards Helen—'to send for the police, but she wouldn't. Nobody would do anything. Nobody.' Her voice had begun to rise ominously.

As they looked at her there came the sound of swing doors being thrust violently open, and heavy feet came running

43

across the hall. Bert Heyward knocked and burst in simultaneously, closely followed by a woman in an overall. He was panting and white-faced.

''Scuse me, Miss,' he gasped, with a bewildered glance at Constable Freeth, 'it's Miss Baynes. Terrible thing's 'appened up to the studio. Mrs Bennett started to clean, and when she shifted that puppet theayter, Miss Baynes fell out, stone dead. There's a great bash on 'er 'ead.'

A horrified silence was broken by a peal of laugher from Madge.

'She's had Festival hospitality till after breakfast on *Monday*,' she crowed, and rocketed into hysterics.

How extraordinary it feels, Helen Renshaw thought, sitting at her desk, not to have the slightest idea of what is going on in the School, or the right to ask.

There had been a period of feverish activity. Constable Freeth had vanished with Bert Heyward, returning with the key of the studio in his pocket to monopolise the telephone in the secretary's office. In his absence Helen had hastily summoned Sister Littlejohn, who had appeared in a matter of minutes and dealt with, and removed Madge Thornton. In the meantime, Joyce Kitson had found Jean Forrest and handed over Mrs Bennett and Mrs Hinks. Constable Freeth had looked in to say that Inspector Beakbane of the Linbridge Constabulary was on his way, and departed again to keep guard over the studio. A call to the Chairman of the Governors had produced the information that Sir Piers Tracey was out on the golf course, but that his wife would go over and find him at once.

For the moment there was nothing further to be done. Better to make an effort to think clearly and face things which would keep nagging . . .

There was the sound of a fast car coming up the drive. It drew up on the gravel sweep, and two men in plain clothes got out. Helen heard Joyce Kitson cross the hall, and a man's voice. There was a knock on the door.

'Come in,' she called.

'Inspector Beakbane, Miss Renshaw.'

He looked more like a farmer . . . Brawny, with an impassive face and bright blue eyes. An outdoor man. About fifty-five.

'Good morning, madam,' he said politely. 'Very sorry to hear about this. Just to put you in the picture, Dr Wallace, the police surgeon, is on his way. When I've had a word with him, I'd like one with you, if it's convenient.'

'Certainly, Inspector,' she answered, 'you'll find me here. Please tell me if there is anything I can do.'

He thanked her and went off. Almost at once a second car drew up, and another man, presumably Dr Wallace, got out and came into the house. Someone must have been waiting for him : she heard voices, and then footsteps dying away. An uneasy silence descended once more. Resting her head on her hands, Helen had a sudden horrific vision of the inevitable arrival of the Press.

A telephone call to say that Sir Piers Tracey was already on the road to Meldon did something to dispel the sense of an all-enveloping nightmare. The return of Inspector Beakbane was almost welcome. Anything, she thought, to get moving, to get the preposterous, grotesque business cleared up as quickly as possible.

He told her gravely that the nature of the injuries precluded accident and suicide, and that he was treating the case as one of murder, and as she had expected, his first question was about Beatrice Baynes's next of kin.

'As far as I know, her only surviving relative is a great-nephew, a Mr George Baynes,' she told him. 'I think he lives in London, but am not sure. Unfortunately, the person who would know, a Miss Madge Thornton, is a godchild of Miss Baynes, and when she heard the news she collapsed, and was taken to our sick-bay. She is on the teaching staff here. Her mother has just died, and the two shocks were too much for her. Would you like to ring up the Sister in charge?'

The call disclosed that Madge Thornton was now asleep, after being given sedatives, and that the doctor had banned all visitors until further notice.

'I think we must try the deceased lady's house, then, madam,' the Inspector said, putting down the receiver. 'Constable Freeth has told me of the events which led you to call him in, and I'll send my sergeant over right away to have a look round and search for Mr Baynes's address.'

After a brief absence he came back again, and sat down in a chair by the desk.

He told her that he felt she was in a position to give invaluable background information. 'You see,' he went on, 'this is a much more complicated business than a murder in a private house. We've got to get the hang of a much wider setting, if I can put it in that way. I understand the deceased was an old pupil of this School, and lived just opposite the entrance?'

'That's quite correct,' said Helen. 'She was here at School just at the turn of the century, and has kept in close touch ever since.'

'Dr Wallace has given a provisional opinion that she died during Saturday night. Assuming for the moment that she was killed on the premises—of course we're keeping the fire-escape in mind—can you suggest why she should be in the studio at that time?'

'It depends on what you mean by Saturday night, Inspector. Perhaps I had better explain a little about last Saturday.'

She outlined the Festival programme, explaining that Beatrice Baynes had not been eligible for an invitation to supper. 'But of course there was nothing to prevent her coming over here again after supper, although it doesn't seem very likely. She was elderly, and had been out all day, and I know that she took some friends back to her house when she left here at

46

about six. There was an art exhibition in the studio, but she had already seen that.'

In response to his request she provided the names and addresses of the three guests at the sherry-party. The Inspector then began to question her about the locking-up arrangements at Meldon.

'Bert Heyward, our resident caretaker, is responsible for it. Normally in the summer term he begins at nine o'clock, starting with the Assembly Hall and working through School Wing—where the studio is—to this house. But Saturday was not a normal day, so he may have been earlier or later. He's most reliable, and I'm quite sure no doors were left unlocked all night.'

'I'll be taking a statement from him later,' said Inspector Beakbane. 'Once the locking-up was done, madam, would it be possible for anyone to get from this house into School Wing?'

'There are connecting doors on all three floors. Those on the first and second floors are kept permanently locked, and haven't been opened for years. The one on this floor is locked by Bert Heyward when he comes through, and he puts the key inside the case of the grandfather clock in the hall. I think this is fairly generally known as far as the School goes. The connecting doors between this house and New House are never locked, in case of an emergency at night. Perhaps if I drew a rough plan?'

'Thank you very much, madam,' he said, studying the sheet of paper. 'I take it,' he went on, 'that quite a few people were sleeping on the premises on Saturday night, although most of the guests were here only for the day?'

'About fifty, I should say. Roughly twenty-five Old Girls, the fifteen members of the Sixth Form, and those of us who are resident staff. I can get you an accurate list.'

'That would be very—'

There was a knock on the door.

'Colonel Patch and Sir Piers Tracey, Miss Renshaw,' Joyce Kitson announced.

The Chief Constable of Upshire strode into the room with outstretched hand.

'Good morning, Miss Renshaw,' he said. 'I needn't say I'm distressed. A shocking thing to happen—here, of all places. Morning, Beakbane. You know Sir Piers from the Bench, of course. He's chairman of the Meldon Governors. We met on the doorstep.'

Greetings were exchanged and two more chairs drawn up. At Colonel Patch's suggestion the Inspector gave a précis of the situation.

'If I may,' Helen interposed as he ended, 'I think there are one or two other things I ought to tell you about.'

'Please go ahead, Miss Renshaw,' said the Colonel.

She briefly described Madge Thornton's visit to her flat on Sunday, and the arrangements she had made for her welfare with Sister Littlejohn.

'I just can't forgive myself for not having taken some action about Miss Baynes,' she said miserably, 'but it really didn't seem called for at the time, and you know, Sir Piers, how difficult she could be.'

'You acted as any reasonable person would have done,' he said, observing her strained face, 'and have absolutely nothing to reproach yourself with, has she, Patch?'

'Nothing whatever,' replied the Colonel. 'In any case, Miss Renshaw, even if you had rung us up there was no justification for police enquiries at that stage. And if we had felt that her not turning up at Applebys last night was suspicious, we certainly shouldn't have started off by searching the school, should we, Beakbane?'

'No, sir. We'd have contacted hospitals for an accident case, and so on. The delay's unfortunate, of course, but it's easy to see how it's come about.'

'I expect you'd like to talk things over,' said Helen, taking herself in hand and rising to her feet. 'I'll go and get that list

48

of the people who slept here on Saturday night for you, Inspector.'

When she returned five minutes later there was an atmosphere of decision in the room. The Chief Constable and Inspector Beakbane bent over the list which Joyce Kitson had produced.

'Well, this would have clinched it in any case,' the former said. 'About forty possible witnesses scattered all over the country by now. You agree, Beakbane?'

'Absolutely, sir. We just haven't the manpower for a job like this, and I know the Super would say the same.'

'I'll ring him, first, of course, and then get on to the Yard right away, and ask them to send someone down. I'd better mention your name, Tracey, as you know the A.C., and tell him Meldon's one of our pigeons. No, Miss Renshaw, the phone in the secretary's office will do perfectly well. We'll leave you two to have a chat.'

'Well, my dear, we've weathered some storms over the past twelve years,' said Sir Piers, moving into the chair vacated by Inspector Beakbane, 'and we shall weather this one, but I wish the woman had got herself murdered somewhere else . . . You're looking very knocked-out, not unnaturally. You want a shot in the arm. Got any brandy in the place?'

'There's some brandy up in my flat, but I'm all right really.'

Ignoring this statement he went in search of Joyce Kitson, and presently came back with a glass on a tray.

'Get this inside you,' he said.

As she sipped the brandy Helen began to feel better.

'Do smoke,' she said.

Sir Piers lighted a cigarette.

'What's particularly on your mind?' he asked. 'Afraid of being a suspect yourself? You'd have bumped her off long ago if you were going to!'

'No, not really, although I suppose I am one potentially. It's Madge Thornton, first and foremost, I think. She's been very odd and overwrought ever since she came back from her mother's funeral, and she was definitely in an hysterical state on Sunday. And when Bert Heyward came in and blurted out about the body, she made a mad remark and went sky-high.'

'H'm. Where is she now?'

'In the Sanatorium. Under sedation, and no visitors allowed.'

'And what else?' he asked, reverting to his original question.

'Ann Cartmell must have been up in the studio quite late on Saturday, doing a final clear-up. Clive Torrance was coming in after supper to advise about some entries for a competition. Of course she didn't murder Beatrice Baynes, but it's well known that Beatrice had had the knife into her, and she was most offensive about her work at the A.G.M. on Saturday. Ann's the highly-strung type who'll probably go to pieces when the police question her. She's due to fly to New York on Thursday, by the way, to take up that scholarship she's been awarded. And then there's Bert Heyward. He must have gone in to lock the fire-escape door on the inside.'

Sir Piers smoked in silence.

'The only possible course is complete frankness with the police,' he remarked at last. 'You must tell them about Miss Cartmell. I doubt if she'll get away on Thursday, unless it can be proved that Beatrice was still alive after she had left the premises. What's the present *terminus ad quem*?'

'About seven o'clock, I think.' She went on to tell him about the sherry party, and the telephone calls she had made.

A knock on the door heralded the return of Colonel Patch.

'I've been on to the Yard,' he told them. 'They're sending down a Chief Detective-Inspector Pollard and the usual support, and they say they ought to get here about three. Now we're—'

'Just a mintue, Patch, Miss Renshaw's thought of a few more things which seem relevant. I'll go and get on to the other Governors,' he said to Helen, 'and draft a stock answer for Mrs Kitson to give parents and other people who ring up.'

'Thank you so much. And we'll get lunch laid on for everyone.'

'That's most kind,' said the Colonel. 'And it would be a convenience if we could have somewhere for an office.'

'Of course. Would the library be suitable? It's just across the hall.'

Time went on in a curiously disjointed way. The imperturbable Jean Forrest provided a series of lunch trays in unusual places. Unfamiliar footsteps passed and re-passed the swing doors into School Wing. Instinctively the Meldon community drew closer together. The Senior Mistress who had left for home that morning returned at once on being contacted by Joyce Kitson. The school doctor looked in, ostensibly to report on Madge Thornton. Incoming telephone calls were handled with tact and brevity in the secretary's office, and very few allowed to go through to Helen Renshaw. Jock Eccles, instructed to shut the gates and keep out unauthorised visitors, assumed his second-best suit and a more than usually militant expression.

Soon after half-past two Sir Piers came in to tell Helen that the crime reported from the *Announcer* was driving from London in a fast car.

'I know Broadbent, the editor,' he said, 'and offered them the exclusive story. The others will all turn up, of course, and hang about for scraps, but it won't be so trying if the scoop has already gone. I'll cope with him when he arrives, so don't worry.'

She asked him if he knew what was happening.

'They're waiting for the Scotland Yard people. Then Patch will go off, and Beakbane too, when he's handed over. Miss Cartmell has been told to come back, so she'll appear some time this evening. Lives in Bath, doesn't she?'

'Yes. Isn't that a car coming up the drive?'

He went over to the window.

'Scotland Yard,' he said a moment later. 'Four of them.'

'Four?'

'The detective-inspector, his sergeant and a couple of technicians, I imagine. For photography and finger-prints.'

'This is the sort of thing that happens to other people, isn't it?'

He came across the room and sat down again.

'History suggests,' he said, 'that Meldon possesses a quite remarkable resilience.'

She had just time to smile back at him when Joyce Kitson announced Chief Detective-Inspector Pollard of Scotland Yard.

Five

'The Figure of Beatrice, by Charles Williams.'
List of Missing Library Books

'I'D BETTER SEE 'em off,' said Inspector Beakbane, as the stretcher party manoeuvred out of the studio door. 'Always gives a good impression in a posh set-up.' He grinned at Chief Detective-Inspector Pollard and went out with a touch of jauntiness in his step.

It'll be O.K. if I watch out, thought Pollard, even if he is twenty years older than I am. Perhaps he'll come off the defensive as we go along.

Dismissing Beakbane from his mind he stood with his back to the door, concentrating intently on the studio. Immediately facing him was the door leading to the fire-escape. To the left of it a table stood against the wall, stacked with an assortment of jars, vases, boxes and other oddments. To the left again, a paper press with drawers underneath . . . His gaze moved on anti-clockwise to the folded screens stacked in the corner, and on again over the easels and stools under the windows in the west wall . . . A lot more junk on the window-sills. The puppet theatre had stood in the corner on his left, its back to the wall behind him. The tug with which the cleaner had pulled it out had swivelled it round through ninety degrees, so that it now faced him. It was a flimsy affair of hessian over strips of rough wood, about six feet high. The powerful light being used by Detective-Constable Strickland, who was finger-printing the inside, showed behind the gentle-moving small curtains, giving a macabre impression of a performance about to begin. The effect was heightened by a Mephistophelian flash as Detective-Constable Boyce took a photograph. Sergeant Toye, sprawled on the floor examining the linoleum through a lens, might have been struck by a thunderbolt. He glanced up at Pollard.

'Looks as if an army's tramped over the place, sir.'

'It has,' replied Pollard. 'A monstrous regiment of women for most of Saturday, and God knows how many people today, before we got here. Carry on, all the same. If the marks on those heels weren't made by dragging, I'll eat my hat.' He looked towards a pair of good, but wellworn black shoes with low cuban heels.

The door opened to re-admit Inspector Beakbane.

'There's nothing more for us here at the moment,' Pollard told him. 'Let's leave these chaps to it and go down to the library, I'd be jolly glad of a re-cap up to date.'

A tea-tray awaited them on the table in the bay opposite the door.

'Bit of all right,' remarked Beakbane. 'Ashtrays, too. Shall I be mother?'

He poured out two cups, dropped three lumps of sugar into his own, held out a packet of cigarettes to Pollard, and opened the folder he had been carrying under his arm.

'Deceased,' he said, without further preamble, 'saw off three highly respectable old schoolmates from the house opposite the gates just after seven on Saturday evening. We've checked with two of them through the Whitesands police : they live down there. As far as we've been able to discover, no one—except the murderer, that is—saw her again until she shot out of that Punch and Judy show affair with her head bashed in, at about twenty to eleven this morning. Dr Wallace, our police surgeon, gives it as his provisional opinion that she was killed before midnight on Saturday. He's doing a p.m., of course, but I doubt if he'll be pinned down any closer after all this time.'

'Odd that nobody noticed her absence on Sunday. Or wasn't it?'

'In some ways, no. She lived on her own, and her daily woman didn't come on Sundays. Actually, it *was* noticed—there are one or two fishy bits of evidence here, including signs of a break-in at the house, which we're pretty well convinced are phoney.' The Inspector expelled a mouthful of smoke, and went on. 'One of the teachers here, a Miss Madge Thornton, is deceased's godchild. She can't be questioned at the moment on doctor's orders : she went sky-high on hearing about the murder, and is in the sick-bay under sedatives. But she told Miss Renshaw that she went over there late on Saturday evening and couldn't get an answer. When deceased didn't show up at church on Sunday morning, Miss Thornton went to the house again—Applebys, it's called—saw the milk and paper on the door-step, still couldn't get answer, and panicked. She came over here, knocked up Miss Renshaw—she's got a flat upstairs—and begged her to contact the police.'

'Which she didn't do, I take it?'

'No. Apparently relations were pretty tricky between them, because of the changes she's made since she took over the school. Brought things up-to-date : girls allowed out with boy-friends, and so on. Deceased was an old scholar herself here, you see, a long way back. Miss Renshaw said in so many words that she didn't want to trigger off an unnecessary row by interfering, and that it seemed obvious that deceased was out seeing as much as she could of her old pals who'd come for the Reunion. So she calmed Madge Thornton down, and got the School nurse to keep an eye on her for the rest of the day and give her a sleeping-pill. She says she's been worried about Miss Thornton, who only came back from her mother's funeral last Friday, seeming very upset and nervy. Time of life, too, I daresay. Cool customer, Miss Renshaw,' added the Inspector. 'Gives me the jitters a bit, between ourselves. Reminds me of the head teacher at my board school who used to scare the guts out of me.'

'Possible suspect?' enquired Pollard, intrigued.

'Given a motive, I wouldn't put it beyond her. Plenty of

brains, and used to keeping her head screwed on . . . Motive's the only hope in clearing up this case, as you'll have seen for yourself. Anybody about the place from seven o'clock onwards on Saturday night could've done it. There were about sixty of them, counting the helpers at the supper, and there's always the possibility that an outsider got in, before they locked up for the night. Look at this . . .'

He produced the rough sketch-plan made by Helen Renshaw, and explained the normal locking-up procedure, and the possibility of internal access to School Wing at a later hour by anyone who knew where the key of the door leading from Old House was kept overnight. The two men sat smoking in silence while Pollard considered.

'A lot hangs on where the murder was committed,' he said. 'Was she slugged in the studio, or somewhere else and carried there afterwards? If somewhere else, the murderer must either have known about the puppet theatre or felt that it was safer to hide the body inside than in the grounds. He—or she—may have thought that the school was closing down for the holidays and that it wouldn't be found for some time. We can't get much further until my chaps have finished upstairs. Not that I'm very hopeful of the floor after all that tramping about. The path outside leading to the fire-escape's like iron after this dry spell, too. There's nothing for us there.'

Inspector Beakbane grunted.

'A strong woman could have carried her. She was a bare four feet eleven inches, and I doubt if she weighed much over seven and a half stone.'

'Still harking back to Miss Renshaw? She's the build for it, all right. About the break-in, phoney or not, it looks as though there's a connection, doesn't it? If there is, the boys ought to be able to clinch it. What time was the locking-up done on Saturday night?'

'I think Bert Heyward, the resident caretaker, is lying. He's supposed to start off at nine, but Saturday night wasn't normal, and he says he was a bit late. When I tried to pin him

56

down he got flustered and said he hadn't noticed the exact time, and that he might have been ten minutes behind schedule. I suggested that his wife might know, and he tried to put me off, saying everything was at sixes and sevens that night because of this Festival, as they call their old scholars' reunion. I reckon he was a good deal later.'

'Or possibly didn't bother to go up to the top floor at all?'

'In that case someone else locked and bolted the fire-escape door on the inside. Mrs. Bennett, the cleaner who found the body, opened it up herself this morning.'

'I'll put Toye on to him,' said Pollard. 'Assuming that Heyward did his round, is anyone else known to have been in the studio after seven on Saturday evening?'

'Two people, anyway. The art teacher,' Inspector Beakbane consulted his notes, 'a Miss Cartmell, and a Mr Torrance, some high-up to do with pictures. He'd come in to help choose some of the kids' work to go in for a competition. Miss Cartmell went home for the holidays yesterday, but we rang up and she's coming back this afternoon. Miss Renshaw gave me Mr Torrance's address : some gallery or other in London. Here we are—the Do-may-ni Gallery.'

'Yes, I know it,' Pollard said. 'It's off Regent Street. Smart work getting the girl back so quickly.' He sat for a few moments with hands thrust in his pockets and chair tilted back, staring out of the window at the park. 'A rum feature of this case,' he went on, 'is what Beatrice Baynes was doing after seven p.m. on Saturday. She must have had quite a tiring day for an old bird in the seventies, and then taken some buddies home for a drink, you say. You'd think she'd have been glad to get her feet up at home. But I simply can't believe she was murdered in her own place, and carted across a public road, past the Lodge, and right up the drive to the studio. Out of the question in daylight, and if it was done after dark, how did the murderer get into the studio? Unless he was in cahoots with Bert Heyward . . . As he lives on the premises, I suppose he could have gone up to the studio during Sunday or early on Monday and locked the fire-escape door then. Would he have the stamina for the job, or any possible motive?'

'Not the stamina, I shouldn't think. Bit weedy. He was in a Jap prison camp in the war, poor chap, Freeth says. As to motive, well, it doesn't seem likely, on the face of it, unless she'd found out something to his disadvantage and she was threatening to tell Miss Renshaw ... chaps that've been through what he must've do go off the deep end sometimes, and that's the truth.'

'Was she well-off?'

'Yes. Pretty warm, Freeth says. Lived quietly, but the lolly was there all right. Lots of it. My sergeant found her solicitor's address, too, by the way; Mr Yelland of Linbridge. He's a partner in an old-established firm : a very decent sort. I rang him, and said someone would be coming along.'

Inspector Beakbane passed over another sheet of paper.

'Handing it to me on a plate, aren't you? No, seriously, I'm dashed grateful to you for covering such a lot of ground. I'd better drop in on him at an early date, and find out who gets the lolly. It may turn out that the next-of-kin nephew's crying out for a bit of our attention. The report from our people on how he reacted to the news ought to come along this evening. I hope the pub where you've booked us in has got a night porter—come in!'

The door opened to admit Detective-Sergeant Toye. Although impassive he conveyed an air of subdued triumph.

'Perhaps you'd care to come up and take a look, sir?' he said to Pollard.

'What have you got?'

'The heel-marks, sir, just as you thought. Only traces : they've been walked over a good bit, and cigarette ash trodden in. But they're perfectly clear beside the table for about six inches, and again roughly in the middle of the room, say a couple of inches, and in a curve over in the corner, where she must've been swung round into the puppet theatre. Boyce has photographed the lot, and we've noted the measurements.'

'Nothing coming from either of the doors?'

'Not a sign, sir. I've been over every square inch.'

'We'd better give that table the full treatment. It looks as though she might have been knocked out beside it.'

'It's a fair headache, sir. Covered with paint stains, and what-have-you, and no end of junk stacked on it. I've ringed one or two stains which look a bit fresher. The fire-escape rail's one mass of superimposed palm prints, Strickland says.'

'Right,' said Pollard. 'Jolly good work. I'll be along when I've settled one or two things with the Inspector.'

Detective-Sergeant Toye withdrew.

'I'd better be getting along too, and putting in a report to the Super,' said Inspector Beakbane, getting up. 'The inquest'll be fixed by now. The Linbridge coroner always takes evidence of identity and adjourns, unless it's absolutely straightforward. Cuts both ways. See you later, then, or early tomorrow. This great barrack fair gets me down,' he added, looking round the magnificent room. 'Feel I want to search all these cubby-holes every time I come in. Lumme, what do girls want with all these books? You and I could teach 'em all they need to know without a single one, I bet!'

The two men grinned at each other.

'Decent picture, though,' said Pollard, going over to examine an excellent reproduction of Velasquez Infanta. 'My wife teaches at a College of Art, so I've picked up a bit.'

'Come off it,' said the Inspector. 'You're educated up to the place, you are, and I hope you enjoy it, that's all. I don't know one flaming picture from another—except that simpering kid in a blue bonnet by the door, and that's only because you London cops never found out who pinched the original from some museum or other.'

'Touché,' said Pollard.

They went out amicably.

After prolonged scrutiny of a small, irregular stain through a powerful lens, Pollard straightened himself up. He experienced the hunter's thrill at the first trace of a quarry's spoor.

'Blood, I think,' he said, 'and a minute bit of hair embedded in it. When you've done, Boyce, we'll get it up for the lab boys . . .'

He watched anxiously as Sergeant Toye carried out the delicate operation of removal, and sealed away the result in a sterilised container, the under-layer of his mind aware of the complexity and potential publicity of the case . . . the biggest job he'd handled on his own.

'What do you make of it, Strickland?' he asked, noticing that the young constable was bursting with a suppressed idea.

'It's how it comes to be just there, sir. There'd've been more of it if she'd fallen and cut her head open, and that would've been on the edge, surely? I was thinking maybe the murderer put down whatever he'd slogged her with, and the blood on that made the mark.'

'So was I,' said Pollard. 'Go up one. But where's our old friend the blunt instrument now?' He peered at the assorted objects on the table. 'You've been over all this lot, Strickland, I suppose?'

'Yes, sir. A lot of blurred old prints, and some clear fresh ones—the small ones, same that keeps cropping up. They look like a woman's.'

'The art teacher's, I expect. I'll get hers this evening; she's coming back. I'm afraid there's the heck of a lot of work ahead of us tonight.'

'You've helped me a lot,' Inspector Pollard said. 'I'm grateful to you for being so frank.'

'Well,' replied Helen Renshaw, 'the strained relations between Miss Baynes and myself were common knowledge. You would soon have got on to them.'

'Tell me something about what she was like as a person, apart from this obsession with the affairs of the School.'

Helen considered.

'Quite able. She had never been stretched by marriage or a

career and that was the root of the trouble, I think. She often reacted to any opposition with outbursts of temper, as frustrated people are apt to do, but they blew over quite soon and in a good mood she could be entertaining ... she had vitality. She was generous over money, on her own terms. She had plenty to spare, but I do know of several instances in which she gave away considerable sums anonymously.'

'What about this godchild, Miss Madge Thornton, who's had a collapse?'

To Pollard's surprise he sensed a sudden slight constraint in Helen Renshaw.

'Miss Thornton is one of our music mistresses,' she said smoothly. 'Not an inspiring teacher, but as she had been here some years when I arrived and had got the post through Miss Baynes, I decided it was the lesser evil to let her carry on. There were plenty of bigger issues I had to fight over. With regard to her collapse this morning, she unfortunately heard the news in a very brutal way, blurted out by the caretaker. She was already upset by her mother's death a week ago, and worried by Miss Baynes's continued absence, and the shock was obviously the last straw.'

'Quite,' agreed Pollard, feeling his way. 'Most unfortunate, as you say. Was she very devoted to Miss Baynes?'

'Oh, yes. She was often over at Applebys in her free time.'

'How did you feel about the relationship in view of the general situation?'

Helen shifted slightly in her chair.

'It was bound to present some difficulties,' she said. 'As you will see, Miss Thornton is rather lacking in confidence, and was dominated by Miss Baynes, who was disappointed in her, I think. I gather that she had paid for Miss Thornton's education—here and at college—and hoped that she would turn out a success.'

'I see. Miss Thornton was really a projection of herself, in which she encountered still further frustration.'

He noted Helen Renshaw's quick glance of approbation.

'Exactly,' she replied.

He made a show of consulting his notes.

'About your caretaker, Bert Heyward. Do you consider him a steady, reliable sort of chap?' Naturally, the exact time of locking-up on Saturday night is important.'

'He's been here for nine years, and I've never found him anything but reliable over his duties. He doesn't show much initiative or forcefulness, partly for health reasons, I think. He was a prisoner of war in Malaya, and has never really got over it. He may have been late in locking up on Saturday after all the unheaval, but I'm quite sure it was done eventually.'

No constraint on this issue, Pollard noted . . .

'You say Miss Baynes habitually snooped on everyone, and wrote letters of complaint to the Governors and yourself, trying to discredit your régime. Was Heyward one of the sufferers?'

'Not very often. She had less opportunity of snooping on him. The gardeners were sitting targets : she couldn't—or wouldn't—understand that we can't keep up the grounds as they were kept fifty years ago.'

'She had unrestricted access to the grounds, I suppose?'

'Oh, yes. All O.Ms have, and to some extent to the buildings, but they are expected to use their discretion in term-time, of course.'

He turned over another page.

'I shall be seeing Miss Cartmell after this. Can you give me any line on her?'

Without hesitation Helen gave him a full account of the circumstances of Ann's appointment, and its successful outcome.

Interesting, he thought, as he listened. She's anxious about this one, for some reason, but not definitely scared as she is about the Thornton woman. He cast about in his mind, and decided on a direct approach.

'Was Miss Cartmell one of the chief snoopees?' he asked. Helen Renshaw looked up quickly, half-smiling at the absurdity. 'If you're convinced that she had nothing whatever to do with the murder, as you clearly are, the more you tell me about her the better. I shall be able to question her much more intelligently and worry her less. Contrary to popular belief the police aren't out for an arrest at any price, you know, Miss Renshaw. A wrong one in this case could easily put paid to my own chances of promotion.'

To his relief, this technique was successful. He listened attentively to an account of Beatrice Baynes's particular hostility to the changes in the art department and her various attempts to discredit Ann Cartmell, culminating in the scene at the Annual General Meeting on Saturday.

'You will find her rather rattled, of course,' Helen Renshaw concluded, 'and very agitated in case she can't get off to America on Thursday. After all, a scholarship of this sort is a big thing to anyone in her position.'

'Naturally. Of course I can't promise anything at this stage—I don't even know when they've fixed the inquest—but we'll do our best for her, under the circumstances. Just one more question. This Mr Torrance : has he any official connection with Meldon? It strikes me as a little unusual that anyone of his standing should bother about schoolgirls' entries for a competition.'

'Nothing official,' Helen replied. 'He's simply continued to take an interest in the art department since he found us Miss Cartmell. It sounds rather ungrateful when he does so much for us, but he's a conceited man, and gets a kick out of the success of his protegées. I'm quite aware that we're simply a means to an end.'

'Is Miss Cartmell?'

'I don't think she's sufficiently mature. I suspect she is flattered by his interest and has a romantic passion for him.'

'Is it reciprocated?'

'I think it's most unlikely. Mr Torrance is a highly-sophisticated gentleman.'

Inspector Pollard smiled as he put his papers together.

'Now I really have done. Thank you once more for all your help.'

To Detective-Sergeant Toye and his assistants, busy at Applebys, the trail of the intruder was as obvious as that of a bull in a china-shop. From the clumsy attempts to obliterate footprints outside the kitchen window, by way of the trail of inadequately-wiped and overlooked fingerprints from the larder to the bureau in the dining-room, his progress stood out like a sore thumb, as Detective-Constable Strickland put it.

'Blooming amateur,' he commented, plying his insufflator.

Sergeant Toye agreed, but as he investigated the bureau he mulled over certain odd features of the break-in. The theft of food was usual enough, but the bee-line for this one particular drawer in the bureau was highly suggestive. The others hadn't even been touched, let alone wiped. The fingerprints were on the shopping-list which he'd retrieved from the floor. Unless the thief was familiar with deceased's habits, it was odd, to say the least of it, that he'd made straight for the right drawer, the second one down, without even trying the others. As to the key, of course, anyone standing by the bureau could see into the jug . . .

No prints on the other things in the drawer. Sergeant Toye, examining a cheque book, saw that fifty pounds had been drawn to Self on the previous Friday. There was no trace of the money. Going upstairs he encountered Detective-Constable Strickland and Blair coming out of Beatrice Baynes's bedroom, carrying their equipment, and learnt that there were no signs of the intruder having entered it. After a brief search Pollard discovered a handbag of very good quality in a drawer. Among other things it contained four pounds in a note-case, and loose change in a purse . . . I don't believe she'd run through forty-six pounds or more between Friday and going to that meeting on Saturday, he mused. If she was going to spend at that rate, she'd've drawn out more. There had been cheque stubs for what looked like monthly household bills . . .

As he scrutinised the room, he noticed a pair of shoes lying on the floor in front of a chair. Smart of the boys to have printed these . . . Just the same size as the ones on the corpse, but newer and smarter-looking. It looked as though she'd changed into an older and more comfortable pair when she came in. Perhaps her feet were hurting her, poor old girl.

He went downstairs to the dining-room again, reflecting that the odds were that somebody had lifted a nice little wad of notes very neatly, and sitting down at the bureau he studied some bank statements, raising his eyebrows. The whole house smelt of money, of course. Not the easy-come, easy-go sort, but a big, steady income, and always plenty in the kitty. The old style : nothing showy, but everything of the best. Replacing the contents of the drawer, he went into the adjoining drawing-room. Silver everywhere, period stuff if he knew anything about it, and a smashing little clock . . . It wouldn't have taken a split second to lift that as well as the snuff-box the daily woman said had gone . . . The front-door bell rang, and he went to let in his superior officer.

'I've rung through to Linbridge for a car, to get Strickland and Boyce on to a London train,' Tom Pollard said as he came hastily into the house. 'The sooner all these dabs are sorted out and checked up the better. One of the most urgent things is to find out if the ones down here are in the studio lot too. Tell them to finish up as soon as they can, and then I'd like to go through the place with you.'

They progressed from the kitchen and larder to dining-room, and stood in front of the bureau while Sergeant Toye summarised his findings and deductions.

'You're on to something there, Toye.' Pollard was invariably generous to his subordinates. 'Whoever made a dead set for that one drawer knew that Beatrice Baynes would have put the lolly there, if "Bank" on the shopping-list meant she'd just cashed a cheque.'

'Someone who pinched the money and then thought up the faked break-in?'

'You know, Toye, I'm not sure that break-in was a complete fake.'

'I don't get you there, sir.'

'Well, take the question of the grub. Inspector Beakbane says the daily woman is a highly respectable local body who did most of the cooking, so she'd know pretty well what was in the larder. She swears that a small loaf and a big slab of cheese have gone, and half a veal and ham pie she made on Saturday morning. Beatrice Baynes wasn't in to lunch, remember. A bottle of milk's gone too. It's a bit thorough for a fake. Looks as though somebody was genuinely hungry.'

'It doesn't hang together somehow, does it? I mean anyone who'd know the ways of the house all that well isn't likely to need to pinch grub.'

'The person who seems to have spent a good bit of time over here is Miss Baynes's goddaughter, the lady who's collapsed and mustn't have any visitors by doctor's orders.'

'Bit odd, that collapse, don't you think, sir? A godmother's not like a proper relative.'

'Odd is the operative word for the whole case, to date,' replied Chief Inspector Pollard thoughtfully.

Six

'9.0 p.m. Start Locking-up Round.'
List of Caretaker's duties for the summer term

SERGEANT TOYE, WISHING to approach the Heywards' flat unobserved, took a circuitous route round School Wing and through the gardens. Behind the Hall he came upon what appeared to be the former stables. An iron staircase led up to living-quarters over them. He noted that the windows were clean and the curtains bright and fresh. A vase of flowers stood on one of the sills. He ascended quietly and pressed a bell-push. There was a vibrant burr, silence, and sounds of muffled altercation. He leant against the rail, whistling gently, an unobtrusive figure in a blue suit. His round pale face and horn-rimmed spectacles gave him a usefully innocuous aspect, partly belied by the shrewd eyes behind the lenses.

A door slammed inside. A second later the front-door was flung open and a woman came out, half closing it behind her. She looked about forty, a plump, rosy country-woman with a militant expression. Toye recognised the maternal type on the defensive.

'Police, aren't you?' she demanded, 'whatever clothes you've got on? Well, then, let me put you right before you come inside, seeing as we can't keep you out, and start bullying my husband about what time he locked up Saturday night. That Beakbane upset him proper this afternoon. He can't take it. No more could you, if you'd been taken by the bloody Japs and bin in one o' those camps and half-starved. His stummick's never got properly right since. He'll tell you five different times in five minutes, he'll be that flustered. If you want to know when he locked up, ask me. Twenty to ten it was when he got up from supper. Nine's the time in term-time, and 'tweren't term no longer, and we didn't sit down to our bit of supper till close on nine, what with all the clearing up in School. Miss Renshaw wouldn't've expected Bert to do his round before we had a bite to eat, seeing he'd bin on duty since seven in the morning. Considerate lady, Miss Renshaw is, and always reasonable. And if you don't believe me, ask Maud Hinks, the lady as found Applebys broke into. She'd bin helping too, and came up for a bit of supper along of us. Not that I'd say Bert was late if I weren't speaking the truth, knowing it's only commonsense. And if anyone thinks my Bert's mixed up in the murder, they want their heads looking at. He's that soft he can't even kill a spider.'

She paused for breath.

'We know all about your husband's war service,' said Sergeant Toye tranquilly. 'Here's my official card . . . And we've already heard from Miss Renshaw what a reliable pair you both are. What I've come round for is to ask for a bit of help in fixing times. It doesn't matter in the least when your husband locked up, so long as we know the time as near as possible. You see, no one could get in from the outside once the outer doors had been locked, could they? May I come in and have a word with him?'

Mollified, she let him into the flat.

'We're in the middle of our tea. You'd better come through to the kitchen . . . Maybe you could do with a cup yourself.'

Bert Heyward, looking white and strained, sat hunched over a plate of ham and eggs. He glanced up nervously and sketched the movement of rising.

'Don't disturb yourself, Mr Heyward,' said Toye, sitting down opposite to him. 'Sorry to call at such an inconvenient time, but we've been over at Applebys trying to link up the break-in there with what happened up here, and it's important to get times clear. I hadn't expected you'd've locked up so early on a day like Saturday.'

Bert paused, an impaled piece of ham halfway to his mouth, and stared at Toye. 'Early? Nine's my time. I was late: forty minutes. I got proper muddled with that chap badgering me, but what the wife's says's right. It was her and Maud Hinks as told me to get crackin'.'

' 'Tweren't term no longer,' reiterated Mrs Heyward stoutly. 'There's a bit more ham and plenty of eggs if you could do with a bite, Sergeant.'

Inspector Pollard often remarked that Toye was a kind of human chameleon with a remarkable facility for blending into an environment, an aptitude which stood him in good stead on this occasion. Within a short time Bert began to relax, and the atmosphere became positively sociable. The excellent ham and eggs were followed by homemade cake and jam. Eating heartily and complimenting his hostess on her cooking, Toye brought the conversation round to Saturday by remarking that they'd left London in such a hurry there had only been time for a sandwich. It looked like being a puzzling case with no end of work . . . Unconsciously, the Heywards began to assume the role of helpers.

Festival was one of the hardest days in the year, he learnt. Not that Mrs Heyward didn't get extra for helping in the kitchen, but all that washing-up three times over was killing in spite of the machines . . . Yes, Bert finished up earlier, as soon as he and Jock Eccles had cleared away the extra seatings round the hard courts, and taken in all the odd chairs people brought outside and then walked off and left, without a thought as to how they were to get back. Then he'd got the Hall to put to rights from the meeting. Always had a good look for cigarette ends : you couldn't credit how careless some folk were, for all they'd been to a posh school. Yes, they always enjoyed a bit of hot supper at the end of the day, but Bert knew she wouldn't get home till round about half-past eight, so he'd got on his bike and gone down to the Plough for a beer. That would be about ten to seven. He'd sat yarning with the chaps and come away again at quarter-past eight. He'd noticed the time, thinking about his supper . . . Yes, he'd passed Applebys about twenty past the hour . . . No, he hadn't seen Miss Baynes about, but Miss Thornton was coming away . . . She was often over there to see Miss Baynes, who was her godmother, they'd been told. Shy, Miss Thornton was. Never much to say for herself, but a nice lady. No wonder she'd gone into a fit when she'd heard . . . Bert was that upset when he got to Miss Renshaw he never noticed Miss Thornton and Maud Hinks. As for Mrs Bennett, she said she'd never get over it to her dying day, a corpse tumbling out on top of her like that . . . Yes, it was a quarter after ten when Bert got back—a fifteen-hour day.

Toye made a mental note that Bert's arrival and departure at the Plough could probably be confimed, and skillfully led the conversation to the subject of Beatrice Baynes. The Heywards agreed that she was a nosey-parkering old besom who behaved as though the place belonged to her. Always poking about the grounds and prying into what wasn't her business. What Jock Eccles said about her you couldn't hardly repeat, but then he'd had her living on his door-step, you might say. No, she hadn't been much bother to them, Bert's work being more indoors. Not that there wasn't a good side to her, same as there was to most. Maud Hinks who worked over at Applebys . . .

No great animosity there, thought Toye, unless they're a pair of first-class actors, which I don't believe. Still, you never quite know with these war victim chaps . . . He'd got to call on Maud Hinks, he told them, to check up one or two points about the break-in . . .

With the loan of Bert's bicycle as a crowning achievement, he set off shortly afterwards for Trill, timing himself carefully. The noise emanating from the Plough and the cars outside, some with London number-plates, suggested that the village and the Press were in active conference. He decided to leave the Plough until the following morning, and went on to Number Two, Church Row.

Maud Hinks was at home, and received him with the manner of one well-accustomed to interviews with the police. Toye, with his usual attention to detail, asked her a few unnecessary questions about the larder at Applebys, and passed easily to the events of Saturday evening at Meldon. Without the slightest hesitation she confirmed that Bert hadn't gone off to lock up until twenty to ten. She'd chipped him herself, saying he'd get the sack if he sat there on his backside much longer instead of getting on with his job . . .

Mounting Bert Hayward's bicycle once more, Sergeant Toye rode back to Meldon, noting that it took him just under five minutes to reach Applebys.

Driving back to Meldon through the afternoon, Ann Cartmell's dominant feeling was sheer exasperation. What on earth was the point of dragging her back? There was nothing about the studio Jean Forrest and Bert Heyward couldn't tell the police . . . She wondered once more what sort of fatal accident could possibly have happened up there? Could somebody have monkeyed with the pottery kiln in the storeroom, and been electrocuted? Anyway, it was switched off all right : the last firing had been a fortnight ago . . . The Inspector who had rung her up had been so stupidly cagey. She still didn't know who had been killed. Surely not Mrs Bennett who always did the cleaning? She'd never have touched the kiln, anyway . . . she was terrified of it!

The spell of fine weather was breaking up. After ten days of sparkling sunshine the dark green foliage of trees against a dull grey sky depressed Ann, sensitive as she always was to light and colour. Even the prospect of Thursday seemed to have lost some of its power to thrill. Suddenly her mind went taut as an alarming idea occurred to her. They couldn't keep her from leaving, just to give evidence at an inquest, could they? Surely not, when it was absolutely obvious she'd nothing to tell them? Seriously disturbed by the thought, she drove on mechanically, completely forgetting that she had meant to stop somewhere for tea.

Turning in at Meldon just after six, she pulled up sharply, astonished to see that the drive gates were shut. Almost at once Jock Eccles came out of the Lodge and proceeded to open them for her with an air of portentous importance, wearing a suit instead of his working clothes.

'Why on earth are the gates shut, Jock?' Ann asked, leaning out of the window as he closed them again behind her car.

'Why, tae keep oot unauthorrised pairsons. Journaleests an' sic.'

'Journalists?' she echoed blankly.

'Aye. 'Tis a case of murder, ye ken.'

'But who's been murdered?' she gasped, the blood ebbing from her face.

'Yon,' he said, with an expressive backward jerk of his head towards Applebys. 'Have ye no' hairrd? She came tummlin' oot o' yon wee puppet the-ayter in the stujio with a great dunt in her heid . . .'

As Ann walked shakily into the entrance hall of Old House a tall man in plain clothes came out of the library and spoke to her.

'I expect you're Miss Ann Cartmell, aren't you?' he said pleasantly, 'I'm Chief Detective-Inspector Pollard of New Scotland Yard, and in charge of the enquiry. We're very sorry to have to bring you back. If you're not too tired, perhaps we could have a talk right away?'

Five minutes later she faced him across the table in one of the library bays, and found herself surprised that he looked so ordinary. Rather big-built and loose-knit, fairish and with a nice, unremarkable face. It wasn't until he began to talk that she sensed a kind of completely assured authoritativeness about him. Ann eyed him uneasily, answering his questions about her position in the School rather breathlessly. He asked her if she knew what had happened.

'Only what Jock said as I came in. Jock Eccles, at the Lodge.'

'What did Jock say?'

'He said that Miss Baynes had been—been murdered. And that she was—was in the puppet theatre up in the studio.' She shivered uncontrollably, and turned her face away.

'Have you had any tea?' Pollard asked unexpectedly.

Ann shook her head. He got up and went out of the room, returning within a few minutes to say that some tea would be arriving shortly. He began to talk easily about the library pictures and his wife's work as an art lecturer. When a knock came at the door he got up again and took in the tray. Ann murmured thanks and poured out a cup of tea with a hand that shook, conscious of being observed.

'Try two or three lumps of sugar,' he suggested. 'You've had a nasty shock. And try not to mind answering a few questions.'

She looked up quickly and burst into speech.

'I don't. It isn't that. It's that I'm so worried about Thursday, in case I'm not allowd to go. I'm flying out to New York, to take up a scholarship at a summer school. My seat on the plane's booked . . . It means absolutely everything to me—I don't know a thing about all this.'

'Somebody's been murdered, you know, Miss Cartmell. Death's very final : much more so than being a few days late for a summer school.'

'I know you think I'm completely self-centred,' she said, with an agitated gesture, ruffling up her hair. 'I'm not, really. Of course I'm sorry that such a ghastly thing's happened to anyone. But I'm not going to pretend I'm sorry Miss Baynes is dead. She loathed me. She's been absolutely bitchy to me ever since I came. She insulted me and my work in front of the A.G.M. on Saturday, just because I didn't teach on prehistoric lines, like the woman who was here before me, and was a friend of hers. She was always snooping and trying to make trouble for me.'

'Don't you think we ought to try to find her murderer as a matter of principle?' Pollard asked, deciding to ignore this lavish display of motive on Anne's part.

'Well, yes, I suppose so. I can't help you, though.'

'I think you may be able to help me quite a lot when you know all the facts.'

He gave her a brief account of the results of the enquiry up to date, and watched her eyes widen with horror.

'Do you mean she—she might have been there all the time? When I was talking to Mr Torrance? . . . When the *girls* were there?'

'It's possible, but by no means certain. The police surgeon has only made a tentative estimate of the time of death so far. Now, Miss Cartmell, without realising it at the time you may possibly have noticed something of great importance. I want to go through the whole evening, from seven o'clock onwards.'

The shock of realising the intersection of the tragedy and her own actions cleared Ann's mind, and she began to answer Pollard's questions clearly and sensibly. No, she had not been to the studio on returning from the staff house, but gone straight to the dining-room where people were gathering for supper. She had deliberately chosen a seat facing the window in order to watch for Mr Torrance.

'Did you notice the time of his arrival?' asked Pollard, taking out his note-book.

'It must have been just on eight. I remember noticing it was five to, and then someone spoke to me and distracted my attention. When I looked out again Mr Torrance was just going in at the door—the one at the foot of the stairs going up to the studio.'

'How long was it before you joined him?'

'About two minutes, I should think. Just after I saw him Miss Renshaw got up and said grace—the short Latin one. I slipped out through one of the french doors, and ran across the Quad and upstairs.'

'You seem to have been in a great hurry.'

The note of amusement in his voice riled her.

'It was extremely good of Mr Torrance to come in at all. I

74

didn't want to keep him waiting out of common politeness. After all, he *is* somebody.'

'Quite. When you got up to the studio he was already there, I take it?'

'Of course he was. He was looking at the paintings, which I'd got mounted on screens for him. He . . .' Her voice trailed off, and she stared at Pollard incredulously. 'You can't—you really can't imagine he can have killed Miss Baynes in two minutes? It's ludicrous. He couldn't possibly.'

'Not possibly. The suggestion is yours. Did Mr Torrance know Miss Baynes?'

'I shouldn't think he'd ever heard of her,' replied Ann sulkily, conscious of having made a fool of herself.

'You yourself had never mentioned her hostility towards you?'

She seized the opportunity of hitting back.

'I shouldn't bore a man like Mr Torrance with petty school gossip.'

'So when you had arrived in the studio,' Pollard went on, maddeningly unruffled, 'you both got down to the job of selecting the competition entries. Now I want you to think very carefully, Miss Cartmell. Did you register anything in the least noteworthy while this was going on? A movement on the fire-escape, for example?'

A trace of anxiety passed over Ann's face. Could anyone have been listening?

'I don't remember noticing anything,' she told him, after a fractional pause.

He pressed her again, urging her to think herself back into the scene, and watched a subtle change come over her. A kind of sleekness.

'No,' she said, a slight tinge of complacency in her voice. 'I noticed nothing.'

'When the paintings had been chosen, did you and Mr Torrance go down together?'

'Yes. He had offered to take the parcel back to London for

me, and I had to collect the entry form from the secretary's office.'

'Did you notice the time as you went down?'

'No, not then. But it was just before twenty to nine when he drove off from the front-door, so it must have been about half-past eight.'

'It took you nearly half-an-hour to choose the paintings?'

'We had some personal conversation after we finished,' she told him rather grandly. 'Mr Torrance was one of my referees for the scholarship.'

Personal conversation my foot, thought Pollard. Advanced necking, if I know anything . . . He glanced through his notes.

'Did you return to the studio after Mr Torrance had left? I think you mentioned some girls just now?'

'Yes,' Ann replied. 'Two Sixth-formers were waiting for me in the Quad, and offered to come up and help. There wasn't much to do, but I thought Bert Heyward would be starting to lock up quite soon and was quite glad to have them. Their names are Nicola Stainsby and Rachel Rivers, if you want to know.'

'Were the three of you together all the time in the studio? Try to remember what you all did. For instance, did anyone go near the puppet theatre?'

She repressed a shudder.

'No, thank goodness. It's right over in the corner, out of the way. We don't use it much—only in the winter terms. The girls folded the screens and put them over in the opposite corner, and sorted a lot of waste paper, while I collected my own gear to take home. Then they helped me carry it down to my car, in the car-park. If you want to know the time, I can tell you exactly. It struck nine as we went across the Quad, and I remember thinking I'd just done it before locking-up time.'

'And then you drove off to the staff house. Did you go straight there?'

'Yes, except for stopping in the drive to offer someone a

lift. A Miss Thornton, one of the staff, who'd been at supper.'

'Did she accept?'

'No. She said she was on her way to Applebys : Miss Baynes was her godmother.'

'You didn't by any chance see Miss Baynes or anyone else as you went past the house?'

'Not Miss Baynes, but now I do remember seeing a man coming out of the porch, and wondering casually who it was.'

'Can you describe him?' Pollard struggled to keep the excitement out of his voice.

Ann shut her eyes and tried to concentrate.

'I really hardly took him in. It was just a glimpse as I began to accelerate. I've got a sort of impression that he was quite young, with brown hair and wearing a green shirt. Rather hikerish.'

Pollard painstakingly established the circumstances of her arrival at the staff house, and the communal packing of the young members of the staff ending with a brew, as she called it, about half-past eleven.

'Well,' he said, 'I think that's all for the moment, Miss Cartmell. Tomorrow morning I'm going to ask you to help me in a way that may cost you rather an effort, but I feel sure you'll manage it. I want you to come up to the studio with me, and I don't want to tell you why until we get there.'

Ann swallowed.

'There isn't . .' she began.

'Of course not. Everything is quite normal, except that the puppet theatre has been taken away, and my fingerprint expert has made rather a mess.'

'All right,' she said, with the sudden resilience of youth. 'I suppose I'll have to, sooner or later. I wonder what Miss Renshaw will do?'

Suddenly she was back in the thick of her immediate anxieties, and looked at him beseechingly.

'I can go home afterwards, can't I? I've got to pack. I *shall* be able to go on Thursday, shan't I?' she pleaded desperately.

'I can't answer that question this evening. No one wants to delay you unnecessarily. In any case, we shall help you all we can.'

Pollard escorted her to the door and watched her crossing the hall, a kind of despairing tautness in her bearing . . . A figure stirred in a corner, and Sergeant Toye rose and came over and joined him.

'Looks as though the brutal police have been grilling her, doesn't it?' said Pollard as they went into the library. 'She's in love : that's the trouble. With this bloke Torrance who got her the scholarship to America. She's in a tiz in case she's kept back to give evidence. It doesn't seem to have occurred to her that she might be a suspect herself. She just isn't interested in the murder, even if it did happen in the room where she works. Actually, she doesn't seem to have been alone there for a single moment from about six o'clock onwards. Did you call in at the sickbay?'

'Nothing doing tonight, sir. The patient's not to be questioned till tomorrow morning—doctor's orders. Badly shocked, the nurse said.'

'Let's pack up here for tonight, then, and go along to our pub in Linbridge and get something to eat. Unless you wangled a meal out of the Heywards while you were pumping the poor boobs?'

'Ham and eggs,' Toye told him sedately. 'Done to a turn, and home-made cake to follow. And one or two useful bits of information.'

'You can keep those until I've fed. I've got mental indigestion already.'

Seven

'I give and bequeath to the Governors of Meldon School the sum of ten thousand pounds free of legacy duty, subject to certain conditions' . . .

Last Will and Testament of Beatrice Agatha Baynes

THE WHITE HORSE at Linbridge was an eighteenth-century coaching inn which reflected the leisurely tempo of life in the small town. There was nothing functional about its lay-out or décor : it suggested, in fact, a rather shabby private house which had somehow become involved in the hotel business. Pollard's room had a curious assortment of miscellaneous furniture, including a basket chair, an immense frowsty wardrobe in dark oak, and limp net curtains. Descending to the dining-room he found a turkey carpet and chairs with well-worn leather seats. Only a few of the tables were occupied, and he wondered absently if the place could possibly pay. He was led to one by an elderly waitress dressed in black with a muslin apron, and ordered a steak and lager. A sabbath calm descended, broken only by distant voices behind the service door.

When the food eventually arrived it was unexpectedly good. Old-fashioned domestic cooking, he thought, propping a newspaper against a monumental cruet stand, and trying to get his mind off the case. He ate with enjoyment, following up the steak with cherry pie and cream, but deciding against possibly dubious coffee. As far as he could see, no one was showing the slightest interest in him as yet.

On leaving the dining-room he went in search of Sergeant Toye. The latter was in a corner of the bar with an evening paper, and showed him a short paragraph giving the bare facts of the discovery of the body. They made for the writing-room, a small bleak place on the first floor. It smelt unmistakably of dry rot. Pollard flung open the window which looked on to a blank wall, and ejected a number of dead flies which were lying on the sill. The writing table bore an unsullied blotter, an ink-stand with dried-up ink and one pen with an encrusted nib. Remarking that it didn't look as though they'd be disturbed this side of doomsday, Toye fetched a chair from the passage, and the two men got down to work.

Jane Pollard called her husband a compulsive tabulator. When on a case his invariable method was to get the results of fieldwork on to paper as quickly as possible. In this way the confused mass of statements and impressions which, in the raw, merely gave him mental indigestion, was reduced to assimilable columns of related facts. These lists, made on sheets from pads which he carried round with him for the purpose, were known to his colleagues and subordinates as Pollard's washing bills, and had become a standing joke. As a case progressed they were duly amended or rewritten. Sergeant Toye, trained in the technique, was now equally addicted to it. On this occasion they pooled their information and proceeded to build up a detailed timetable with marginal comments :

SATURDAY

7.05 p.m.	Beatrice Baynes sees off friends from Applebys.	Confirmed.
7.18 p.m.	Ann Cartmell arrives at Meldon and goes straight to dining-room.	Unconfirmed.
7.30 p.m.	Festival Supper.	
7.59 p.m.	Clive Torrance goes into School Wing.	Could he have arrived earlier?

8.01 p.m. approx.	Ann Cartmell joins him in studio.	
8.20 p.m.	Bert Heyward sees Madge Thornton leaving Applebys.	? Confirm by Thornton.
8.30 p.m. approx.	Ann Cartmell and Clive Torrance come down from studio and collect form from office.	? Confirm by Secretary.
8.38 p.m. approx.	Torrance drives off.	? Confirm by Secretary.
8.41 p.m.	Cartmell returns to studio with two girls.	? Confirm by girls.
8.59 p.m.	Cartmell and girls leave studio.	? Confirm by girls.
9.02 p.m.	Cartmell offers lift to Thornton in drive.	? Confirm by Thornton.
9.03 p.m.	Cartmell sees man in porch of Applebys.	
9.06 p.m. approx.	Cartmell arrives at Staff House and packs with friends until brew-up at 11.30 p.m. approx.	?Confirm by friends.
9.50 p.m.	Heyward locks fire-escape door of studio on inside, and landing door on outside.	Unconfirmed.

The two men sat smoking in silence, contemplating the time-table.

'Reactions?' suggested Pollard presently, and they began to make jottings independently, with long pauses for thought. Apart from an occasional passing step and a distant clashing of pots and pans the little room was completely silent. Faint smells of cooking came wafting in at the window. Finally they exchanged notes, and after discussion drew up a second list:

Madge Thornton : Seen leaving Applebys at 8.20 p.m., and going there by her own admission just after 9 p.m., but otherwise unaccounted for. Why did she make two visits to Applebys within an hour?

Ann Cartmell and Clive Torrance : Alone in studio from 8.01 to 8.30 approx. Possibility of A.C. paying it an earlier visit before supper, and C.T. during supper, using the fire-escape entrance, which cannot be seen from the dining-room.

Bert Heyward : Admits being in studio about 9.50 p.m. when he locked up. It would be useful to get evidence other than his wife's that the locking-up round took its normal time and course.

Person(s) Unknown : The studio was empty and accessible from School Wing and the fire-escape for considerable periods of time :
  7.05—7.59 approx.
  8.30—8.41 approx.
  8.59—9.50 approx.

Also accessible at any time during the night from Old House to anyone knowing where the key of the connecting door(s) was kept.

Toye picked up the sheet of paper and stared at it. Pollard swore suddenly.

'This looks like being one hell of a case, doesn't it? Wide open as far as opportunity goes, and not a whiff of a motive so far.'

'Must have been a motive, cutting out a homicidal maniac dodging around, or Bert Heyward having a brainstorm.'

'Too right. Well, let's take the usual ones. Financial gain. Who benefits? Only the solicitor chap can tell us for sure, but we can make a few guesses. What about this great-nephew who seems to be the next-of and only kin? Could he be the man Miss Cartmell saw coming away from Applebys just after nine? Mr George Baynes will certainly have to be interviewed about his ploys on Saturday evening. Then we seem to hear an awful lot about this godchild of Miss Baynes, Madge Thornton, and she might have been down for something in the will. Her mother died recently, and perhaps an allowance has stopped.'

'Teachers do pretty well these days,' objected Toye. 'More likely she was helping her mother.'

'If you know a better 'ole than conjecture at the moment, old son, lead me to it.'

'I'll try a bit of my own, sir. What about the school? Wouldn't deceased have left it something handsome, seeing she was so nuts about the place?'

'You mean the headmistress or one of the Governors might have done her in to get some money for new buildings? Beakbane rather favoured a case against Miss Renshaw : he's got traumatic memories of his schooldays. Ingenious, Toye, and theoretically possible under opportunity, but would it have been the unpremeditated affair this looks like? Let's try the sex motive.'

'Torrance and Cartmell?'

'Yes. Miss Baynes decides to take an evening stroll, drops in at the studio, and surprises them in an advanced embrace. She threatens to tell all, and Torrance kills her. Cartmell suggests the puppet theatre as a handy disposal unit. Unconvincing, I'm afraid, don't you think?'

'Well, yes, sir. Not a situation that would lead to a murder these days, especially with people in a good position like this Mr Torrance, even if he's a married man. Even if Miss Cartmell got the sack, she'd find a new job fast enough, teachers being so scarce.'

'Absolutely sound. And I'm convinced that girl knows nothing whatever about the murder. She's amazingly naïve in some respects, and she'd've given herself away twenty times over when I questioned her, especially if she was trying to cover up for her boyfriend. Of course, Torrance could have done the job without her knowing anything about it. Suppose he arrived at 7.35, and went up to the studio by the fire-escape, which can't be seen from the dining-room. He would have had plenty of time to commit the murder, hide away the body, go out the way he came, and turn up in the Quad at the time Miss Cartmell expected him. But how did he know Miss Baynes was going to be there? If they'd made an appointment, it would have been at Applebys, surely? And what about motive?'

'Might be something going a long way back,' Toye suggested.

'Well, if it is, we've bloody well got to unearth it, that's all ... What's your considered opinion of this Heyward chap?'

'Much what yours is about Miss Cartmell, sir. But psychological grounds aren't factual evidence, and you can't rule out mental instability altogether. Suppose, as you were saying just now, deceased went for a stroll, only later — say just before nine. She'd see the locking-up hadn't been done, and could've gone up and sat in the studio to catch Heyward out when he did turn up. Maybe threaten to report him. He might have gone for her in a sort of black-out.'

'What seems so unlikely to me is that an old girl like Miss Baynes would be gallivanting round as late as that, after the sort of day she'd had. And this applies even more strongly to any idea of her turning up somehow after locking-up, and being murdered by somebody getting through from the rest of the school. All that strikes me as fantastic.'

Toye agreed.

'All the same,' he said, 'there are still the earlier times when the studio was empty, as far as we know. Leaving Mr Torrance out of it, she could have gone for a stroll during the supper, say, and surprised a casual thief up there, who hit out and killed her without meaning to. After all, someone did break into Applebys.'

84

'The hell they did! That break-in bothers me as much as anything in the case. On the face of it, there surely must be a connection with the murder, but when you start trying to work it out you're up against one snag after another. I ask you, would a chap who'd just got away with about fifty quid and a dollop of grub go wandering about the school afterwards? Or if he'd just killed an old woman who'd chanced on him up in the studio, would he be likely to hang around a few hundred yards away, and try his hand at a spot of housebreaking? Then there's the decidedly phoney touch about the break-in itself : the theft of the grub and the theft of the money don't match up.' Pollard stubbed out a cigarette and sat frowning, his chair tilted and his legs straight out in front of him.

'Do you think there's any chance of something a bit more definite about the time of death?' asked Toye.

'Not much. Not in court, that is. We might get an unofficial opinion. Well, let's push round to the station before we go and see the solicitor. I shall get claustrophobia if I stay in this undersized morgue much longer.'

Inspector Beakbane was off duty, and the Scotland Yard men were received by Superintendent Martin of the Linbridge Constabulary. The Super was a tall, cadaverous man with a hooked nose and hooded eyes, suggesting a large bird of prey. Distant at first, he responded to Pollard's request to run over the latest developments with him, and listened attentively. He remarked that there was no sense in overlapping, and that the most useful thing that the Linbridge Force could do was to trace the man seen coming out of Applebys on Saturday evening. A pity there were so many people about on Saturday with a big affair on at the school : a stranger was less likely to attract attention. Still, they could do their best. The Inspector would want to know about the inquest. It was fixed for twelve noon the following day, and they could count on its being adjourned after identity had been established. And would he ring this number at Scotland Yard, and ask for Detective-Constable Longman . . . ?

Pollard knew Longman, a keen and promising youngster recently seconded to the C.I.D. Waiting for his call to go through, he surmised correctly that he had been given the job of contacting George Baynes. Longman apologised for the delay in reporting back to Linbridge, explaining that he had gone to the address given him only to find that Mr Baynes was out at his job and nobody knew where he worked. It was a scruffy sort of place off the Edgware Road, one of those tall terrace houses gone to seed, and now let out in single rooms called service flatlets . . . Pollard's interest was sharply alerted.

Longman had eventually found a Mrs Bragg who lived in the basement and did the cleaning. She'd been hostile at first, but on hearing that he'd come to contact Mr Baynes about a family bereavement, thawed and became quite chatty, wondering if it was his rich old auntie down in the country who was going to leave him a fortune one of these days. He, Longman, got the impression that George was a favourite with her, and tried to lead her on a bit. It seemed that he was a lively young spark with a hole in his pocket, but always a joke and a pleasant word for her, even if he did leave his room in a shocking mess.

Returning at half-past five, Longman had waited about until he saw a young man come along the street and go into the house. He'd followed him up to his room before Mrs Bragg had a chance to get talking. On being shown a police card Mr Baynes had looked decidedly scared, more than folk usually did. Longman had then broken the news of the murder. He was convinced that Mr Baynes's immediate reaction was genuine incredulity and distress. Then, quite suddenly, he'd seemed to get panicky, and was clearly greatly relieved to hear that he was not called upon to go down to identify the body. On being asked casually when he had last seen Miss Baynes, he'd said without hesitation that it was at Whitsun,

86

when he'd stayed with her. Then he'd asked a lot of questions about the time and place of the murder, which Longman had been unable to answer.

Asked for a description of George Baynes, the constable said that he was average height or a bit below, lightly built, with a narrow face, sticking-out ears and brown hair. Pollard congratulated Longman on his report, and asked to be put through to his Chief's office. Here he made arrangements for George to be shadowed, and for appointments to be made for himself to see both George and Clive Torrance during the latter part of the following day. Reinvigorated, he sprang to his feet and hurried out to the police car where Sergeant Toye awaited him.

Mr Yelland of Yelland, Yelland, Frayne and King, Solicitors, occupied a pleasant house on the outskirts of Linbridge, and escorted Pollard and Toye to his study.

'Sit down and make yourself comfortable,' he said, indicating a pair of leather armchairs in front of his desk. 'Presumably I'm not a suspect, so I hope you'll take a spot of something. What about some nice cold beer out of the fridge?

'Of course I'm not the old family solicitor as far as Miss Baynes is concerned,' he went on, when they were settled with glasses and cigarettes. 'She only transferred her business to us in '37, when she came to live at Trill after her mother died. But she deposited a lot of papers with us, and I've been trying to dig out anything that might possibly be relevant to this fantastic affair. I expect it's the terms of the will you are chiefly interested in?'

Pollard assented, and added that he hoped there would not be any difficulty.

'Under the circumstances I feel that it's in the interests of justice to tell you anything you want to know, Inspector.' Mr Yelland took up a sheet of paper and glanced briefly at it. 'Miss Beatrice Baynes was a wealthy woman,' he said, putting the paper down again, and clasping his hands in front of him, 'even for these days. She lived well within her considerable income, and had a shrewd head for investment. The post-war appreciation of her capital more than kept pace with inflation. It's early days to name a figure, but I don't think that £120,000 will prove to be very wide of the mark. After payment of death duties and other charges on the estate, I mean.'

Pollard whistled softly.

'A tidy sum,' the solicitor agreed. 'You'd be surprised how many of these old ladies there still are, sitting very pretty and keeping quiet about it. Well, to revert to the testamentary dispositions of Miss Baynes, made in 1951, about £20,000 goes in legacies to old friends and servants and charities. The Governors of Meldon get £10,000 — I'll come back to that later, if I may. The residuary legatees get two-thirds and one-third respectively. They are Mr George Baynes, a great-nephew, and Miss Madge Thornton, a godchild. She is — or was — a music mistress at Meldon. A trust has been created in each case.'

Pollard and Toye made hasty mental calculations.

'Say £60,000 and £30,000,' continued Mr Yelland. 'Neither can touch the capital, which is tied up on any children they may have. If either dies childless the capital reverts to the other's trust fund. If both eventually die without legal issue, it goes to specific charities.'

'Had Miss Baynes any other relatives who are excluded as beneficiaries?' asked Pollard.

'I thought you'd want to know that,' replied Mr Yelland with a touch of self-congratulation. 'Hence my researches into the Baynes archives. The short answer is, no.' He turned over the pages of notes in front of him. 'The family fortune was founded by Miss Baynes's grandfather, in the middle of the last century. He was a manufacturer of various kinds of hardware at Warhampton. He left the business to his only — repeat, only — child, Arthur, father of Beatrice and her two brothers Clarence and John. Arthur carried on successfully, and made still more money. Unfortunately, the only one of his children to inherit his commercial acumen was Beatrice, and in those days, of course, it was unthinkable that a woman could run a manufacturing concern. Clarence was bone idle and merely interested in spending money, and John had academic leanings and was sent to Oxford just before the '14 war. At the same time Arthur sold out very profitably, and retired on the proceeds. John joined up and was killed on the Somme in 1916. He was unmarried. Arthur himself died in 1920. Clarence and Beatrice were left legacies, and were appointed residuary legatees after the widow's life interest in the estate. Surprisingly, the money wasn't tied up, although Clarence had a son, born in 1907, Edward Baynes, who eventually became a not very successful chartered accountant, and the father of George. Old Mrs Baynes died in 1936, and Clarence had run through almost every penny of his inheritance by his own death in 1951. In the meantime, Edward Baynes and his wife were both killed in the London Blitz in 1941, leaving George, then aged eight. Clarence took him over, much to the fury of Beatrice, who — with some justification — considered him quite unsuitable for bringing the boy up. In fact, she consulted my father about taking legal action in the matter. After Clarence's death she saw a lot more of George, and did her utmost to get him established in a worthwhile profession, but with very little result. He's about four-fifths Clarence to one-fifth Beatrice. She has consistently refused to give him an allowance in the hope of forcing him to buckle to.'

'What I can't get over,' said Pollard, 'is this Miss Thornton getting such a hefty proportion of the life interest. After all, the godchild relationship is usually a pretty nominal one. Do you mean that she isn't even a distant connection?' He gazed at the rough genealogical table which he had scribbled down while the solicitor was talking:

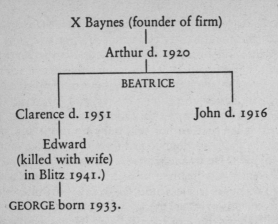

X Baynes (founder of firm)
|
Arthur d. 1920
|
BEATRICE
|
Clarence d. 1951   John d. 1916
|
Edward
(killed with wife)
in Blitz 1941.)
|
GEORGE born 1933.

'If she had been,' replied Mr Yelland, 'I feel sure that Miss Baynes would have mentioned it. She had strong family feeling, partly, I think, because she had so few relatives. I can remember her remarking on one occasion when she was adding a codicil to her will, that, as both her parents were only children, she hadn't a single first cousin. The sense of family even overcame her vigorous disapproval of George's fecklessness, as her will shows. I have always imagined that Madge Thornton must be the daughter of an old friend. At any rate, some years ago Miss Baynes mentioned in passing that Mr Thornton had died.'

'Mrs Thornton died only last week,' said Pollard thoughtfully.

'Perhaps Mr Thornton was an old flame.'

Sergeant Toye cleared his throat.

'Excuse me, sir, you said something about going back to the legacy of the school.'

'Quite right, Sergeant. We must stick to the facts, although I don't think this legacy can possibly have any relevance to the enquiry. It is to the Governors of Meldon, and the terms of the bequest specify that the money is only to be used for capital projects which have the unanimous support of the governing body. Very neat.'

'I'm not sure that I'm with you,' said Pollard, 'unless it's an indirect hit at Miss Renshaw?'

'Oh, you've got on to the feud, have you? Yes, Miss Baynes felt that she could count on a few diehards lingering on among the Governors, possibly as long as Miss Renshaw herself remains at Meldon, and that they could be relied on to obstruct any of the latter's more up-and-coming ideas. Miss Renshaw can fairly be said to have saved the place from extinction, you know. It had got hopelessly stuck in a rut before the war and was going down-hill fast. Miss Baynes was there as a girl, and the slightest change in anything was anathema to her. She had an absolute fixation about the place. I don't know how Miss Renshaw has survived having her living just across the road all these years. However, she has won hands down, and Meldon's now doing exceedingly well. I'm sending my own girls there.'

'You mentioned a codicil just now,' said Pollard after a pause. 'Has Miss Baynes made any recent alterations in her will?'

'It's virtually the same as when it was first drawn up. The codicil you refer to was a bequest to an additional charity in which she had become interested. There was never any suggestion that she was considering alterations in the main provisions, although she remarked more than once that an assured income would almost certainly do George more harm than good.'

'Do you think that Mr George Baynes and Miss Thornton knew the extent of their expectations under the will?'

'I think that is in the highest degree unlikely, Inspector. Miss Baynes was a woman who kept her own counsel.'

Eight

'Visitors : on arrival please ask for Sister.'
                    Notice on the door of Meldon Sanatorium

SISTER LITTLEJOHN WORE the uniform of a famous London hospital with a starchy and uncompromising air. Pollard struggled against the sensation of being a patient under observation.

'Doctor Dodd has already visited Miss Thornton this morning,' she stated. 'He has agreed to you seeing her for a short time, but only on the understanding that the interview stops at once if she shows signs of getting upset. Those are his orders, and it's my duty to see they're carried out, Inspector.'

'Quite,' he said, casting round for an approach. I accept that, of course.'

Earlier in Pollard's career, the Assistant Commissioner had referred to him in his absence as a personable young man. This had regrettably leaked out, and there seemed little hope of ever living it down at the Yard. Occasionally, however, he found it worth while to cash in on this asset. Leaning back in a corner of Sister Littlejohn's settee he smiled at her, as she sat primly in an armchair.

'You know I haven't only come here to see Miss Thornton,' he told her. 'It's going to be an enormous help to discuss one or two matters with someone of your experience and knowledge of the set-up, Sister, if you can spare the time.'

He thought he detected the faintest bridling movement as she replied that she would be glad to help in any way she could, and folded her hands on her aproned lap.

'May I just check up on one thing before I tell you what is really in my mind?' Pollard consulted his notebook. 'Inspector Beakbane understood from Miss Renshaw that after Miss Thornton had been to her flat on Sunday morning in a very overwrought state, she herself rang you up, and that as a result you were kind enough to befriend Miss Thornton later in the day.'

'That's quite correct, Inspector. Not in any professional capacity, but just in a friendly way, as you say, apart from giving her a mild sedative to take when she went to bed. I took her out in my car for a picnic tea, and then had her back here to supper.'

'Very good of you, if I may say so, when your term's work was officially over. Now, this is where I feel you and I speak the same language, Sister. The thing that puzzles me about Miss Thornton is that hysterical outburst on Sunday morning. That wasn't after she'd heard the news of the murder in such an unfortunate way, but twenty-four hours *before* the body was discovered, and anything up to about eighteen hours *after* the old lady was killed. You'll see what I'm thinking? I needn't tell anyone like you that some people react to an appalling discovery by persuading themselves that they haven't made it . . . a sort of nervous self-protection, isn't it? Do you think it's possible that Miss Thornton saw something of the murder? She might conceivably have come on the body, and been so terrified that she couldn't admit it, even to herself.'

Sister Littlejohn nodded slowly several times, giving Pollard a long look of complete understanding.

'That's a very interesting idea, Inspector. Very interesting indeed. I must say it had never struck me.' She relapsed into thought, while Pollard noted that the possibility of Madge Thornton's being a potential suspect had obviously not struck her either. 'No,' she said at last, 'I really don't think anything of that sort could have happened to her. I'm sure there would have been some sign of it in the way she talked and behaved

93

when she was with me. She was worried, certainly, but I can't say she showed any sign of having had a dreadful experience.'

'Was it just Miss Baynes's absence that was worrying her, do you think?'

'Funny that you should ask me that, Inspector.' Sister Littlejohn unconsciously settled herself in her chair for a good talk. 'From what Miss Renshaw had said over the 'phone, I got the idea that Miss Thornton was afraid the old lady had met with a motor accident, or something like that. But it seemed to me that she was very anxious to see Miss Baynes about something, and it was not being able to find her that was the trouble. I put it down to the fact that there was a lot of business to see to in connection with Mrs Thornton's death. Miss Thornton hasn't had much experience of that kind of thing. Unworldly, I should call her. And there aren't any brothers or sisters to help her.'

'I wonder,' said Pollard cautiously, 'if they had had a row?'

Sister Littlejohn looked almost startled.

'Oh, I don't think that's likely. Miss Baynes was a very dominating person. In fact, some of us used to think it was a shame the way she'd often snub Miss Thornton, who'd never try to stand up for herself.'

'Was that why you didn't encourage Miss Thornton to go round to Applebys again on Sunday evening?'

She gave him a quick, admiring glance.

'You don't miss much, do you, Inspector? Well, we can't afford to in our jobs, can we? Yes, it's quite true : I tried to keep her off the idea. You see, at that time I naturally thought Miss Baynes was having a day out with her old friends, and would probably come home tired and not in the mood to hear about all Miss Thornton's problems, and might quite likely be very short with her. After all, it didn't look as though there was anything so urgent it couldn't wait till Monday morning.'

'I seem to have heard a lot about the godchild relationship,' said Pollard. 'Would you say they were fond of each other, although the old lady was so domineering?'

Sister Littlejohn seemed to find this question difficult.

'Well, yes and no. Miss Baynes was good to Miss Thornton in her own way : lovely Christmas and birthday presents, and so on. I shan't be surprised if she's been remembered in the will, either. And Miss Thornton was very patient with her, and did a lot of little things for her. But I wouldn't say they were wrapped up in each other. I think it was more that Miss Thornton didn't seem to have many friends, and Applebys was somewhere to go at weekends and so on.'

Pollard decided that he had probably exhausted this source of information.

'This has all been most helpful,' he told her. 'I wonder if you could just do one more thing for me? We need Miss Thornton's fingerprints. They'll be all over Applebys and we want to be able to eliminate them. Can you get them on a clean medicine glass or something of the kind? It might be better than risking upsetting her by asking for them in the usual way.'

'Why, of course, Inspector. That's very simple. I'll just give her a tablespoon of plain water to take. She's not the questioning kind of patient.' She gazed at him, her eyes intent with interest behind her spectacles. 'Surely the brute who did this dreadful thing must have left some prints in the studio? That'll help you to catch him, won't it?'

Pollard was amused by the triumph of human curiosity over professional correctness.

'The trouble is that a room like the studio which is used by a lot of people gets simply smothered in prints, all on top of each other. My experts have been hard at work on them, of course. Then there's the question of whether the murderer's prints are in our records.'

'You simply can't tell what will happen these days with such awful men about, can you? In my opinion the mental

95

hospitals are discharging cases far too early. And between ourselves, Inspector, I think they're a great deal too casual about the locking-up here. All these fire escapes—it's just asking for trouble. I'm very careful over here, I can tell you, isolated as we are. When I first came I insisted on safety catches being put on every window. Not that we've had any trouble up to now, apart from village boys getting into the park now and again, but better safe than sorry, I say . . . Now, if you'll just wait here, I'll run along and see to that little job for you.'

Left alone, Pollard sat and considered a possible case against Madge Thornton. Assuming that the murder was committed in the studio, her movements were at present unaccounted for during much of the time that the room had been empty on Saturday evening . . . He hoped that Sergeant Toye, now at the Staff House, was managing to establish the time of her return there after the second visit to Applebys . . . It seemed to him that there were intimations of possible motives. After all, Yelland could only give it as his personal opinion that she hadn't known about her expectations under the will . . . Smouldering resentment at years of petty snubs and humiliations suddenly bursting out, when general control was weakened by the shock of her mother's death? A bit far-fetched, perhaps, but cases of the kind had been known . . . A serious row between the two women? But what could it have been about? Miss Renshaw and Sister had sketched substantially the same portrait of Madge in relation to her godmother. It would clearly have needed tremendous provocation to goad her to the point of making a violent physical assault . . .

He was roused from his reflections by Sister Littlejohn's return. The plan had worked beautifully, and Miss Thornton was all ready to see him. She really seemed much more like herself this morning, but they'd be keeping her for a day or two longer, to make sure she was properly on her feet again. Until after the funeral, probably.

Pollard, who had been debating with himself whether a watch ought to be kept on Madge Thornton, was considerably relieved by this information. They went along a passage smelling of antiseptics and stopped outside a door with a glass panel.

'I'll be in the surgery just opposite, doing up the medicine glass,' she murmured in his ear. 'Here's Mr Pollard to see you, dear,' she announced cheerfully, flinging the door open. 'He just wants a little chat with you while I'm busy in the surgery. He can't stay more than a few minutes.'

Madge was up and dressed, sitting in an armchair by the window. As Pollard crossed the room she looked up at him nervously, and his trained perception registered a complex of emotions behind her trepidation, of which fear was only one. He was immediately struck by the fact that she was well-built, and rather clumsy-looking, with big feet and strong hands ... a better build for it than Renshaw, he thought, remembering Beakbane ... Pollard had married an exceedingly attractive woman, and it seemed incredible that anyone could be content to make so little of herself ... that large face, with its neglected, roughened complexion, and the lank, straw-coloured hair which looked as though she cut it herself. Rather curious light eyes, which watched him apprehensively. And that awful shapeless cardigan, a sort of sandy colour, bunched over a cotton frock ... When she spoke in answer to his conventional greeting, it was a pleasant surprise to find that she had a rather deep, agreeable voice. As she made no attempt to ask him to sit down, he seated himself opposite to her, and began to make general conversation, gradually working round to her position at Meldon.

'I hate my work here,' she said abruptly. 'Except the gardening.'

'Gardening?' he asked, puzzled.

'Yes. I run the girls' gardens. That part's all right.'

It came to him that this large, awkward woman would look perfectly at home in gardening kit, with a foot on a

97

spade . . . He asked her why she hadn't become a professional gardener if she preferred that kind of work to teaching music.

'Aunt Beatrice didn't approve. She said it wasn't a suitable career. She was paying for me, you see.'

Educated her, and has left her a life interest in £30,000, thought Pollard.

'I suppose Miss Baynes was an old friend of your parents?' he asked.

'I don't know about a friend.' She spoke rather sullenly, dragging out the word. 'She'd always known them, I think, right back in her Warhampton days.'

It occurred to Pollard that Mr Thornton might have been an employee in the Baynes business, and that Madge could have a social inferiority complex.

'I'm so sorry to have to come and bother you when you've had so much trouble just lately,' he said gently, 'but I think you may be able to help me a lot. You must have been more intimate with Miss Baynes than anyone else at Meldon. Would you try to put your mind back to last Saturday? I don't suppose you went to the Festival supper, did you? It must have been a very trying day for you.'

'Oh, yes, I did. We all have to — to entertain the Old Meldonians. I'm one myself, but I count as staff now.'

Reflecting that she would hardly lie about something which could be verified so easily, Pollard asked if she had seen Miss Baynes on her first visit to Applebys, at about twenty minutes past eight.

'No, I didn't. The door was locked, and there was no answer when I rang.'

'Did you see anyone about?'

'Only Bert Heyward. He went past on his bike, just as I came away.'

'What did you do then?'

'Oh, I just wandered about in the park. I thought Aunt Beatrice would be back soon, and I'd wait.'

'Did you meet many people?'

'No. I kept away from the school and the gardens. I didn't want to talk to anybody.'

'But you must have wanted to talk to Miss Baynes very badly, if you went over to see her again?'

Watching Madge intently, Pollard saw her clasped hands tighten until the knuckles whitened.

'That—that was different. I'd hardly seen her since I got back from the funeral.'

'Wasn't Miss Baynes at your mother's funeral?' he asked in surprise.

'No.'

Could this be relevant to the theory that there'd been a row, he wondered?

Madge confirmed that Ann Cartmell had offered her a lift in the drive, and said that the second visit to Applebys had been as abortive as the first. She had gone round to the garden and called, but Aunt Beatrice hadn't answered. Her choice of words struck Pollard as slightly odd. Had she any reason to believe that Miss Baynes had been there all the time? He asked if she had been surprised at her godmother's being out.

'Yes, I was,' she said. 'Aunt Beatrice hardly ever went out in the evening.'

'But at this stage you weren't worried about her?'

'Worried? Oh, no,' she replied, with an inflexion in her voice which he was unable to interpret.

'How disappointing for you it must have been,' he remarked, 'when you wanted to spend a little time with someone you were fond of.'

The sudden anger in the pale eyes was unmistakable, as she clapsed and unclasped her hands. Pollard experienced a feeling of triumph : beyond any doubt something had happened to arouse indignation like this . . .

'I expect you were glad to get back to the Staff House and go to bed,' he went on. 'Did you manage to get a lift?'

'No. I walked.'

'Did you go straight back from Applebys?'

'Why should I?' she demanded angrily. 'It was a lovely evening and I'd a perfect right to walk in the park if I wanted to.'

Damn, he thought, she's beginning to feel cornered. She'll go off again in a minute if I'm not careful . . .

'It must have been very pleasant strolling there,' he said easily. 'Did you by any chance see anyone coming away from the school, or from Applebys, while you were about?'

Exasperatedly he saw her grasp the arms of her chair, and rise a little in her seat. Then her eyes became blank, and she began to laugh, a high-pitched hysterical laugh . . .

The door opened, and Sister Littlejohn came swiftly and competently into the room.

Pollard locked the cardboard box containing the medicine glass into his car, and went into the entrance hall of Old House, bracing himself for another difficult feminine interview. Ann Cartmell promptly appeared in the doorway of the secretery's office, giving a totally unexpected impression of lightheartedness. He apologised for keeping her waiting, and suggested that they go into the library.

'You're feeling a bit better about things this morning, aren't you?' he asked.

'Oh yes, much better. Mr Torrance rang me from London late last night. He tried Miss Renshaw first to find out where I was, and she gave him the Staff House number. He says I mustn't get into a flap in case I have to be a day or two late getting to New York. He's sure it won't be more, and that a seat on a 'plane could be wangled somehow. He's going to cable his friends about meeting me just the same if I'm held up, and thinks I'll be able to stay with them after the summer school instead of before, if necessary.'

Pollard registered the facts of the situation previously unknown to him.

'Your course doesn't begin this week, then?'

'No. Isn't it lucky? I was going to spend the weekend with these friends of Mr Torrance in New York until Tuesday evening, and have a super time sight-seeing. It was awful to think if missing it, but now it looks as though it'll come off after all.'

'Are they artists, too?' he asked casually, marvelling at her childlike self-centredness.

'Mr Torrance says they both paint . . . He told me someone from Scotland Yard was going to see him today. Will it be you?'

'It might be. Now, shall we go up to the studio? There's nothing there to upset you, as I said last night.'

At the request of the police Jean Forrest had held up the cleaning of School Wing. It was empty and silent, the air close and still. As Pollard walked along the echoing corridor with Ann Cartmell, he glanced into the deserted classrooms and reflected that few places were more dead than school buildings during the holidays. They went up the stone staircase at the far end, and came to the studio door which was locked and sealed. He inspected and broke the seal and inserted a key. Going in first, he held the door for Ann, and at once indicated the empty corner on the left.

'You won't ever have to see the puppet theatre again, of course,' he told her in a matter-of-fact voice, and went across to open the fire-escape door. 'Let's have some air, shall we?'

The studio looked both squalid and dramatic. Dust and finger-printing powder lay everywhere, and easels, stools and screens had been hastily thrust into wildly irrelevant positions by the investigators. The table by the wall facing the door was strewn with the various objects which had been left stacked upon it. There was a curious random pattern of white chalk circles . . .

Pollard beckoned to Ann and made a gesture towards the table.

'Have you ever played Kim's Game?' he asked.

She nodded affirmatively, looking at him in bewilderment.

'Well, then, has anything been removed from here? Try to remember what was stacked together before my chaps disturbed it all.'

She gave a despairing exclamation.

'But I'm hopelessly untidy—I never know where things are!'

'Just take your time, and don't get fussed over it. You'll be surprised at what you can remember.'

He moved away, making himself as inconspicuous as possible, and embarked on an imaginative reconstruction of the actual murder. Suppose Beatrice Baynes had come up the fire-escape—whether casually or by appointment could wait for the moment. The murderer, X, is also there. They confront each other at the table, just where Ann Cartmell is standing now. An angry scene develops. X, infuriated, snatches up some heavy blunt object with a rounded edge, and smashes it down on the old woman's fragile skull . . . She slumps to the floor, while the killer, panic-stricken, looks round for somewhere to conceal the body, unconsciously putting the weapon down on the table . . . Obviously the puppet theatre is the place . . . He—or she—heaves up the body, but not quite soon enough to avoid those short, telltale marks of dragging made by the victim's heels. It is comparatively light, and not too difficult to carry across the room, but has to be put down again while X pulls the puppet theatre clear of the wall. Quite safe to touch the rough canvas : it won't take prints . . . Now the stowing away of the body inside. This takes a bit of manoeuvring, and the heels drag again . . . Then the contraption is pushed back against the wall . . . All X will have to do now is to snatch up the weapon and make an unobtrusive exit . . . So easy to overlook that tiny blood-stain where it has rested on the table . . . Obviously the puppet theatre is the place . . . broad shoulders and strong hands was quite a convincing figure. . .

A slight sound made him turn round. Ann Cartmell, looking pale and upset, had taken a step towards him.

'There *is* something missing,' she said, and swallowed. 'A stone we use for a paperweight.'

'What sort of stone?'

'Like one of these.' She showed him a cardboard box containing flat, water-worn stones from four to six inches in diameter, of the type found on shingle beaches.

'But how can you be sure that one of these has gone? They look much the same.'

'The missing one was rather special. It had veins of quartz or something, which made a pattern like the Sphinx. The girls called it the Sphinx — one of them brought it back from a holiday at Westward Ho!'

'But are you quite certain it was on the table last Saturday? I don't want you to think I question what you are saying, but you told me just now that you were bad at remembering where things were, didn't you?'

She looked at him steadily.

'Yes, I'm absolutely certain. When I came up after tea to take down the exhibition, I used it to weigh down a pile of paintings. A breeze had got up, and was coming in at the fire-escape door, and things were blowing about.'

Pollard took a deep breath.

'Can you remember noticing it when you were here with Mr Torrance, or when you were doing the final clear-up with the two girls?'

She closed her eyes, and thought intently.

'I'm so sorry,' she said at last. 'It simply didn't register with me again.'

At any rate, he thought, we've established the place and the weapon, almost beyond doubt . . .

'Don't let this distress you too much,' he said, observing the expression on her face. 'It would have happened in any case, I'm afraid.'

Sergeant Toye was in the library, adjusting the timetable made at the White Horse. Handing Pollard some notes, he reported that his luck had been in at the Staff House. Taking Miss Thornton first, her return on Saturday evening had been witnessed by the housekeeper, Mrs Milman, who had come out of her room on the ground floor just after the end of the ten o'clock news on the radio—say at twelve minutes past. Pressed, she had said that Miss Thornton looked a 'bit het up', but added that she'd been like that ever since her mother died. She had noticed Miss Thornton emerging from the bathroom in her dressing-gown about half an hour later. During a conversation with the Senior Mistress Toye had also established that Miss Thornton was present at the Festival supper.

'Then she's unaccounted for during the short period when Miss Cartmell was seeing off Mr Torrance, and again from after the offer of the lift—which she confirms—to the time when Bert Heyward locked up the studio at about nine-fifty, if he did,' said Pollard meditatively. 'I've managed to see her, by the way.'

He was just beginning to tell Toye about the interview when a police car drew up outside the window, bringing Superintendent Martin and Inspector Beakbane *en route* for the inquest, which Pollard did not propose to attend. The four men sat round a table in one of the bays, while Pollard once again outlined a case against Madge Thornton.

'Opportunity,' commented the Super tersely. 'Physique for it, too, from what you say. Motive seems a bit theoretical, apart from the money. Dabs in the right places in the studio might clinch it.'

Toye, invited to proceed, stated that there was overwhelming evidence that Ann Cartmell had returned to the Staff House soon after nine, and been occupied in packing and having a late snack with her friends until about midnight.

'That bears out my conviction that she knows nothing whatever about the murder,' said Pollard. 'I've seen her again this morning. She's a self-centred little piece at present, and looks on the whole business as a tiresome interference with her arrangements for going to America. And if she's out of it, presumably Torrance is, too.'

Toye interposed to explain that he had called at the Lodge, and questioned the head gardener, Jock Eccles, about the time of Mr Torrance's arrival. Eccles had fulminated about a car which had swung in at the gates at a dangerous speed, and gone tearing up the drive. He'd shaken his fist after it from the kitchen window. Somewhere round half an hour later, he'd been in the garden when it came back at the same daft speed, hardly slowing down to turn right into the road. A Jaguar, with a dark man at the wheel.

'Doesn't look as though he'd paid an earlier visit, does it, sir?'

Pollard agreed. The Super, who liked solid, tangible clues, showed signs of restlessness, and reverted to the man seen leaving Applebys about nine o'clock, and the steps he was taking to trace him. On hearing that there was a bare possibility that the stranger had been George Baynes, next-of-kin and cheif beneficiary of the deceased, he became almost voluble.

'Now that makes sense, if you like,' he said. 'If his dabs are the ones in Applebys and they turn up in the studio too, you're home and dry . . . I've brought along the P.M. report for you. It arrived just before we came away. It's what Wallace said in the first place, put in a long-winded way with a lot of technical terms . . . "fracture of the skull in the left parietal region . . . result of blow delivered with great violence . . . fairly narrow, rounded object . . ."'

'Doesn't follow that the assailant was out of the way tall,' said Inspector Beakbane. 'Deceased was only four foot eleven.'

'I think I can tell you what the object was.' Pollard gave the gist of his conversation with Ann Cartmell about the missing stone. Toye suggested searching the garden near the foot of the fire-escape.

'Mightn't have been too big for a man to stuff in his pocket,' replied the Super. 'About the probable time of death, now. All the usual stuff about how impossible it is to say anything at all, and then the mixture as before, more or less . . . not much later than Saturday midnight, and it could have been several hours earlier.'

'I suppose we couldn't hope for anything nearer after nearly forty hours.' Pollard looked at his watch and started putting papers into the brief case. 'I'd better make tracks for London. I want to drop Thornton's dabs in at the Yard before I see Torrance and Baynes.'

Nine

'There have been remarkable developments in the art department.'

H.M. Inspector's Report on Meldon

PRESS CAMERAS CLICKED as Inspector Pollard drove out of Meldon Park. He felt a surge of elation : a hasty glance at the morning papers had shown him the extent to which the case had caught on with the public. His own name had featured quite prominently ... As the police car gathered speed he visualised Jane bringing in the evening papers, perhaps with his photograph on the front page ... her gratification, veiled in banter ... People's heads turning after him in the street, and after them both as he led her into an expensive restaurant to celebrate the triumphant conclusion of the enquiry ... married a good-looker, too, they'd be saying ... Old Crowe, his Chief at the Yard, possibly dropping a hint about the future ...

These agreeable visions were suddenly extinguished by a cold shower of realism. Exactly what had he achieved so far? Bloody little, if anything. Suppressing an inclination to go to the other extreme, and visualise failure and a ruined career, Pollard embarked on a form of self-interrogation which had often yielded dividends in the past.

Had he tripped up over anything? He reviewed the checking of alibis and further enquiries entrusted to Sergeant Toye, and the search for the young man being carried out by the Linbridge police. George Baynes was being shadowed. Madge Thornton was safely under futher sedation and the watchful eye of Sister Littlejohn. The results of the first lot of dabs would be waiting for him at the Yard ... Suppose Thornton's weren't anywhere in the studio, or on the bureau at Applebys? Pollard frowned, as the teasing problem of the relation between the murder and the break-in returned to his mind. If she'd gone for the cash — and she'd almost certainly have known where it was kept — what about the food? She was, of course, in a peculiar state of mind ... Could the young man after all have been someone on the run, and nothing to do with the murder? Extraordinary coincidences did happen ...

He pulled himself up again, and went on to the second question of his self-imposed catechism : what do I know about X, my most promising suspect? As applied to Madge Thornton, it seemed to have distinct possibilities ... A middle-aged spinster orphan — no, she could be secretly married, divorced or a widow — a middle-aged orphan, and a not very successful music teacher, who had been at Meldon some years longer than the H.M. Also, the godchild of the late Beatrice Baynes, who had paid for her education, given her expensive presents, left her a very comfortable income, and yet had been disappointed in her, snubbed her, and failed to attend her mother's funeral, although there must obviously have been some link with the family. Yet, thought Pollard, in spite of this alleged down-trodden status, she showed unmistakable signs of fury when Beatrice had been mentioned, and was hell-bent on tracking her down on Saturday evening, and again on Sunday morning, presumably to have a row with her ... So far, she had produced no alibi for two periods during which the studio was apparently empty : 8.30 p.m. to 8.40 p.m. and from just after nine to approximately nine-fifty. As far as physique went, she could easily have delivered the killing blow, and carried the old woman's small, frail body across the room.

Pollard mulled over the facts, conscious that something was nagging at the back of his mind. He waited, and it suddenly clicked into position. That housekeeper, Mrs — Mrs

Milman. She'd told Toye that Madge Thornton had looked a bit het up, but had been like it ever since her mother died . . . That was it. The psychological disturbance had been sparked off by Mrs Thornton's death. Not just as a result of the actual bereavement, surely? It wasn't as though Madge had been living at home, her whole existence centred on her mother. And it was quite fantastic to suggest that Beatrice Baynes's absence from the funeral could have caused trouble on such a scale. Could Madge have discovered that her godmother had done her parents some really serious injury in the past? And was there any hope of getting it out of her? He'd better follow up this idea from the other end, and have enquiries made about the Thorntons by the Warhampton police.

Am I barking up the wrong tree after all? Pollard negotiated a snarl of heavy lorries and shot ahead, as he considered this third question. What about young Baynes, with his walloping financial motive? Well, he was being shadowed, and would shortly be interviewed . . . Suppose he really had been the man Ann Cartmell saw? He might have come down on Saturday evening, found Applebys locked up, and gone across to the park on the chance of finding his great-aunt, who had decided to take an evening stroll there. For some reason they'd gone up to the studio together, and had a flaming row. He'd killed her, stuffed the body into the puppet theatre and the stone into his pocket . . . Then he could have gone back to Applebys, pinched the money and food, and made his way back to Town by a devious route . . . Almost unbelievably cool, and the most appalling risk right under the noses of the people at the Lodge . . . Still, colossal risks did come off sometimes, and like Madge Thornton, he probably would have known where Beatrice Baynes kept her money.

Pollard had a good memory and began to work out times. The murder could hardly have been committed in the short interval between 8.30 and 8.40 p.m.? It would have had to take place after Ann Cartmell and the two girls had cleared off at nine o'clock . . . Suppose George Baynes had come out of Applebys at a minute or two after nine, and gone over to the park — but he'd have run into Madge Thornton who was coming down the drive. Pollard felt a thrill of excitement. It was the question about whether she'd seen anyone coming away from Applebys that had sent her over the edge. Could the two of them possibly have been in it together? They both stood to benefit handsomely, quite apart from Madge's unknown grievance. Or was she trying to cover up for George? What sort of relationship existed between them? They certainly didn't appear to have much in common . . . His thoughts raced on. At last it looked as though he might be on to something. Anyway, there were a few definite lines of enquiry to follow up, and to tell the Old Man about . . .

Reluctantly Pollard began to devote more of his attention to the traffic and less to his case.

'Don't mind giving us another job to do, will you?' said Sergeant Phillips of the Yard Fingerprint Department. 'It all helps to pass the time. Those puzzle pictures of Boyce's are just too simple.'

'Well, these may help you,' replied Pollard, handing over Ann Cartmell's prints and the cardboard box containing the medicine glass. 'I know you get stuck very easily! Just find out if the dabs on the glass are in either of Boyce's two lots while I go and do a spot of work. I shouldn't think either of the two I've given you are in Records, but you could have a look.'

After a few more exchanges with Phillips he paid a brief visit to his own room. Here he learnt that George Baynes had gone at his normal time to the Kensington estate agency where he worked, and had shown no sign of making a bolt. He had been told to come to the Yard on leaving work. Mr Torrance would be pleased to see Inspector Pollard at the Domani Gallery at any time during the afternoon. Chief Superintendent Crowe was out on an urgent case, but expected back later, and wished to see Inspector Pollard . . .

Lunch — very belated — seemed indicated. Pollard rang up the secretary of the college where his wife lectured, left a message to say that he would be coming home some time that evening, and made for the canteen.

The Domani Gallery was in Wain Street, off the west side of Regent Street. Pollard ran a critical eye over the exterior. The place looked prosperous, and an exhibition seemed to be in progress. He went in, found a reception desk with a temporarily deserted air, and passed on into a large room. Here about thirty people were contemplating paintings and consulting catalogues. He glanced round for someone in charge, and saw a tall, dark man surrounded by a group of young people. They were all trousered, long-haired and sexually indistinguishable, and listening with attention while the speaker commented with great assurance on a startling abstract. Wondering if this were Clive Torrance, Pollard crossed the room and joined the outskirts of the group . . . Well-dressed, he thought, and beginning to put on weight . . . looks as though he does himself well . . .

At this moment the man turned round, saw Pollard and broke off in mid-stream.

'Fly, all is known,' he remarked to his audience. 'Unless I'm very much mistaken, Scotland Yard has caught up on me. I was at the scene of the crime, you know. Am I right, sir?'

'Mr Clive Torrance? Chief Detective-Inspector Pollard of New Scotland Yard,' Pollard replied equably, producing his official card, and noting a subtle change come over Torrance on being addressed in public school English. The young men and women goggled.

'Not the Puppet Theatre business?' demanded a shaggy youth in ringing tones. Heads were turned towards them from all sides. Torrance looked at Pollard, making a gesture of amused despair.

'I do apologise, Inspector. Where the hell is Haynes? In the loo, I suppose. Oh, there he comes . . . Let's go up to my flat, shall we? Unless you'd like to arrest me on the spot, that is, and give the Domani unparalleled publicity?'

This remark was received with hilarity, and a volley of requests for information which Torrance waved aside.

'A terrific thrill for them, of course,' he remarked, escorting Pollard up a flight of stairs. 'God knows what they'll go spreading round about me. In here, Inspector.'

A door marked PRIVATE gave on to a small landing. On the right Pollard caught a glimpse of what looked like a large studio-cum-workshop. Torrance led the way into a sitting-room on the left.

It was a well-proportioned Georgian room with white panelling and good windows, furnished with unobtrusive luxury. Pollard took in the quality of the plum-coloured fitted carpet, the beautiful curtains of a Regency design, and a couple of paintings of the French Impressionist school. Torrance indicated one of two opulent armchairs, remarked that he knew drinks were ruled out, and proffered a choice of cigarettes of the more expensive brands. Lighting up for them both, he sank into the second chair, and gazed at Pollard.

'This really is a god-awful business,' he remarked. 'You know, what's haunting me is the thought that the poor old girl may have been in that puppet show contraption all the time little Cartmell and I were choosing those paintings. Do tell me — if it's permissible to ask — has the time of death been established?'

'Only that it was probably before midnight, or soon after,' replied Pollard. 'After an interval of something like forty hours it's impossible to be very precise, unfortunately.' He observed the man's sensual mouth and chin, and air of aplomb, and felt a flash of compassion for Ann Cartmell's vulnerability. 'Well, I don't think it's very likely that you can help us much, Mr Torrance, but you'll understand that we like to get statements confirmed as far as possible. Perhaps the simplest thing would be for you to run through everything connected with your visit last Saturday?'

'I'll do that gladly, although I'm afraid it's not likely to get you much further.' Clive Torrance crossed his legs and thrust his left arm behind his head. 'First of all, I'd better explain briefly how I come to be connected with Meldon. I found Ann Cartmell for them a couple of years ago. I do a lot of work in connection with art education — arranging courses and summer schools and what-have-you, and she'd just been on one of them. She'd taken a toss in her first job, and was thinking of chucking teaching altogether. I'd got a hunch that she had what it takes to make a good teacher of art, in spite of her immaturity and lack of confidence, and it turns out I was quite right. She's a nice child, and I kept an eye on her down there. For instance, I gave them a lecture as a boost to the art department, and so on. I encouraged her to put in some of the girls' stuff for this Commonwealth Schools show which is coming off in the autumn — it would be a tremendous feather in her cap if Meldon pulled off an award — and I said I'd help with the final selection if I could . . .

'Well, that's the general background, I think,' Torrance continued, expelling a mouthful of cigarette smoke. 'I'm pretty busy, of course, and to tell you the truth the whole business went out of my head until last Saturday. I had a meeting in the afternoon, and then was going on for a short weekend with some friends at a place called Stannaford Magna — it's a village about twenty miles beyond Trill. I was just chucking my things into a bag after lunch when I remembered these blasted paintings, and realised that I'd be passing within a few miles of Meldon. What? Oh, yes, sorry, you'll want the address. Mr and Mrs Gavin Scorhill, Flete House, Stannaford Magna. In the 'phone book, if you want the number.'

'Thank you,' said Pollard, making a note. 'Please carry on.'

'Where was I? Packing. Yes, I don't like letting people down, so I rang Meldon on chance, and found that Ann Cartmell was still there, and hadn't sent the stuff on her own. I told her I could drop in for a few minutes about eight. She said she might still be held up at some Old Girls' supper, and asked me to go straight up to the studio, where she'd leave the paintings out. I'd been there several times, and know the lie of the land. In the end I was a bit late getting off, and didn't arrive at Meldon until just on eight : I remember noticing the clock in the Quad, and she joined me almost at once, and we got down to the job.'

'Almost at once?' said Pollard. 'One minute after you? Two? Five?'

'Well, it's a bit difficult to be as exact as that. I went in,' Torrance screwed up his eyes, 'saw the paintings were pinned up on screens, walked across the room, caught sight of one I liked, and was looking at it when I heard the door open and she came in. Say two minutes. Not as much as five, I'm certain.'

'Artists are often sensitive to all kinds of subtle impressions. Can you remember having any sensation of someone having just gone out of the studio, for instance?'

Torrance looked at him with evident gratification.

'I'd no idea the police appreciated that kind of thing. No — that sounds quite insufferable. Forgive me. I know exactly what you mean, of course, but I honestly can't say I remember getting any impression of anything. I'd come down with a specific purpose, you see, and I suppose my mind was on it. I'm a bit of a single-tracker when professionally engaged.'

'You're quite sure you didn't hear any sound — perhaps a very slight one — on the fire-escape?'

Torrance paused, and shook his head. 'Nothing helpful there, I'm afraid.'

'Right. And I suppose this applies to the whole time while you and Miss Cartmell were both there?'

'Oh, certainly. We were talking pretty well non-stop. I'm quite sure no one actually came in. I can say that definitely, but it's pretty negative, I'm afraid.'

Pollard reflected that a man like Clive Torrance was probably skilled at keeping an ear cocked for untimely arrivals.

'Did you notice the time when you both came away from the studio?' he asked.

'Yes. I was giving her a few tips about her visit to the States — I'd sponsored her application for this summer school over there which she's probably told you about—and then I offered to take the paintings back to London for her and drop them in, and realised that it was later than I thought. It was just on half-past eight. My watch is pretty reliable.'

'And then you went down to your car together?'

'We had to collect an entrance form from the secretary's office *en route*. Oh, wait a minute. I dashed back to pick up a copy of *Artifex,* which she suddenly remembered I'd left behind. She ran on to the office in the front of the building, and I picked her up there. She came out and waved me off. I'd parked in the sacred precincts outside the front door, I'm afraid, instead of going round to the car park.'

'Did you have any difficulty in finding the *Artifex*?' asked Pollard, trying to keep all sign of interest out of his voice.

'None whatever. I'd brought it down with me to read over the weekend, and there happened to be a reproduction in it relevant to something I was saying to her about one of the paintings—I simply can't resist teaching. She must have put it down on the table when she'd looked at it, and it got underneath our discards.'

'Did you by any chance notice a flattish grey stone with a white quartz pattern lying on the table?'

Torrance gave him a sharp look.

'Let me think . . . There was a lot of junk at the fire-escape end of the table . . . vases . . . jam jars . . . a pair of board compasses . . . boxes . . . No, sorry, I can't remember seeing a stone of any kind . . . Was it? . . . Good God!'

'Almost certainly the weapon used, yes.'

'Well, it does rather look as though the body—was there, doesn't it?'

'It's certainly suggestive,' replied Pollard, 'but not conclusive. Even an artist's visual memory is selective to some extent, I suppose.'

'Oh, quite. I've often noticed that with my own. It's rather interesting. Related to one's subconscious, presumably.'

'Had you ever met Miss Baynes?' asked Pollard, accepting another cigarette.

'Not in the sense of having been introduced to her. Of course, she may have been to the lecture I gave at Meldon, but I wouldn't know. She wasn't at the little supper party that Miss Renshaw laid on for me. I'm damned sorry for that woman, and for Piers Tracey, too. He's Chairman of the Meldon Governors, as you probably know. An awfully decent chap.'

Pollard agreed that the murder was extremely unfortunate from the point of view of the school authorities, and closed his notebook.

'Well, I don't think I need take up any more of your time, Mr Torrance,' he said. 'As you were up in the studio, I had better take your fingerprints, if you don't mind. We're trying to get the very large number of impressions sorted out.'

'Not in the least. I shall be interested to see exactly how it's done.'

'By the way,' said Pollard in the course of the operation, 'it's possible that you might be called as a witness at the resumed inquest. Have you any plans for going abroad in the fairly near future?'

'Not until mid-September, at the earliest. I might be going over to Paris for a few days about then. But surely you'll have laid the maniac who must have done it by the heels by that time?'

'We certainly hope so,' answered Pollard, making as though to rise.

'Oh, just one other thing before you go. About little Cartmell. She will be able to go all right, won't she? Even if not on Thursday? Dash it, it's obvious she hasn't the remotest connection with the murder—you've only got to look at the kid. It's just sheer bad luck that it happened in the studio instead of one of the labs or a classroom.'

'I'm afraid that's a matter for my superiors. She is, of course, an important witness, unless it can be proved that

Miss Baynes was still alive after Miss Cartmell left the school premises that night.'

'Well, I must say I think it's damned rotten luck. This summer school would benefit her work immensely, quite apart from the chance to see a bit of the world on the cheap.'

'I quite appreciate that, but I'm afraid it's just one of those things . . . I shall be raising the matter of her going, of course, and I've promised her to see what can be done.'

'I'm glad to know that. If it's a question of a dearer last-minute fare on the only available plane, I've told her that I insist on standing it. She needs a let-up after this beastly business.'

Torrance opened the door, and the two men went out on to the landing.

'Are you a painter yourself?' asked Pollard, as they passed the room opposite.

'Not within the meaning of the act. The history of art and art criticism is more my line. I'm the *Assessor's* art critic, you know, and go on the air quite a bit these days. My hobby's wood carving. Come in here, if you've got a minute.'

As he listened to Torrance enthusiastically discussing the properties of various types of wood from the standpoint of a carver's art, Pollard felt his distaste for him less strongly. The man was certainly a creative artist in this medium : there were some superbly designed and executed specimens of his work.

'Reverting to Ann Cartmell once again,' Torrance said as they went downstairs, 'I suppose I had better tell the friends of mine who were meeting her and putting her up for a night or two, to stand by?'

'I think I should,' replied Pollard. 'What about giving me their name and address, in case we are able to rush her over there at short notice, and can't get on to you?'

'That's very decent of you, Inspector. I'll write it down.'

Stepping out into Wain Street a few minutes later, Pollard had the all too familiar feeling of having spent precious time in thoroughly exploring a dead end.

Ten

'Meldon was founded in 1880, to provide a sound education
for the daughters of professional and middle-class families.'
History of Meldon School

WITHIN MOMENTS OF returning to his room at the Yard,
Pollard was immersed in the reports awaiting him on his
desk. Blood tests confirmed that the sample taken from the
table in the studio belonged to the same group as that of
Beatrice Baynes. Microscopic examination showed that the
minute fragment of hair was identical in all respects with a
specimen from the area of the injury . . . It must have been
absolutely unpremeditated, he thought. No weapon brought
along. Would she have been strangled if the stone or something similar hadn't been so handy? Whoever did it was pretty smart over the disposal of the body, but rattled enough for
the traditional small mistake, the putting down of the
weapon without checking up on bloodstains.

The immensely enlarged photographs of the scratches on
the shoe heels and the linoleum showed a correspondence
beyond any question. Pollard's imaginative reconstruction of
the actual murder returned to his mind. He felt, with gratification, that it must be accurate in all essentials . . . Young
Strickland must be told he'd done a sound bit of deduction
over the bloodstains.

Turning to the detailed report on the fingerprints, Pollard
had the sensation of being pulled up sharply. There was no
trace of Madge Thornton's in the studio. He realised with
discomfort that he had begun to take a good deal for granted

where she was concerned : theorising ahead of his data, in fact. But all the same, it seemed quite incredible that she wasn't linked in some way with the murder. If she and George Baynes had been in collusion, her part would probably have been to get Beatrice up to the studio on some pretext or other. In this case she quite possibly wouldn't have left any prints, since the fire-escape door was apparently open all the evening . . . But surely a crime committed in collusion was more likely to have been carefully planned ahead than unpremeditated? . . . He went on reading. As he had feared, the rough wooden struts and hessian of the puppet theatre had failed to yield a single distinguishable print. Ann Cartmell's were everywhere, and Bert Heyward's on both doors and the window catches, but neither of these sets nor Madge Thornton's were on the bureau or other surfaces in Applebys.

Resolutely putting the reports aside, Pollard tabulated the findings of the interview with Clive Torrance. The statements made confirmed Ann Cartmell's in all respects, except that she had not mentioned Torrance's return to the studio to fetch the forgotten *Artifex*. Probably it had seemed so trifling an incident that she had genuinely forgotten it. All the same, he must establish the vital point as to which of them remembered that the periodical had been left behind, and check over times again, as a matter of routine.

Putting the dossier of the case in order, Pollard pressed a buzzer and summoned Detective-Constable Longman, who reported that George Baynes was in an adjoining waiting room. Shadowing him had been child's play. He'd made no move during the night, gone to work at a normal hour, and stayed in the office except for a brief excursion for lunch nearby. Asked if he seemed nervous, Longman hesitated.

'More worried, I'd say, sir. He seemed too preoccupied to notice anything, going through the streets and on the bus.'

'Well, if you're sure he didn't notice you, sit over there, and take it all down when he's shown in. And get me a nice glossy photograph of an only moderately villainous crook, and wipe it clean of prints. I'm anxious not to put the wind up him at this stage.'

Pollard was immediately struck by a resemblance between George Baynes and his great-aunt. The shape of the face, he thought. A much weaker mouth and chin, though . . . Dark, as Cartmell said about the man she saw, and only about five foot nine. Doesn't look as though he slept much last night . . .

Invited to sit down, George Baynes subsided on to the chair in front of Pollard's desk, and darted an uneasy look in the direction of Longman.

'My secretary,' said Pollard. 'I'm sorry to have had to trouble you to come along, Mr Baynes, but as Miss Baynes's next of kin, we're hoping you may be able to help us a lot in the enquiry. I take it that you are, in fact, her nearest surviving relative?'

'Yes, that's quite right,' replied George, with obvious relief at the innocuous opening of the interview. 'The family's on the way out from the look of it. I'm the only one of my generation.'

'She had no surviving brothers or sisters, then, or nephews and nieces?'

'No. Her elder brother, my grandfather, died in 1951. My father was an only child, and he and my mother were killed in the Blitz. There was a younger brother, but he was killed in the '14 war. Aunt B. hadn't any sisters.'

'But surely Miss Madge Thornton is a connection?' enquired Pollard with simulated surprise.

'Good Lord, no!' ejaculated George fervently. 'No relation at all.'

'Really? The fact that she is a godchild of Miss Baynes seems so much in evidence.'

'*She* was a bit too much in evidence if you ask me. Always hanging round Aunt B. when I was down there. Eye to the main chance, in my opinion.'

'Miss Baynes must have been attached to Miss Thornton, though. I understand that she paid for her education, and gave her very generous presents. It will be interesting to see if she has made provision for her in her will.'

George looked up sharply.

'Do you know anything about the will yet? I couldn't get a thing out of old Yelland, her lawyer, when I rang him up.'

'I expect he feels it would hardly be correct to divulge its contents until after the funeral.'

'Lawyers are always so damned cagey. When on earth will the funeral be? How long are the police going to hold it up?'

'Assuming that the coroner issued a burial certificate this morning, it will be a matter for the executors,' replied Pollard calmly. 'I suppose Miss Thornton's parents must have been old friends of Miss Baynes?'

'I haven't a clue,' said George impatiently. 'It must have been ages ago, anyway.'

'Do you know Miss Thornton well?'

'Hardly my cup of tea!'

'No,' agreed Pollard. 'It must have been annoying for you to have her in and out so much when you were staying with your great-aunt.'

'She nearly drives me up the wall,' George admitted in a burst of confidence. 'And Aunt B. felt the same, if you ask me. She was a one, you know, and liked you to stand up to her. I've seen her hopping mad at Madge's everlasting "yes, Aunt Beatrice", and "no, Aunt Beatrice". Can't think what she saw in her. If the old dear hadn't been so strait-laced, you might have thought Madge was a by-blow of hers.'

Could there possibly, Pollard wondered, be anything in this preposterous suggestion?

'Well,' he said, 'no doubt you'll be hearing all about Miss Baynes's will when you go down for the funeral.'

For the first time since the interview began, George showed signs of unease.

'Oh—well, yes, I suppose so. It takes so long if you haven't got a car. Upsets them at the office.'

Pollard made a pretence of consulting his notebook.

'I'm sure you'll understand,' he went on, in a slightly different tone, 'that in a case of murder the police have to make a large number of enquiries from everyone in any way connected with the victim. You will have seen in the Press that Applebys was broken into in the course of last weekend. We consider this highly significant. We have reason to suppose,'—he fixed his eyes on George's face—'that the person involved had an intimate knowledge of Miss Baynes's habits.'

The young man paled visibly, and moistened his lips.

'Not really?' he said, with an attempt to show keen interest.

'Yes. There were unmistakable indications. Now, Mr Baynes, I want you to look at this photograph very carefully. Take your time . . . Have you ever seen this man working at Applebys? Possibly as a gardener?'

George took the photograph with a hand which was far from steady. Pollard watched him considering his reply.

'I'm not quite sure,' he said at last. 'I've got a rotten memory for faces. There was a chap doing some digging in the garden at Whitsun, but I didn't notice him particularly.'

Pollard took back the photograph by a corner, and dropped it into a drawer.

'Was that your last visit to Applebys?'

'Yes.'

'You are quite sure you didn't go down there last weekend?'

'Absolutely. I was on duty at the office.'

'Not all the weekend, surely? You're at Grant and Wotherspoon, the estate agents, aren't you?'

'Yes. No, I mean, I was on duty on Saturday morning.'

'What did you do after the office closed?'

'Went and had a sandwich and beer at the pub across the road, and then hung about listening to the racing results.'

'Any luck?'

'None. Not even placed.'

'And then?'

George took a deep breath. He's prepared the next bit, thought Pollard.

'I'd begun to feel a bit under the weather. When I got home I was as sick as a dog. Could hardly get to the loo. It must have been the sandwich, I suppose : they hand out such muck at these places. I felt bloody. Went on heaving for hours, and just lying on my bed and sweating.'

'How unpleasant,' said Pollard. 'Wasn't there anybody to get you a hot water-bottle, or anything?'

'Oh, no. There's only a woman who cleans the place after a fashion, but she goes off to her married daughter on Saturdays and Sundays.'

'But what about the other people living in the house? I should have thought one of them might have come to your assistance.'

'They wouldn't have known anything about it. I didn't hear a sound. Most people are away at weekends, and I barely know the other chaps by sight.'

'So you spent all Saturday evening on a bed of sickness?'

'I certainly did! I could hardly sit up. I took a dollop of aspirin, and slept it off. Didn't move till Sunday morning, when I felt like a cup of tea and some toast. I was just about able to crawl round to the local by lunch-time.'

'Well, I'm glad you managed to recover so quickly,' said Pollard, 'although you still look a bit the worse for wear. I don't think I need keep you any longer, Mr Baynes — I expect you'll be glad to get home. Perhaps you won't mind waiting while your statement is typed out for you to read through and sign?'

There was a perceptible pause.

'Er—no, of course not.'

'Just see Mr Baynes to a waiting-room, Longman, and then get his statement done as quickly as you can, will you . . . ?'

'Did he sign it, Longman?' Pollard asked.

'Yes, sir. Skimmed through it and dashed his name down. Very anxious to be off. Pitt was waiting to tail him. Bit amateurish, wasn't it, sir?'

'Difficult to believe he can really think we've swallowed it, isn't it? You dropped the prints in on Dabs?'

'Yes, sir. They said they'd get on to them right away.'

The telephone on Pollard's desk rang, and he accepted a personal call from Linbridge.

Sergeant Toye reported that the inquest had been adjourned after the coroner had taken evidence of identity, and that the burial certificate had been duly issued. The funeral—strictly private—had been fixed for Thursday, and Mr Yelland had wired to Mr George Baynes's private address to ask him to come down tomorrow—Wednesday—afternoon.

'Has he, now?' ejaculated Pollard.

'That's right, sir.' Toye went on to report in guarded fashion that Madge Thornton was again under sedation, that the presumed weapon had not been found, and that a house-to-house enquiry about strangers in the neighbourhood was in full swing. He, Toye, had found out that one of Miss Cartmell's girl helpers lived quite near, and the other one was conveniently staying with her. He was just going over to check up with them . . . Yes, in the presence of the parents, of course.

Pollard was briefly encouraging, and rang off. As he did so, a messenger arrived from Sergeant Blair of the fingerprints department. A report stated categorically that the prints on the bureau and other surfaces at Applebys were those of George Baynes, but that none of his appeared in the photographs relating to the studio at Meldon.

'What the hell!" muttered Pollard. 'When are you taking over from Pitt, Longman?'

'Ten o'clock, sir.'

'Keep in touch, then. It's just faintly possible that I may be making an arrest. And for God's sake, don't let young Baynes give you the slip.'

Chief Superintendent Crowe looked up from an evening paper as Pollard came in. PUPPET THEATRE MYSTERY INQUEST screamed from the front page.

'Publicity in a big way,' he remarked. 'You'll have to bring it off, my boy. Let's hear your report.' He pushed a box of cigarettes towards Pollard, and lighted a pipe in a leisurely way. 'Go ahead,' he ordered.

Years ago Crowe had just scraped into the police by a millimetre of height. Now, not far from retirement, he was still upright and energetic, with a thatch of white hair, and very bright eyes, appropriately capable of a fixed avian stare. This he now directed upon Pollard, who took a deep breath and plunged.

The Chief Superintendent was famous for the apparently irrelevant remarks which he would throw out at the end of a subordinate's report, and also for the sudden unnerving demands for information while it was in progress.

'Wait a minute,' he interrupted, after Pollard had been talking for some time. 'Make out the family tree of this Baynes lot.'

Thanking Heaven that history had been his favourite subject in school, Pollard seized a sheet of paper, and hastily constructed the genealogical table showing the four generations of the family which had emerged in the course of the enquiry. Crowe accepted it with a grunt.

'Go on,' he said, thirty seconds later.

When Pollard had finished, silence descended. Crowe blew

a perfect smoke ring, and watched it slowly disintegrate.

'These middle-class murders mean a hell of a lot of work,' he remarked.

'Sir?' replied Pollard, accepting the gambit.

'The nobs,' pronounced Crowe, 'are news. Thanks to the Press their lives are an open book. In the working-classes the neighbours know everything, and a bit more. The middle classes are much better at covering their tracks. They're reticent, and expert at not attracting attention, all tucked away in their detached houses with a nice bit of garden. You have to dig. Jolly deep, sometimes.'

'Meaning the history of the Baynes family, sir?'

'I've stated a general principle. What do you want done?'

'I thought of enquiries about the Thorntons, to try to establish some kind of link with the Bayneses.'

'Naturally, but can't you think of a shorter cut as well? Time isn't on your side, my boy.'

'Somerset House?'

'Of course. Where can we get Madge Thornton's date of birth, to speed things up?'

'Ministry of Education?' suggested Pollard, in a flash of inspiration.

Crowe grunted approval, and made a couple of notes on his pad, and resumed his unblinking contemplation of his subordinate.

'What do you consider is the most striking feature of the murder?' he asked.

'Its unpremeditated character, sir.'

'Quite. That adds to your difficulties, too, doesn't it? No nice trail of poison-buying under false names, or secondhand typewriters acquired in disguise. Just a handy paper-weight picked up on the spur of the moment. You needn't necessarily have a motive in the ordinary sense of the word. Have you taken steps to get a medical report on this caretaker chap?'

'No, sir,' replied Pollard, mentally kicking himself.

Crowe made another note, without comment.

'Anything else?' he asked.

'Applying your principle of digging deep, sir, it might be as well to make some enquiries about Torrance and Cartmell, although they hardly seem to be in the running.'

'Quite right. We'll put that in train, although it may take a bit of time. Do you want to arrest young Baynes?'

'On the breaking and entering charge?' Pollard hesitated. 'On the whole, I'd rather not, unless you feel I'm taking an unjustifiable risk. He's being tailed, and I don't think he'll make a bolt at this stage. Much too keen to see how he comes out under the will. Seems to me a point in his favour, that. My guess is that he'll go down to Linbridge tomorrow to see the solicitor, and I'd rather confront him with the evidence of the break-in down there. I think he's more likely to give himself away. And if I confront Madge Thornton with *him,* I think there's a good chance she'd crack up, if they were in it together. I still feel that's a possibility, in spite of the lack of evidence of their dabs in the studio, and the fact that it seems to me to have been unpremeditated.'

Crowe considered.

'Who's trailing him?'

'Pitt and Longman, sir.'

'All right. We'll put on a more experienced man to cover the train journey. What else?'

'There's this girl Ann Cartmell, and her scholarship to America. Toye is now checking on a final point, but I think we can take it she's got an alibi for the whole period, although admittedly she was in the studio alone with Torrance for about half-an-hour. I've got a hunch that he'll see to it there's a stink in the Press if we don't let her go.'

'I can't see a man like Torrance laying himself open to being blackmailed by committing a murder in front of a witness,' replied Crowe thoughtfully. 'All the same we can't let her go till we've screened her. Keep them quiet by saying not before Monday. You said this affair she's going to didn't start up till Tuesday, didn't you?'

'Yes, sir,' said Pollard, marvelling at his chief's capacity to absorb detail from a oral report.

'Right. You know where to find me. Keep going—and good luck. This case is giving you a chance a lot of chaps would like to have.'

Eleven

'Stark human tragedy has usurped the stage of the Meldon Marionettes whose delightful performances have so often featured in our pages.'

The Linbridge Echo

'IT WAS JUST after we got engaged,' Jane Pollard said. 'You drove down to fetch me back at the end of the course.'

'Strike me pink!' ejaculated her husband. 'So I did. And you say they were both there?'

'Yes. It was one of the National Art Summer Schools. Clive Torrance was the director, and did some lecturing and teaching. I remember Ann Cartmell quite well.'

Tom Pollard straddled a chair. 'Spill the beans,' he said. 'All of them.'

'Not until you've had a bath and we're at the drinks stage. Actually they don't add up to the smallest hillock, I'm afraid. Just my impressions, that's all. Nothing that a famous detective would consider evidence.' She indicated a scatter of evening papers, and put on a stagestruck expression.

'Come off it!' He cuffed the side of her head and departed in the direction of the bathroom.

The Pollards occupied a small flat near the British Museum, on the top floor of a converted terrace house. There was no lift, and the set-up was old-fashioned, but their rooms were unexpectedly large, and the height above street level reduced traffic noise and petrol fumes. Jane had redecorated the flat herself, and they were gradually collecting pleasant pieces of furniture for a family house later on.

Bathed and relaxed, Tom sat by the window and contemplated his wife. On this warm, close evening she was wearing a green and gold tunic and trousers which she had designed herself. He thought how well it set off her bright auburn hair, creamy complexion and brown eyes, and how, even in repose, she conveyed her dynamic quality and amused, appraising attitude to life.

'To the case,' she said, raising her glass. 'And oneupmanship.'

'Cheers,' he replied.

Jane went to the point with characteristic directness.

'I thought Clive Torrance was ghastly,' she said. 'The most blatantly conceited man I've ever struck. He simply wasn't true at times. Unpleasantly subtle conceit, too.'

'Meaning? I thought it simply hit you in the face when I saw him at the Domani.'

'The conceit's all tied up with perfectly sound things. He *is* an artist, and genuinely keen on the country's art education. A first-class teacher, too. But he gets the wrong sort of kick out of it. I mean, he enjoys the adulation of his protégées much more than seeing them push on into the do-it-yourself stage. And he plays to the gallery, too, which always makes me see red.'

'Yes. There was a demonstration of that this afternoon. How amorous is he?'

'Highly, I'm quite sure, but he doesn't mix business and pleasure. 'He's the kind of man who weighs up asking you to go to bed with him with the possible effect on his reputation if it gets out. Never mind yours. But he'd never take risks on a course, if that's what you're thinking.'

'What about Ann Cartmell?'

'She was rather pathetic, I thought. Very gifted artistically, but desperately unsure of herself. She'd come a cropper in her first teaching job, and all her educational ideals were in bits. She was talking about going into advertising, I remember, but of course she hasn't the personality or drive for it. I gather she has stayed in teaching after all. I wonder how she got taken on by a school in the Meldon class?'

'Torrance got her the job. Apparently their art woman died just before the school year started — it must have been soon after this course you were on. The Chairman of the Meldon Governors had met him, and asked him if he could find somebody at short notice. I gather that ever since, he's constituted himself a sort of unofficial art director of the school. The H.M. has got him nicely sized up, but admits that he's useful. Did he show any special professional interest in Ann Cartmell, as distinct from amatory?'

Jane Pollard stared out of the window.

'No,' she said, 'I can't remember anything in that line either. But it was a big place, and there were quite a lot of us. And oddly enough, I was a bit preoccupied with my own affairs just then.'

'You don't say,' remarked her husband, getting up and refilling her glass. 'What sort of a show is the Domani?'

'Pretty well thought-of. It belongs to a syndicate, but policy and all that is believed to be left to Torrance. It specialises in the work of young artists, but handles other stuff as well. I imagine it's doing nicely.'

'Torrance certainly is. He took me up to his rooms. Lush, but good. He's got a sort of workshop-cum-studio up there, too, and showed me some marvellous paneling he'd carved.'

'He's an artist, all right. He doesn't paint much these days, as far as I know, but he certainly knows how painting should be done, and can get it across.'

'Them as can't, teach,' murmured Pollard.

'I was waiting for that. Let's eat. There's a casserole in the oven.'

Later, when supper had been cleared away, they discussed the case at length.

'Wouldn't it make a gorgeous stage thriller?' Jane remarked. 'That superb opening . . . I often think,' she went on seriously, 'that much more attention ought to be paid to the victim in a murder case. After all, the victim is the *raison d'être* of the crime. He—or she—must have got something, or know something or have done something which sparks off the killer. What do you really know about B.B.?'

'The trouble is that you can only know the victim by hearsay. I've given you a biographical sketch incidentally. The thing about her that sticks out for me is the sheer waste of a human being. I mean, she was able, and a fighter with tremendous staying power, and capable of generosity, and all it came to in the end was an obsessional hostility to changes in her old school.'

'It sounds to me,' Jane said, 'as though it went deeper than that. Probably the only time in her life when she was stretched and fulfilled was when she was at school, and the opposition to the changes was an irrational attempt to protect something she valued enormously. How extraordinary of the parents, though, to send her to a pioneer school, and then simply keep her at home to do the flowers. Too much money, I suppose?'

'I should think so. Not a very congenial family life, either. Apparently she couldn't get on with her elder brother, and the younger one was killed in the First World War, while the Blitz accounted for her only nephew. That left the unsatisfactory George, who may have murdered her. And the goddaughter is quite definiety a flop, and also a suspect. Frustrated at every turn, poor old girl, and finally descending to getting a kick out of snooping.'

'I'm pretty sure that it was the prospect of successful snooping that got her over to the school again after a whole day at an Old Girls' Reunion. You wouldn't know how exhausting they are. Old Boys just sit and guzzle at dinners.'

'I suppose,' Pollard said meditatively, 'that she might somehow have found out that Torrance and Ann Cartmell were going to be up in the studio, and hoped to burst in on what police reports call a compromising situation. But if so, it was a forlorn hope, from your account of Torrance. Even if it had come off, I take it that you'd discount the idea that he'd go as far as murdering her to safeguard his public image?'

'Of course I should. It's a fantastic idea. Personally, I think she was after the caretaker. Perhaps she'd found out that he sits a bit lightly to locking-up in the holidays. If she could report to the Governors that the place had been left open all night it would reflect on the Renshaw régime.'

'The difficulty about this is the timing,' said Pollard. 'Madge Thornton says that she couldn't get an answer at Applebys when she went there at about 8.20. Heyward wasn't due to start on his round until 9.0 Surely B.B. wouldn't have gone over so early?'

'You've only got Madge's word for it, after all. Suppose she found B.B. in, and discovered that she was going over to snoop on Heyward? Madge could have hung about in the grounds, and then followed B.B. up to the studio and killed her. There is the money motive, and the strong probability that something had come to light at the time of Mrs Thornton's death which involved B.B. Do you think there could possibly be anything in that by-blow remark of George's?'

'Theoretically, yes. Madge is in her mid-forties, so would have been born during the First World War. I've wondered if B.B. was allowed to go off and be a V.A.D. or something of the sort? But anyway, the question of Madge's parentage is being looked into . . . One's got to remember that no prints of hers have cropped up in the studio.'

'That's not conclusive proof of her innocence, is it?'

'No, especially as the blasted puppet theatre wouldn't take prints. But think of the fun Counsel for the Defense would have over it . . . Anyway, If Madge is guilty, where does George come in, and why did he break into Applebys? While I was driving up this morning I got quite exctied over an idea that they might have worked the whole thing between them, but the more I think about it, the more unlikely I think it is.'

'Because it seems to have been so unpremeditated, you mean?'

'Yes. I simply can't believe that they were secretly such buddies that they'd team up and murder B.B. the moment an unexpected chance turned up. I wonder . . .'

Jane looked at him.

'Let's call it a day. My head's going round, and you're beginning to look glassy-eyed. How early must I set the alarm?'

Pollard examined a squalid little heap of food scraps which had been brought into Linbridge police station. An empty milk bottle had yielded excellent fingerprints. He passed one of the photographs which he had brought back from the Yard to Inspector Beakbane.

'Sticks out like a sore thumb, doesn't it?' remarked the latter, trying to conceal his gratification under a show of nonchalance. 'Thought our chaps would soon pick him up for you. We'd better get along the bloke who met him, hadn't we?'

'I'd be grateful. This has been an enormous help. How far away was this barn where Baynes dossed down on Saturday night?'

'About a couple of miles out on the Whitesands road. Reckon he got going again as soon as it was light, and just melted into the holiday crowds when he got there. Plenty of trains back to London.'

'Which way would he have gone, do you think?'

'The usual way would be along the Trill road, and then take the left fork just short of the village.'

Pollard, who had a good bump of locality, looked interested.

'Then he could have cut through the park?'

'Sure. Cut off a big corner that way, and less risk of being seen, too. But getting out on the far side might have been tricky. They don't use the gate, and it's kept padlocked. He'd have to get over a pretty hefty wall.'

Pollard reflected that George Baynes looked reasonably athletic.

'Do you think he and Miss Thornton may have met in the park?' asked Toye.

'It's possible. But whether they were in cahoots is another story, and one I find it difficult to swallow. But it's been suggested to me that Miss Thornton may have known that Miss Baynes intended to go over and snoop on Heyward on Saturday night, and followed her there, and that all her subsequent antics were to cover her tracks.'

'Bit risky to go up after her with Heyward due to arrive at any moment, surely, sir?'

'You can't commit murder without taking risks,' replied Inspector Beakbane. 'It often holds me back.'

'Come on, Toye,' said Pollard. 'I've got a feeling we're out-staying our welcome here. Besides, we've got a day's work to do.'

In another room they viewed the timetable together.

'I got confirmation from those girls all right,' said Toye. 'Pair of young baggages, if you like. Mr Rivers sat doubled up in the corner. I thought playing their game was the best line to take. They did their best to date me, if you please. The Cart's Heart Throb's what they call Mr Torrance . . . Still, they were good witnesses, for all that. Absolutely definite that they were with Miss Cartmell the whole time, from when she came into the Quad from seeing him off, to when she drove away in the car, just after nine o'clock.'

'Well, that's one more loose end tidied up . . . And we know that both Cartmell and Thornton were at the supper . . . Any luck with the secretary?'

'I found her a bit sticky, sir. Chip on her shoulder, I'd say.

Said it had been a tiresome interruption, and she hadn't noticed the time particularly. But in the end she agreed that it was about half-past eight, and that Miss Cartmell was only there for a very short time before Mr Torrance arrived. He didn't come in—said goodnight very graciously from the door—and after they'd gone, she'd heard a car start and drive off almost at once.'

Pollard put another tick in the third column of the timetable.

'Let's get cracking,' he said. 'I want to make the most of this breathing space before George Baynes arrives, and we get a report from the Yard on the Baynes-Thornton connection.'

As the police car drew up outside the Staff House, Ann Cartmell came running out, her face anxiously interrogative, an expression which quickly turned to near-despair.

'Oh,' she said, almost in tears, 'nothing more definite than not before Monday? I did hope that now the inquest's over, I'd be allowed to go on Thursday after all.'

'It isn't over, you know,' Pollard told her. 'Only adjourned, for more enquiries to be made. But a lot of ground will have been covered by Monday, and I think the sensible course for you is to go home and start getting your things together. We've got your telephone number, and I'll get into touch with you the moment my superiors come to a decision about your going. And you know you don't have to worry about cheap fares. Mr Torrance told me he was seeing to that.'

Her face lighted up.

'He's wonderful to me.'

Golly, thought Pollard, you poor little boob . . . 'Suppose we hop into the back of the car,' he said aloud, 'while I just make sure there's nothing more I want to ask you before you go.'

Getting out, he opened the rear door for her, and sat beside her with his notebook on his knee.

'Let me see,' he said casually, turning over some pages.

'Oh, yes. Just a small point, but we have to get everything absolutely clear. When I saw Mr Torrance yesterday, he said something about having gone back to the studio to fetch a copy of *Artifex*, on Saturday evening.'

Ann Cartmell looked at him with a sudden startled expression.

'Oh, dear! I forgot to tell you that, didn't I? It must have gone straight out of my head. He'd shown me a reproduction in the August number which he had with him. I must have put it down on the table, and we both forgot about it. It wasn't until we had got down to the Quad that I suddenly remembered, and asked him if he'd picked it up. He wasn't a bit cross, although it was all my fault.'

Pollard suppressed a strong desire to shake her.

'It was you who remembered about it?'

'Yes, fortunately, or he'd probably have gone off without it.'

'Now, I want to get this quite straight, Miss Cartmell. While Mr Torrance went back to the studio, you hurried on to the secretary's office. Is that right?'

'Yes.'

'How long was it before he joined you?'

'Oh, hardly any time. I ran ahead, and luckily Mrs Kitson was still there. She gave me the form, and I only had to fill in the three names : everything else was done. I was just sticking up the parcel when he came to the door. Then we went out to the car together, as I told you.'

With this, Pollard let her go.

'What did you make of that?' he asked Toye, rejoining him in the front seat.

'O.K. I'd say, sir, on both counts. She strikes me as too — well, simple, to have been putting on an act. And it's difficult to see how Torrance could have had a quarrel leading to murder, and stowed away the body and got down to the office in the time. We've got the secretary's evidence that he turned up in a matter of minutes.'

'I agree. Having checked up on that one point about which of them remembered the magazine, I think we'd better start on the interminable job of trying to find someone who saw the two Bayneses and Madge Thornton on their various comings and goings last Saturday evening. Dash it—there were about fifty people who were spending the night on the premises. I refuse to believe that they'd all turned in by about nine o'clock. Let's make for the school, and see if we can get any of them eliminated.'

Twelve

'Behind
The wall,
The wall compounded of fossiliferous limestone,
Voiceless fragments of an earlier creation,
Stands another wall, articulated, ericacaean,
Red-eyed in the agony of the year's springtime,
Impenetrable rampart of rhododendron.'
CORINNA HISLOP. Lower VI (Arts)

From The Meldonian

HELEN RENSHAW was looking older, thought Pollard, noting
the lines of strain about her eyes. As he put the evidence as to
the place and method of the murder before her, he saw that
she had anticipated the request that he was going to make,
and was disturbed by it.

'I can't help realising,' she said unhappily, 'that this may
lead to asking a great deal — in fact, a terrible thing from
some member of the school.'

'On the other hand, Miss Renshaw,' he replied, 'it may well
be the means of completely clearing innocent people.'

'That is true, of course,' she admitted, and reluctantly took
the list of names which he held out to her . . . 'All these
persons slept on the premises last Saturday night, to the best
of my knowledge and belief, but some of them can be accounted for between nine and ten o'clock. That should
simplify your enquiry. For instance, some of the very elderly
were staying at the Sanatorium, and I saw Sister Littlejohn
shepherding them over there from the dining-room, directly
after supper . . . Then my coffee party up here didn't finally
break up until about a quarter past ten . . .

Pollard watched her as she carefully annotated the paper,

and wondered how she would cope with the problem of a murder on the school premises when it came to dealing with the girls next term. When Toye had gone off to interview the resident staff, and contact a series of local police forces by telephone, he remained behind to talk to her about Bert Heyward. He learnt that the fullest enquiries had been made into the man's health and character at the time of his appointment nine years earlier, and he had never shown the slightest sign of mental instability.

'Naturally, if he had, we couldn't have risked keeping him for five minutes in a girls' boarding school,' Helen Renshaw said. 'As I told you, he isn't a forceful personality, but most conscientious and very capable as a handyman.'

'I think you said he hadn't much initiative. Isn't that rather a drawback in such a responsible post?'

She smiled.

'Have you met Mrs Heyward yet, Inspector?' she asked. 'She has more than enough for both of them. We really appointed her as much as him, and it has worked admirably.'

'Yes, I see,' said Pollard. 'My sergeant rather deduced that. Apparently Heyward was upset by Inspector Beakbane's questions.'

'I think some nervousness of authority is a hangover from his concentration camp experiences. I've noticed it myself, and always make a point of dealing with him very gently.'

An interesting point, thought Pollard. How would he react to an unexpected hostile challenge in the half-light, especially if he were feeling slightly guilty about being late?

Thanking Helen Renshaw, and promising to keep her informed of any important developments, he left Old House and walked down the drive. He crossed the road and went in at the garden gate of Applebys, but did not enter the house. Standing in the porch, he tried to imagine the thoughts of Madge Thornton as she had stood there on the previous Saturday evening . . .

I'm furiously angry with Beatrice, he told himself, and determined to see her. I've come back for the second time, and try the front door. No good—the catch is down, so I ring the bell . . .

He listened to the oddly disturbing sound of a bell ringing and ringing in an empty house.

There's no answer, but she may possibly be in the garden, so I go round to see . . .

Pollard went round the side of the house, and looked up at its uncommunicative façade with every window closed. The garden was already showing faint signs of neglect. The grass needed cutting, and the dead roses snipping off. Birds hopped about with an air of being in possession.

I call up at the bedroom window . . . . if she's gone to bed, I'm going to get her up . . . Again, no answer. She must have gone out to dinner somewhere . . . She's hardly ever as late as this. I'm going to wait . . .

Pollard's eye fell on a garden seat. No, he thought. Beatrice might have invited one of her old friends to spend the night, and be bringing her back . . . So I decide against staying in the garden . . . I go round to the front of the house again, and hesitate for a minute or two . . .

He stood just inside the gate and looked across the road at the wall of Meldon Park. The iron railings removed for scrap metal during the war had not been replaced. The wall itself was only about three feet high, and backed by tall rhododendron shrubs. With a sudden feeling of excitement he went over to the school gates and turned right, carefully scrutinising the bushes. Opposite the entrance to Applebys he found two small branches snapped off. They hung limply, their leaves already dry and curling. After satisfying himself that the ground was too hard to take footprints, he manoeuvred through a gap into the narrow space between the rhododendrons and the wall. It was a perfect observation post for anyone prepared to kneel or crouch. Moving cautiously he came on clear signs of a sojourn . . . twigs snapped off, and the carpet of dead leaves scuffed up. Dropping on to his knees he found that the top of the wall was only a little below his eye level, and estimated that he was about three inches taller than Madge Thornton. Examining the branches behind the disturbed area he came on a sandy-coloured woollen thread caught on a broken twig. He disengaged it with care, and put it into an envelope. A painstaking search of the leaves on the ground stirred up a good deal of dust and an acrid smell which made him sneeze, but failed to yield any useful result.

Squeezing his way out to the park again, Pollard stood lost in thought, while automatically brushing himself down . . . Surely, if George Baynes had cut through the park after leaving Applebys, he wouldn't have risked the gates under the very nose of the Eccles family? Much safer to go over the wall and dive into the shrubs, after peeping out to see the coast was clear. And if Madge was still keeping the house under observation he must have landed almost on top of her. Was this the explanation of her hysteria when he had asked her if she had seen anyone coming away from Applebys? If the encounter had taken place, *could* it have led to their joining forces to murder Beatrice?

Going back to the road, Pollard walked along close to the wall, looking for any traces of George's passage. Not more than a dozen yards beyond the place where he had found the woollen thread there were several more snapped-off branches suggesting that someone had pushed through in haste. He leant over the wall and saw signs of a heavy landing : a deep heel print in a patch of bare earth.

After a second dusty and fruitless investigation among the dead leaves, he began to make his way back to Old House, thinking furiously. Since Ann Cartmell had overtaken Madge in the drive just after nine, it didn't look as though the latter had been in her spy-hole between her two visits to Applebys. She might not, therefore, have seen George arrive. But if she took up her position after her second call, she might quite well have seen him leave : she hadn't turned up at the Staff house until about ten-twelve . . . The strand of wool of that hideous sandy colour was pretty conclusive evidence that she had been there at some stage, but it could have been in the afternoon, perhaps? She might have hoped that Beatrice would come home for a rest after lunch . . .

Pollard switched his thoughts to George Baynes. Was it possible that he had come down by invitation? Madge didn't seem to be in Beatrice's confidence as far as the latter's plans went. He might have found a note in the porch, hidden by arrangement, and telling him that his great-aunt had gone over to the studio. He could have followed her there, had a quarrel and killed her in a sudden blind rage . . . Not a very convincing idea, surely? How well did he know the lay-out of the school, in the first place? Mot men were extremely chary of invading female institutions . . . Then of course, if he'd arrived just before nine and gone straight over, he'd have met Madge coming down the drive . . . One kept on coming back to Madge . . . He'd simply got to see her again, and must tackle the doctor.

Arriving at the front door of Old House, he went in and found Toye in the library, who reported that he had drawn a complete blank with Joyce Kitson, Jean Forrest and the various matrons. None of them had anything to report about the Bayneses, Madge Thornton, Bert Heyward or the purlieus of the studio between nine and ten on Saturday night or round about half-past eight either. George Baynes, met off the London train by Sergeant Toye and diverted to the police station, came in protesting indignantly.

'I've come down to see Yelland by appointment,' he blustered. 'It's the ruddy limit hauling me off like this as if I was a ruddy criminal. We've got important business to see to. Surely you can wait for an hour, whatever it is you want to see me about?'

'Murder invariably takes priority over other business,' replied Pollard. 'Sit down, Mr Baynes. This may take a little time. Mr Yelland has been told that you will be late for your appointment. You are, of course, within your rights in refusing to answer any questions except in the presence of a solicitor.'

There was no mistaking the alarm on George's face as he subsided on to a chair, muttering that he had no need of a solicitor and making a creditable attempt to glare at Pollard.

'As you please,' said the latter. 'Sergeant Toye, I think Mr Baynes may wish to amend the statement he made to me yesterday. I put it to you,' he went on, looking steadily at George, 'that everything in it relating to your actions between Saturday afternoon and roughly midday on Sunday is pure fiction.'

'Try to prove it then,' snapped George, with uncertain truculence.

'We have, Mr Baynes. Up to the hilt.'

'If you think I'm going to fall into that old trap, you're doomed to disappointment.'

'Very well, Mr Baynes. I'll do the talking, if you'd rather have it that way. I put it to you that you were in a pretty tight corner financially last Saturday afternoon, and that your unlucky bet or bets brought matters to a head. You simply had to have some cash, and decided to appeal to your great-aunt. As you were broke, I expect you hitch-hiked to somewhere within walking distance of Applebys, probably where the minor road over the hills to Trill leaves the London road.'

Pollard broke off, and nodded to Toye, who rose and went out of the room, returning a few moments later with an elderly man of the farm labourer type.

'Good afternoon, Mr Aggett,' said Pollard. 'Do you recognise the gentleman who is sitting opposite to me?'

The man favoured the discomfited George with a searching stare.

'Aye, I met 'un Saturday night on the road up over Glintridge. On me way 'ome from the Plough, I wur. Roun' ten to nine, must've bin.'

'Are you quite sure?'

'Aye. 'E be spruced up now, but wur dressed loike one o'

they 'ikers when I seed 'un, wi' a green shirt an' pack on 'is back. But 'tis same chap, I'd take me bible oath. Know 'un anywur wi' they stick-out lugs o' his'n'.'

'Thank you,' said Pollard hastily. 'Have you any comment to make, Mr Baynes?'

'The fellow's nuts. I was ill in bed on Saturday night.'

''Ere!' broke in Mr Aggett indignantly. ''Oo's sayin' I'm a liar?'

When he had been escorted out, and Toye had returned and resumed his seat, Pollard looked at George.

'Shall I go on, Mr Baynes? I put it to you that you arrived at Applebys just before nine o'clock, but found the front door locked and could get no answer when you rang the bell. You were seen coming out of the porch in your green shirt at about five minutes past nine.'

'Can it be that one or two other chaps in the country wear green shirts?'

'Undoubtedly, but let me go on with my reconstruction. You got through quite a lot before you vaulted over the wall and crashed through the bushes, didn't you? I'm not quite sure of the exact order of events, but perhaps it was something like this. You found that the kitchen window was open and got into the house. You went to the drawer in your great-aunt's bureau where you knew she kept her money, unlocked it with the key which she kept in the jug on the top, and stole about fifty pounds. You also helped yourself to a valuable snuff box from the drawing-room. You were hungry enough to raid the larder and take some food and a bottle of milk. It is never easy to remove all traces of one's fingerprints, but you were quite remarkably inept at it. Really, you made it too easy for us.'

'You haven't got any fingerprints,' said George hoarsely. 'I suppose this is one of the ways the police try to trap people into admitting things.'

'You left impressions on that photograph you handled at Scotland Yard, Mr Baynes.'

George swallowed, but said nothing.

'The only thing we're not quite clear about,' Pollard continued in a conversational tone, 'is whether you broke into Applebys before or after you murdered Miss Baynes.'

There was a violent crash as George Baynes leapt to his feet, sending his chair flying backwards.

'It's a bloody lie,' he shouted. 'I never set eyes on her the whole time.'

'Sit down,' ordered Pollard brusquely, as Toye, who had also sprung up, replaced the fallen chair. 'Now that you find you can't deny being at Applebys last Saturday, I suggest that you make a truthful statement this time. Perhaps you don't realise that it's an offence to try to mislead the police?'

George Baynes, now ashen-faced, looked at him steadily. When he spoke, it was with unexpected dignity.

'All right,' he said. 'I admit what I told you yesterday wasn't true. What I'm going to say now, is. But before I start, I want to say that I never saw Aunt Beatrice from first to last, and that I'd sooner have chucked myself under a bus than done her any harm. We didn't see eye to eye over a lot of things, but I was fond of her, and she was my only living relative.'

'What you have just said will be included in your statement,' replied Pollard. 'Now, I suggest that you start from the point at which you were listening to the racing results on the radio.'

He followed intently as George described his sudden decision to go down to Applebys and ask for an advance on his birthday cheque, and how he had tried in vain to get through to his great-aunt on the telephone. George confirmed that he had hitch-hiked, arriving at the crossroads at 8.20 p.m., and his encounter with Mr Aggett. Arriving at the school gates, he had seen the parking notice and deduced that something was on at Meldon. He had found Applebys locked up, and just as he was going away from the front door, had seen a girl drive out of the gates and turn along the road to Trill.

'What did you do next?' asked Pollard.

'I went round to the garden. You can't always hear the bell if you're out there. But there was no sign of Aunt B., so I peered into the dining-room and drawing-room windows. While I was doing that I heard the gate click, and skipped behind some bushes.'

'Why did you do that? I should have thought that you would have gone round to the front door again, expecting to see Miss Baynes.'

'You didn't know Aunt B.,' replied George, with the first gleam of humour he had shown. 'I'd come down in hopes of touching her, and was terrified of queering my pitch. I wanted to get a clue on the sort of mood she was in.'

'What happened then?'

'I heard the front-door bell ring and wondered who on earth could be calling at that hour. Aunt B. liked to doss down awfully early, and evening visitors weren't encouraged. After a bit I heard someone coming round to the garden, and Madge Thornton appeared.'

'Were you surprised?'

'Completely baffled. I'd taken it for granted that Aunt B. was over at the school, but I realised that she couldn't be, because Madge would have known about it, and was almost certain to have been there herself. So I decided that Aunt B. must have gone out to supper, probably with some old pal.'

'What did Miss Thornton do?'

'Dithered a bit, and peered in at the windows as I'd done, and then called up at the bedroom window. Nothing happened, so in the end she went away again. I waited till I heard the gate, and then popped out.'

There was a pause.

'Go on, Mr Baynes,' said Pollard crisply.

'All this will sound pretty unconvincing,' George Baynes said unhappily, "but it's the honest truth. My one aim was to step off on the right foot when Aunt B. came back. Sometimes the thing that paid off best with her was cheek. I was jolly hungry, so when I found the kitchen window was open, I nipped in and vetted the larder and the fridge. There was plenty of grub about, but my tongue was hanging out, so I thought I'd take a look round and see if there was any sherry going : there usually was. The drawing-room door was open, and there was a decanter and four glasses on a side table. They'd been used, so I felt sure I was right about her being out to dinner. I took the decanter and went on into the dining-room, with the idea of taking some grub in there . . . I wish to God I hadn't . . .'

'What gave you the idea of stealing the money?' asked Pollard bluntly.

George looked extremely uncomfortable.

'I picked up a shopping list which had fallen on to the floor, and saw she'd been to the bank . . . I — I knew which drawer she kept her loose cash in — she never made any secret of it. The key was always on the top of the bureau, in a china jug. I unlocked the drawer, and saw a great wodge of notes lying there, and . . . well, I just lost my head. I mean, I knew she'd masses more, and, well, it seemed as though it would save an awful lot of bother . . . Are you going to arrest me for housebreaking?'

'That remains to be seen. Go on.'

George shifted uncomfortably.

'Well, I thought the best thing would be to make it look as if there'd been a break-in. I swiped a snuff-box from the drawing-room — I haven't flogged it, by the way — and grabbed some food and a bottle of milk and legged it out of the window. I was expecting Aunt B. to turn up at any moment: it wasn't a bit like her to be out so late. I thought I'd cleaned up all my prints.'

'What time was it when you left the house?'

'Half-past nine. The clock in the hall struck just as I was getting out of the kitchen window.'

'What did you do next?'

'I hung about for about five mintues, trying to decide whether it was better to lie low in the garden until it was darker, or make a dash for the Whitesands road. In the end, I began to feel a bit edgy and decided to clear off and cut through the park.'

'Weren't you afraid of being seen from the Lodge?'

'I didn't risk the gates. It's perfectly simple to get over the wall. I had a good look and then streaked across, a bit downstream from the Lodge. Then I made off in what I knew was more or less the right direction.' George broke off suddenly.

'Go on, Mr Baynes.'

'The next bit sounds even more improbable.'

'Well, let's hear it.'

'You won't believe me, but I was followed. It was nearly dark, and the ground's rough with a lot of tree roots and clumps of stuff. I tried to hurry, but I was terrified of coming a purler and dishing an ankle.'

'Did you see the person you say was following you?'

'No. It was too dark for that. But I could hear whoever it was stepping on dry twigs, and trying to run. Whenever I stopped, the noise stopped, but not soon enough, if you know what I mean. I got a bit panicky because I wasn't sure of the best way of getting out on to the road : there's a high wall on that side. In the end I found a gate into some fields, and shimmed over that, and ran like blazes.'

'Did the noise of snapping twigs and so forth go on until you got clear of the park?'

'Yes, but they seemed to fall behind a bit, as though I was getting ahead.'

'I put it to you,' said Pollard, after a lengthy pause, 'that this last part of your statement is pure invention, and that in actual fact you came upon Miss Baynes taking a late stroll in the park. For reasons of her own she asked you to go up to the studio with her, by way of the fire-escape. When you were up there you decided, in view of the fact that she was almost bound to discover that you had robbed her, that it would save an awful lot of bother—to use your own expression—if you killed her.'

This time George Baynes neither shouted nor blustered.

'I suppose you have to put that sort of thing to people,' he said. 'All I can say is that I didn't meet Aunt B. or anybody else, and that everything I've told you this time is the plain truth.'

'Why did you make for Whitesands?'

'Because I thought mixing in with the holiday crowds was the safest way of getting back to town without being spotted.'

'Even Whitesands is hardly crowded in the middle of the night.'

'I didn't try to get there until breakfast time the next morning. I dossed down in a barn on the road. I was flat out, and slept like a log when I'd eaten the food I'd brought with me.'

Sergeant Toye got up to answer a knock on the door.

'Excuse me, sir,' he said to Pollard, on returning to the room. 'There's a call for you from the Yard. Would you care to take it in the Super's office?'

Thirteen

'The school has retained the extensive park of the eighteenth-century house.'

The School Prospectus

THE MINUTES DRAGGED past. George Baynes sat hunched at the table, staring at the discoloured green distemper on the walls and the dreary little yard beyond the window. Sergeant Toye read through his notes and kept an unobtrusive eye on George. At intervals distant voices and footsteps punctured the silence.

At last Pollard returned, coming into the room with a brisk step and an atmosphere of purpose.

'I'm afraid we must ask you to remain here for the present, Mr Baynes,' he said. 'I shall have other points to clear up with you later today. They're just bringing you a cup of tea.'

'Am I under arrest?' asked George thickly.

'No. You are assisting the police in their enquiries into the death of Miss Baynes.'

A red-faced young constable entered with a steaming cup and a couple of biscuits. Giving a significant nod in the direction of George, Pollard went out followed by Toye.

'That was the Yard,' he said. 'It turns out that Madge Thornton is a Baynes all right. On the wrong side of the blanket, though. They've discovered that she's the illegitimate daughter of John Baynes, the one who was killed on the Somme in 1916. The mother was a music student, and died in childbirth. The child was posthumous, and legally adopted by the Thorntons in December 1916. Thornton was an accountant in the Baynes firm at Warhampton, who'd stayed on with the new management when Arthur Baynes sold out and retired.'

Toye stared at him.

'I never thought of that one,' he said. 'Quite a lot falls into place now, doesn't it, sir?'

'Yes. I think, myself, that Madge came on her birth certificate or some letters among Mrs Thornton's papers last week. It's easy to understand how she'd feel. Imagine it, Toye. Realising how she'd been conveniently disposed of, and never acknowledged. You know, I can't help wondering if Beatrice fixed the whole thing. There's a ruthlessness about it which doesn't suggest grand-parents, somehow ... Beatrice certainly paid for the child's education and training. And then made it quite clear to the unfortunate Madge what a disappointment she was, making her more clumsy and gauche than ever. That blighted George Baynes in there being supercilious, too. And all this on top of the psychological tension of being an adopted child, not nearly as intelligently handled in those days as it is now.'

'It doesn't make it look too healthy for Miss Thornton, does it, sir?'

'It certainly doesn't, added to the financial motive. My guess is that she came back from the funeral absolutely determined to have it out with Beatrice. Festival would have held things up : quite possibly some of Beatrice's friends had already arrived. Saturday evening was the first reasonable chance of seeing her. Hence the two visits to Applebys within an hour, and what I'm convinced was a watch on the house from behind the wall of the park. We'll have to get hold of that cardigan, unless she admits to having been there ... I've just phoned the doctor, by the way, and managed to get him to agree to my seeing her now. You'd better come along too, but let's just take a look at the timetable first.'

They spread it out on the table.

'If she went over to her spyhole after drawing a blank at 8.20,' said Toye after a few moments, 'why did she come out again and go off in the direction of the school? Miss Cartmell overtook her going down the drive soon after nine.'

'Let's assume for the present that she didn't go straight to ground. Suppose she wandered up to the school to fill in time, saw Beatrice on the fire-escape, where she'd been listening in to Cartmell and Torrance having a passionate encounter, followed her into the studio, challenged Beatrice and killed her in sudden uncontrollable rage? No, I don't think it's a physical possibility, do you, if she didn't start off from Applebys until 8.20?'

'No,' agreed Toye, 'especially with Mr Torrance going back for that magazine.'

'Let's wash it out then, and assume that she went back to the school after the second visit to Applebys, say about a quarter past nine. It's difficult, I admit to account for her going up to the studio . . . she'd just seen Ann Cartmell going off and must have known that the place would have been cleared up for the holidays. Still, suppose she vaguely wandered up and found Beatrice lying in wait for Bert Heyward . . . Plenty of time to have a flaming row, commit the murder while beside herself, hide the body and then cool off in the park before going back to the Staff House . . . Good God, somebody simply must have seen these people coming and going! You might find out if any reports have come in yet.'

Toye returned a few minutes later, empty-handed.

'We'd better go and tackle Madge Thornton,' said Pollard, 'and it looks like being a pretty dicey job.'

On this occasion Sister Littlejohn was strictly professional, and made no attempt to conceal her disapproval of the presence of Sergeant Toye.

'I don't like this at all,' she said. 'If my patient has another upset like the last one you gave her, Inspector, it may have much more serious results. But if Doctor Dodd has given his permission, I suppose I must let you in.'

'It's possible,' Pollard told her, 'that I may be able to do

153

something to set her mind at rest this time.'

'I hope so, I'm sure,' she replied in a disbelieving tone. 'This way — she's still in the same room, and please try to make your visit as short as possible, won't you?'

Madge Thornton was in bed, propped up with pillows and engaged in doing a jigsaw puzzle. She was wearing the hideous sandy-coloured cardigan as a bed jacket.

'My word!' exclaimed Sister Littlejohn, assuming her ward-side manner and giving the quilt an unnecessary tweak. '*Two* gentlemen visitors for you this time, dear. Just ring your bell if you want anything — I'm only in the next room.'

She swept out. Madge made a nervous, clumsy movement, dislocating the jigsaw.

'Bad luck,' said Pollard, 'when you'd done such a lot of it. Suppose we let Sergeant Toye put it together again for you? He's a dab at them.'

Toye unblinkingly removed the tray and himself to a table in the window, and Pollard seated himself on a chair by the bed. Madge looked anxiously from one to the other.

'Mr George Baynes came down here from London this afternoon,' he remarked in a conversational tone, watching a startled expression come over her face. 'A young man whose behaviour has naturally placed him under grave suspicion. After first telling me a string of the most outrageous lies, he now admits to having been here last Saturday evening. Inevitably he is in a very awkward position. I have taken the rather unusual course of coming to see you, Miss Thornton, in case you are able to clear him.'

A chain reaction was perceptible in Madge's big, light eyes. Surprise was followed by relief, which gave way to unmistakable gratification at this slight recognition of her personal importance. She did not reply, however, but looked interrogatively at Pollard.

'Did you know that he was coming down?'

She shook her head.

'Would it surprise you to learn that Miss Baynes had invited him?'

'Yes,' she said without hesitation. 'It was Festival weekend, and Aunt Beatrice wouldn't have wanted him staying in the house. If she invited anyone it would have been one of her O.M. friends.'

'You're quite certain that you didn't see him when you paid your second visit to Applebys?'

'I'm quite sure I didn't.'

'We know,' Pollard said, watching her carefully, 'that he must have arrived only a few minutes ahead of you.'

She looked puzzled.

'But where was he then? I went round to the garden ... Did Aunt Beatrice let him in after all?'

'After all? What do you mean by that, Miss Thornton?'

Madge coloured, and was silent.

'Well, let's leave that problem for the moment, shall we, and see if you can help me over another? According to Mr Baynes, he left Applebys just after nine-thirty, but at present we only have his word for it. It is perfectly possible that he left earlier, met Miss Baynes taking an evening walk in the park, was invited to accompany her to the studio for some reason, and killed her there before the caretaker arrived to lock up School Wing at 9.50.'

'No,' Madge said, in so deep and vibrant a voice that Toye looked up quickly from the jigsaw puzzle. 'He couldn't possibly have done that.'

'Do you mean that you saw him take some course of action that completely rules it out? You were watching Applebys from behind the wall of the park, weren't you? You left us your signature, you know : a strand of wool from that cardigan you're wearing now.'

This time her cheeks flamed.

'I suppose you think I behaved like a — a housemaid?'

Pollard was amused by this socially obsolete expression. An echo of Beatrice, I bet, he thought ...

'I think,' he said, 'that you wanted to see Miss Baynes very urgently last Saturday evening, but that you also wanted to be quite sure that she returned to Applebys alone. What you had to discuss was presumably a private matter, and you didn't know if she had invited one of her old friends to spend the night. So you decided not to wait in the garden, and took up a position where you could see her come back.'

It was immediately obvious that his deductions had been correct, and that she was impressed by them.

'Reverting to Mr George Baynes,' he went on, 'did you actually see him come away from Applebys?'

'Yes.'

'And did you notice the time?'

'It was about five and twenty minutes to ten. I'd kept on looking at my watch because I was so surprised that Aunt Beatrice was staying out so late.'

'Did you see where he went on leaving Applebys?'

'He — he jumped over the wall into the park. Quite close to where I was.'

'And then?'

'He started off quickly. Not towards the school, though. He kept over to the right of the park.'

'Were you surprised to see him?'

Madge nodded vigorously.

'Just for a moment I couldn't believe my eyes. Then I was furious.'

'Why furious?'

'Because I thought that he and Aunt Beatrice had been in the house together all the time, and hadn't let me in . . . I always hated it when he came down. He despises me. So did Aunt Beatrice. I used to feel out of it, and yet I couldn't stay away somehow.'

Interesting Pollard thought. Almost as though she had had some instinctive knowledge of the blood tie.

'What did you do when Mr Baynes had struck off into the park, Miss Thornton?'

Madge once again showed signs of embarrassment.

'I—er—followed him. I wanted to speak to him.'

'You followed him to the studio, perhaps?'

'No. I don't see how I can prove it to you, but neither of us went anywhere near the school building. George was cutting through the park, a long way over on the Trill side.'

'If you wanted to talk to him, why didn't you call out to him?'

'I was afraid someone might hear. It was all so queer I didn't seem able to think clearly. I just started off after him. I felt sure I'd catch him up when he tried to get out on the far side. I didn't think he'd know that the gate on to the Whitesands road is kept locked.'

'And did you catch him up?'

'No. He went so quickly, and found the old iron gate into the fields. I heard the squeak it always gives, so he must have got out that way. It was too dark to see anybody when I got there . . . So he couldn't possibly have been to the studio. I could hear him ahead of me all the time, and it must have been quite ten to ten by then.'

'What did you do next, when you saw that there was no hope of catching up with him?'

'I just went home. I walked, of course, I haven't a car. Aunt Beatrice said it wasn't necessary as she had one. It seemed such a long way . . . I felt terribly tired, and so puzzled by everything I felt I couldn't face trying Applebys again that night'—She suddenly broke off and started in horror at Pollard. 'It wasn't George who broke into Applebys and took the snuff-box, was it?'

'I'm afraid it was. He admitted it to me this afternoon. He also took about fifty pounds in cash.'

'But—he—I *must* know. Please tell me the truth. He didn't kill Aunt Beatrice in Applebys?'

'I think we can accept the fact that she was killed in the studio,' he told her.

'Then George didn't do it,' she exclaimed in tones of

heartfelt relief. 'He couldn't have. And if he took the money and the snuff-box, Aunt Beatrice couldn't have been in the house while he was there, could she?'

'It doesn't look like it. Why,' Pollard asked, with a sudden deliberate switch of subject, 'did you want to talk to Mr Baynes so very much?'

He waited for her answer, with the sense of having arrived at the crux of the interview.

'I—er, had something to tell him. Something private.'

'I expect it was the same thing that you wanted to discuss with Miss Baynes, wasn't it?'

In the silence which followed he could almost feel Toye's anticipation as he sat apparently engrossed in the jigsaw puzzle. It was broken at last by what was hardly more than a whisper from Madge.

'What do you mean?'

'Well, Miss Thornton, all births are recorded at Somerset House, you know.'

'So you know everything . . . Even who I am?'

'Not quite everything,' he said gently, 'but you have fitted in several missing pieces for me. Would you like me to tell Mr Baynes what you wanted to tell him yourself on Saturday night?'

Her eyes filled with tears.

'He'll hate me being a relation. He thinks I'm just awful—ugly and clumsy and stupid. What the girls call a drip. I was feeling so angry then. I wanted to tell him he'd no right to look down on me. But now I feel it won't make any difference, really.'

'When he knows that I couldn't make you admit that you'd seen him when I first questioned you, and that your evidence has helped to clear him of a possible charge of murder, I think you'll find Mr Baynes's attitude very different,' said Pollard grimly. 'Besides, there's another side to it, isn't there? You're his only living relative as far as I know, and it looks as though he's going to need a good deal of help and moral support. If he's finally cleared of the graver charge, as I hope he will be, you won't wash your hands of him because of the thefts, will you?'

He watched Madge struggling with the utterly unfamiliar concept of a situation in which she was at an advantage in regard to George.

'No, of course not,' she said at last, wiping her eyes and blowing her nose vigorously. 'If he wants to have anything to do with me, that is. It won't surprise me if he doesn't, even if he is in trouble . . . Yes, I think I should like you to tell him. I feel I don't know how to put it.'

'I'll be very glad to do that for you, Miss Thornton. Will you tell me how you have just found out that Mr John Baynes was your father?'

She nodded, and hunted in a handbag for an envelope which she gave to him.

'I found this when I went home last week. It was with some papers belonging to my adopted mother.'

The letter was written on expensive paper headed with an engraved address in Leamington Spa. The date was December 10th 1916, the ink faded but the handwriting strong and decisive.

Dear Mrs Thornton,

I am writing to confirm that one of the nursing-home staff will be bringing little Madge to Warhampton next Thursday by the train arriving at 12.15 p.m.

Now that everything has been arranged, I am indeed feeling thankful that my poor brother John's child will be in the care of you and your husband, so long associated with our firm. I know that I can rely absolutely on your complete discretion : neither the child nor my parents must ever hear the sad story.

With kind regards,
Sincerely Yours,
Beatrice A. Baynes.

Pollard looked up to find Madge watching him.

"I've always realised I was a — bastard,' she said, with

obvious relief at putting her sense of humiliation into words at last. 'But I wish I knew something about my real mother, all the same.'

'I can tell you that she was a music student. That's where your musical talent comes from, you see.'

'I haven't real talent. I'd like to stop teaching music. I'm no good at it. I only get girls who aren't any good, either. If they give me anybody promising by mistake, the parents always write and ask if she can change.'

'Perhaps you will be able to give it up now ... You understand that the police have to try to get all statements confirmed, don't you? So I'm going to ask you if you saw anyone go past while you were watching Applebys on Saturday?'

'The only person I knew was Miss Craythorne, the Senior Mistress. She drove past about twenty past nine, going back to the Staff House. I expect she'd been to Miss Renshaw's coffee party ... I feel a lot better,' she went on, apparently inconsequently. 'In spite of everything, I think I'd like to go to Aunt Beatrice's funeral tomorrow. I mean, it's no good going on being angry with people for ever, is it, especially when they've died?'

'No good at all. I think you are being very wise, and generous, too, if I may say so. I suggest that you — or Sister — ring up Mr Yelland and find out what the arrangements are.'

The door opened to admit Sister Littlejohn.

'Excuse me, but Mrs Kitson has just rung through to say that Miss Renshaw would be glad if Inspector Pollard would go over to school as soon as he can, and that it's important,' she announced, unable to conceal the gleam of excited interest in her eye. 'In any case, I think my patient has been talking quite long enough.'

'Miss Thornton tells me that she is feeling a lot better,' Pollard could not resist saying to her, as they left after a hasty leave-taking from Madge.

'What's your reaction to that little lot?' he asked Toye when the Sanatorium door had closed behind them.

'I think she was speaking the truth, sir, and Mr Baynes too, for that matter. Of course they could have agreed on the story between them, although I can't see the two of them working in together, somehow.'

'Neither can I,' said Pollard as they walked across the car park. 'In fact I think it's a psychological impossibility.'

Fourteen

'Old Meldonians are making their contribution to society in
many and varied spheres.'

The Headmistress's Speech Day Report

A SPRUCE ESTATE car had arrived during their call at the
Sanatorium, and was standing outside Old House. Pollard
eyed it speculatively, wondering if its presence implied a
quick response to one of the enquiries sent out that morning
about those in residence at Meldon on Saturday night. He
waited in the library with Toye, while Joyce Kitson went to
report their arrival to Helen Renshaw. Looking round at the
shelves he felt that years had elapsed since he had first entered
the room just over forty-eight hours earlier . . . There was a
curious elusiveness about the case . . . a sense that whoever
you succeeded in catching up on would turn round and face
you, and prove not to be the person you were looking for
after all. Young Baynes, for instance, with his lies and seem-
ingly improbable story of being followed across the park . . .
Pollard looked at Toye who had taken down a copy of *Murder in the Cathedral*, and whose normally smooth brow was
furrowed in perplexity.

Footsteps in the hall announced the return of Joyce Kitson.
Miss Renshaw would see them at once in her flat, she said,
and led the way upstairs. As they were shown in, Pollard was
astonished to see a nun in a white coif and black habit, par-
taking of afternoon tea from a tray. Helen Renshaw rose and
took a step forward. He thought he could detect relief in her
face.

'Sister Felicity,' she said, 'may I introduce Chief Detective-

Inspector Pollard and Detective-Sergeant Toye of Scotland Yard? Sister Felicity of St. Anne's Convent, Middlebridge, Inspector.'

Pollard took an instant liking to Sister Felicity's rather sallow, lively face, with its upturned nose and alert brown eyes, which were fixed on him with undisguised interest.

'Well, well,' she said, when the introductions had been made, 'I never thought that I'd meet a real, live Scotland Yard detective. If it wasn't for this terrible tragedy, I should be really enjoying myself.'

Helen Renshaw suggested tea, which Pollard politely declined.

'Perhaps it would save time,' she said, taking the hint, 'if I explained that Sister Felicity is an Old Meldonian, who had permission from her Mother Superior to come to Festival and stay overnight.'

'It was the last week-end of my annual Rest fortnight,' broke in Sister Felicity. "We all have one, to keep in touch with our families and friends.'

'Sister was one of the group who came up here to have coffee with me after supper last Saturday evening,' Helen Renshaw went on, a faint flicker of amusement passing over her face. Pollard reflected that she was in a better position than he was to observe Toye's reactions. 'She left with a friend shortly before nine. Perhaps it would be simpler if she herself takes up the story here? Shall I leave you?'

He assured her that it was unnecessary, and turned to Sister Felicity, sitting erect and full of pleasurable anticipation.

'I'm most grateful to you for coming over here so promptly,' he told her. 'I gather you have some information for us?'

'Mother instructed me to say that she much regrets the delay. Unfortunately we went into Retreat on Monday, and have been out of touch. Completely. But when the police called today just after Sext, Mother naturally went to the parlour. Knowing that I had been here last Saturday night, she felt obliged to break my silence.'

She paused, as if to emphasise the magnitude of the step taken.

'A very proper decision, if I may say so,' said Pollard, feeling his way.

'Exactly. Mother maintains that the religious life should be based on practical common sense. Among other things, of course. When I told her that I had visited the studio on Saturday evening and sat with a friend on the little platform at the top of the fire-escape, she suggested to the very nice sergeant of police who had called, that I should drive over here at once. All our sisters under fifty have passed their driving tests,' she added.

Pollard had a sharp sense of an impending crisis in the evolution of the case.

'I'd like you to describe exactly what you did after leaving the coffee party here,' he said. 'Everyone who visited the studio after seven o'clock last Saturday is an important witness. Sergeant Toye will be taking notes, and afterwards he'll transcribe them, and we'll ask you to read your statement, and if you agree that it is accurate, to sign it.'

Sister Felicity folded her arms inside the voluminous black sleeves of her habit, and proceeded with a combination of great seriousness and childlike enjoyment. One of her special pleasures in attending Festival, she explained, was a meeting with her greatest friend outside the Community, Hilary Fleming, who had been at school with her, and was now married and living in Manchester. Dear Miss Renshaw would quite understand that while they had greatly enjoyed coming up to coffee in her lovely flat, they felt they still had a lot to say to each other, and were among the earlier leavers, as just a minute or two to nine. As neither of them had managed to see the art exhibition during the day, they had decided to go up to the studio on the chance that the work had not yet been taken down.

'Just a minute,' interrupted Pollard. 'Which way did you go? Through School Wing itself, or across the Quad?'

'Across the Quad, Inspector, going out of the door from the entrance hall downstairs.'

'Take your time over this question, Sister, won't you? Did you meet anyone, or see anyone about in the Quad, or on the stairs up to the studio?'

Sister Felicity closed her eyes.

'We didn't actually meet anyone,' she said decisively, opening them again, 'but as we went out into the Quad I noticed two of the girls carrying a lot of odds and ends and talking to an O.M. or one of the staff. They were just disappearing under the archway leading to the car park. Nobody else, I'm quite sure. Shall I go on?'

'Please do.'

The two friends had gone up the staircase to the studio, only to find it stripped and tidied for the holidays. The door on to the fire-escape was open, and they had wandered out to find a magnificent sunset in progress. Fetching a couple of stools from inside, they had settled down to enjoy the spectacle, and have a long, leisurely conversation. It was a very warm evening, and they had sat on while the splendour built up to its zenith and slowly faded, until at last a sheet of white mist over the playing fields below made them realise that they were beginning to feel a bit chilly.

Pollard struggled to keep his mind strictly on the course of Sister Felicity's narrative. Its full implications must wait for the moment.

'Weren't you surprised,' he interrupted, 'that no one had come to lock up School Wing?'

Yes, they had both remarked on it. Then, just as they switched on the light and were putting the two stools away, there had been the sound of a door being locked and bolted, and footsteps coming upstairs, and Bert Heyward came in... Yes, she knew Bert Heyward well by sight. She came to Festival regularly. He'd seemed quite surprised to find them there, and they'd had a little chat while he locked the fire-escape door, and then they had all gone out together into the corridor. Yes, she distinctly remembered him locking the studio swing doors on the corridor side.

'Which way did you and Mrs Fleming leave School Wing?'

'Along the top corridor, and down the stairs at the Old House end. The door at the bottom of the studio stairs had already been locked, you see.'

'Did you hear Bert Heyward return to the studio by any chance?'

Sister Felicity, who clearly saw the implications of the question, looked Pollard squarely in the face.

'I'm quite sure he didn't, Inspector. He was only just behind us, opening each classroom door, and flicking on the light to make sure all the windows were shut. He was just behind us on the stairs too, and went off along the first floor corridor, doing the same thing. By the time we were out in the Quad, making for New Wing where our rooms were, he was working back to Old House on the ground floor. The lights were going on and off one after the other.'

Mentally consigning Bert Heyward to uttermost perdition, Pollard thanked Sister Felicity for her clear statement, and sent Toye down to the library to type it out. As they waited, he questioned her about the possibility of anyone having entered or left the studio while she had been sitting on the fire-escape platform.

'I'm quite sure that would have been impossible,' she said without hesitation. 'Those swing doors on the corridor make a special little thud when they open and shut. And we weren't talking loudly. People were still about, down in the gardens, and crossing the Quad, you see. It was such a lovely evening. But we could go and try, couldn't we? You and Miss Renshaw could be talking outside, and I'd come in and go out as quietly as posible.'

Rather taken aback by this practical and matter-of-fact

suggestion, Pollard agreed that the experiment would be worth making ... After that unspeakable fool Heyward never mentioned these women, he thought, I'm leaving absolutely nothing to chance.

A rather silent trio walked through the echoing emptiness of School Wing, and up the stairs to the studio, still locked and in a state of squalid disorder. Sister Felicity clicked her tongue.

'Don't worry,' she said briskly to Helen Renshaw. 'Re-decoration, and a move round of the equipment, and they'll soon forget all about it. The young are so resilient ... Any-way, it's a thrill to them ... we had a murder at my school ... a splendid bit of one-upmanship among their contem-poraries.'

Helen Renshaw agreed rather wryly. Pollard stared at them, and wondered if women would ever cease to surprise him in one way or another.

Out on the platform Helen Renshaw asked how much longer the police would need the studio. He was replying when they heard the distinctive sound of the swing doors opening.

"It's impossible to do it more quietly,' Sister Felicity said, after the third experiment. 'Try it yourself, Inspector.'

Pollard tried.

'It's conclusive,' he said, as much to himself as to them. 'No one entered or left this room from the arrival of Sister Felicity and Mrs Fleming just after nine, until Bert Heyward came in to lock up ...'

'You again?' said Mrs Heyward, opening the door and find-ing Toye outside. 'You know tea-time, don't you? Come along in.'

As on his earlier visit Bert Heyward was seated at the kitchen table, this time consuming fish and chips. He looked up without a trace of apprehension.

'Ain't you caught the chap yet?' he enquired. 'You Lunnon blokes an' all?'

'Not yet,' replied Toye patiently. 'Thank you, Mrs Heyward, but I daren't stop even for a cuppa : the Inspector's hopping mad. I just want to clear up one point. When you got up to the studio to lock up on Saturday night,' he said addressing himself to Bert, 'was anything out of the ordinary at all?'

'Well, the electric was on, and two Old Girls up there. Bin sittin' out on the escape, so they said. But you wouldn't call that anythin' out of the ordinary for Festival. You comes on 'em all over the place, talkin' their 'eads orf.'

A pregnant pause was broken by an explosion from Mrs Heyward.

'Bert Heyward! You great daft stupid lump!'

'What's wrong now?' demanded her husband, setting down his knife and fork with a clatter. 'One of 'em was that Sister in nun's get-up. She comes every time. Nuns don't go round murderin' folk. Anyway, I never gived either of 'em another thought from that day to this. Nobody ever arst me if I'd found Old Girls up there . . .'

Mrs Heyward gave Toye a long look compounded of exasperation, apology, and utter relief . . .

In the library Pollard listened to Toye's account of his second visit to the Heywards, and relieved his feelings by fluent and uninhibited comment on the mentality of Bert. Toye apologised miserably.

'I ought to have asked the direct question, sir.'

"We've both tripped up. I ought to have spotted it myself from your report . . . We've wasted the heck of a lot of time, but it's no good moaning over it . . . If this Mrs Fleming confirms Sister's statement, as she doubtless will, we're just about back where we started.'

'There's still that bit of time between eight-thirty and

eight-forty, sir. George Baynes is cleared, but Madge Thornton still hasn't an alibi. There's only her word for it that she was strolling about the park.'

Pollard extracted the latest version of the time-table, and pushed it towards Toye.

'Let's have a look at this bit,' he said, stabbing with a finger.

approx.
8.30	Mrs Heyward returns home.
	Cartmell and Torrance come down to Quad.
8.32	Torrance returns to studio (A.C. and C.T.)
8.33	Cartmell reaches office (Kitson)
8.35	Torrance reaches office (Cartmell and Kitson)
8.38	Torrance drives off (A.C., Kitson, and Eccles)

'Eccles . . .' Pollard flicked through his notes. 'In his statement to you he said he saw Torrance drive away while he was in the Lodge garden. It's just possible he saw Madge come across from Applebys at 8.20 . . . You know, Toye, we seem to have overlooked this chap . . . Let me see, yes, Miss Renshaw said Beatrice Baynes was always snooping on the gardeners. Wasn't there something about it in your report on the Heywards?'

'Yes, there was sir. They remarked on how tough it was on Eccles to have her living so near, and he seems to have spoken his mind about her pretty freely.'

'What did you make of him yourself?'

'He's a truculent customer. A red-headed Scot, bald on top. Canny though. I don't see him committing an unpremeditated murder, somehow.'

'We'd better look into his movements on Saturday evening, all the same. Let's push off and find him . . .'

Jock Eccles, run to earth at the Plough, was both truculent

and unco-operative. When offered the choice of sitting in the police car or being taken to Lindbridge police station he boarded the vehicle with muttering resentment, and sat down heavily. When asked where he had been between seven and eight o'clock on the previous Saturday evening, he demanded angrily if he were being accused of the murder.

'If I were charging you, you would have been cautioned,' Pollard told him. 'You are simply being asked to help the enquiry by answering a simple question. Where were you?'

With great difficulty it was established that Jock had finished his clearing up at the School by about a quarter-past six, and had returned home, got his bicycle, and come along to the Plough for a drink.

'When did you go back to the Lodge?'

'I didna luk at my watch.'

'How long had you been back before that Jaguar went up the drive?' asked Toye.

'Just a wee while.'

'I think we all could do with a drink,' said Pollard, with a glance at Toye, who got out of the car and went into the Plough.

If not exactly mellowed, Jock became slightly less aggressive after some refreshment. While affirming that a man couldn't be expected to know the very minute he stepped outside his door, he volunteered the information that Bert Heyward came along on his bicycle shortly afterwards, having stayed on at the Plough for a game of darts.

'Did you see anyone else you know?' asked Pollard as casually as he could.

'Ay. Mistress Thornton came oot frae Applebys and crossed ower to the gates.'

'Did you speak to her?'

'For why should I be bletherin' wi' the puir body just hame fra' her mither's graveside?'

Asked if he had noticed in which direction Madge had gone, Jock gave Pollard a long, hard look.

'If she'd murrderrt the auld yin up in the stujo, ye couldna blame her, but she dinna gang that way a' aw'. She was awa' doon the parrk to the wee path that rins to the Staff Hoos. I watched her a while, draggin' her step wi' her heid doon . . .'

'The landlord says Eccles was there, right enough,' Toye reported, 'and Heyward too. They turned up at unusual times because of Festival. They're both regulars, you see.'

Pollard grunted, and they drove to Linbridge police station in silence.

'I'm sorry to have kept you so long,' Pollard said, striding into the room where George Baynes still sat in an apathetic huddle. 'It was unavoidable. You'll be glad to get away for a meal, I'm sure. I've rung Mr Yelland, and he'll look you up at the White Horse after dinner.'

George blinked.

'You mean I can go?'

'Yes. As far as the death of Miss Baynes goes, I'm not making a charge, largely as the result of your cousin's statement.'

'My *cousin*?'

'Miss Madge Thornton. She's your first cousin once removed, the daughter of your late great-uncle, Mr John Baynes, who was killed in the First War. She wasn't born in wedlock, incidentally . . . Perhaps I had better explain.'

'What happens about the breaking and entering charge?' asked Inspector Beakbane, when an unusually subdued George had departed.

'God knows,' replied Pollard wearily. 'I couldn't care less at the moment. Two days of blood, toil, tears, and sweat, and we're back where we started.'

'You want a drink,' said Beakbane. 'When you're my age, my lad, you'll know you can't start properly on a case till you've cleared the ground.'

Fifteen

'During the summer term the pupils make occasional expeditions to Whitesands where they enjoy the stimulating sea bathing under careful supervision.'

School Prospectur (1885 edition)

POLLARD WAS A strong swimmer, and striking out soon left the few belated bathers in the shallows far behind. The water was deliciously cool, and smelt tangy and salty. The sun had finally disappeared for the day behind a bank of stratus cloud scored by thin parallel lines of bright gold. Overhead was a vast aquamarine emptiness. At last he stopped swimming, rolled over on to his back and floated tranquilly, staring upwards . . . Water did something to you when your mind was so scribbled over with facts and impressions that there seemed no hope of ever sorting out your data, scrapping the irrelevancies, and distinguishing the real pointers. A merciful process of obliteration set in, giving you to some extent a fresh start. Gently rising and falling with the swell beneath him, Pollard relaxed. He watched first one star and then another come out in the deepening blue-green vault above him, until he lost count and felt a sudden desire for the world of men and action. Turning over again he made for the shore with a powerful crawl stroke, and saw the Whitesands esplanade leap into loops and festoons of light from end to end. Then his feet encountered warm, yielding sand, and seconds afterwards he stood on the beach and shook himself like a dog.

Ten minutes later he emerged from a bathing cabin, handed in his hired trunks and towel, and went in search of a meal. The esplanade and streets were full of strolling holidaymakers who had eaten and were streaming out of the hotels and boarding-houses. Pollard made his way through the crowds with some difficulty, and found a half-empty grill room, where he ate ravenously. Then he rang Jane from a public call-box.

The conversation brought her very near, the sounds of the flat coming across as a background to her voice. They were invariably discreet when he was out on a case, and had a simple code. 'Ground floor,' he replied in answer to an enquiry about where his hotel room was situated, and so conveyed a complete lack of progress.

Without comment Jane remarked that the art teachers' refresher course on which she had been engaged ended the next day, and that from then on the flat would be continuously manned. He replied that he had no plans at the moment, but was undoubtedly returning to London in the near future.

'On no account overlook the importance of the leading role in the play when you're casting the parts,' she said just before they rang off. 'Try to get right inside the character and think her thoughts.'

With the words still echoing in his ears Pollard replaced the receiver. It was at the precise moment when he turned to emerge from the stuffy and constricting telephone kiosk that he knew intuitively that the living Beatrice Baynes had experienced the same kind of constriction in the narrow confines of the puppet theatre. Startled at the strength of this impression, for he was not a fanciful man, he stood for so long with his hand on the door that an irascible face materialised and peered at him. Coming out with a hasty apology Pollard set out for the car-park, guided through the streets by his subconscious mind and surprised to find himself standing by his car, key in hand. He got in and hesitated. Ideas were flooding into his mind and he must have solitude in which to evaluate them. The prospect of Linbridge police station and his depressing little bedroom at the White Horse was intolerable. Making a quick decision he switched on the engine and threaded his way through the town to the suburbs and open country beyond. Driving slowly he saw a lane which seemed to lead up to the ridge of hills behind Whtiesands, and chanced his luck. It held. He met no other car and climbed quickly until the gradient flattened out at the top. A gate giving on to a carried hayfield stood conveniently open. He turned the car in, bumped over a few yards of rough ground, and turned off the ignition and lights. Air full of delicious country scents and tiny muted sounds came in at the window. Far below, Whitesands scintillated to the water's edge, beyond which sea and sky became indistinguishable. Was that a ship or a star? He sighed contentedly, lit a cigarette and began to order his thoughts.

In retrospect it was astonishing that he had never visualised Beatrice Baynes snooping from inside the puppet theatre. He had assumed, without giving the matter any real thought, that she had been on the fire-escape, if eavesdropping on Clive Torrance and Ann Cartmell, or simply sitting in the studio if lying in wait for Bert Heyward. It was now established beyond any reasonable doubt that Bert Heyward was not the murderer, so therefore one could tentatively work on the hypothesis that Cartmell and Torrance had been Beatrice's target . . . Of course, she could hardly have failed to attract notice if she had been hanging about on the fire-escape. There'd have been quite a lot of people about in the Quad and the grounds. The puppet theatre gave cover, and far better facilities for seeing and hearing. He'd been a clot not to think of it before . . .

Pollard lit another cigarette, and hoisted his left leg up onto the passenger's seat. He could visualise that small, determined figure coming into the studio and glancing sharply round, so intent on her unpleasant little scheme that she was oblivious of its squalidness . . . She'd manoeuvred herself into the tall hessian-covered box, and adjusted the curtains to give herself an adequate view of the room without running the risk of being seen . . . Utterly grotesque behaviour in a woman of her generation and education . . . Jane was right, though : Beatrice's mentality was baffing, but after all, it was her murder he was investigating, and he must make an effort to piece her together from all the sources available to him.

Beakbane had been the first, presumably primed by Constable Freeth, for the Inspector had said that he himself had never seen her. A wealthy old girl living just across the road, he'd remarked, as they walked through School Wing towards the studio. A tartar . . . some bee in her bonnet about the School . . .

Fair enough, thought Pollard. Beakbane's comments and the set-up at Applebys underlined a built-in assurance, based on an established social position and plenty of money. The ample, solid comfort of the house returned to his mind. Sitting pretty, Yelland had said . . . All this reinforced by an aggressive character and quick temper. The sort of overbearing old woman a village bobby would hope not to get embroiled with . . . But none of these things had deterered the murderer. Did this suggest that he was a stranger? Or someone mentally unbalanced?

There had been a faintly surprised look in the glazed eyes . . . the astonishment registered in the last fraction of consciousness that a violent physical assault could happen to *her*. He remembered how the body had looked so small that it might almost have been one of the puppets, exccpt that nothing artificial could ever look as lifeless as a body which had once breathed and moved. She'd been lying in a theatrical sprawl, almost tragi-cosmic, with the pointed toes of the rather old-fashioned shoes pointing upwards and outwards, and one arm flung out in a violent gesture of abandon, just as she had crashed out onto the floor at the feet of the horrified Mrs Bennett, the whole attitude a travesty of the personality indicated by the decorous clothes. Then a closer look had shown the cleaner the brutally-shattered skull. Tragi-comedy had become undiluted tragedy.

Helen Renshaw's account of Beatrice had been objective

and analytical, as if she were discussing a problem pupil. She had effectively conveyed a dynamic, frustrated elderly woman, no longer dangerous because impotent to put the clock back. Surely Beatrice must have known this : she was very far from being a fool, according to both Helen Renshaw and Yelland. Perhaps, Pollard thought, she had compensated by telling herself it was a point of honour to carry on the losing battle.

Several people had mentioned the outbursts of temper. Yes, Beatrice would have had little instinct of self-preservation in face of threats or an attack. Even if there had been a chance, it probably never occurred to her to try to escape. And she was undoubtedly a fighter : the initial challenge might well have come from her.

Pollard shifted his position. Dimly he felt that he was groping in the direction of what actually happened in that scene of savage violence which had ended Beatrice's life.

Surely the person who could do more than anyone else to fill out her personality for him was Madge Thornton, inarticulate though she was. Her whole life had been shaped by her godmother's mentality. How utterly ruthless and how secretive Beatrice had been about the relationship between the two of them. What had Yelland said? Miss Baynes was a woman who kept her own counsel, wasn't it? Family feeling had been relentlessly sacrificed to family pride. Even in this modern age of changing moral standards there didn't seem to have been the slightest sign of compromise and an acknowledgment of the blood tie. A most extraordinary rigidity, thought Pollard, and all of a piece with her hostility to the changes at Meldon. All the same, the unconcealed disappointment in Madge showed that family feeling still ran strongly below the surface ... So did the practical toleration of George's deficiencies ... But she had found it bitter that Madge, a Baynes, was a dreary failure, a tolerated academic drudge at Meldon whereas a chit like Ann Cartmell could bring distinction to the School ...

Pollard metaphorically sat up. Of course this made Beatrice's virulent dislike of Ann even more explicable. The girl had not only revolutionised the art department, one of the last strongholds of the old order, but her ability and popularity and personal attractiveness only served to make the unfortunate Madge Thornton's lack of these things more conspicuous, at any rate in Beatrice's eyes . . .

He carefully stubbed out his cigarette, tossed it through the window and lit another. Had he given enough attention to this almost pathological hatred of Ann Cartmell? It had rather tended to get submerged in Beatrice's overall hostility to the new régime, hadn't it?

Pollard considered the account given to him by Helen Renshaw of the extraordinary scene at the Annual General Meeting. Surely, he thought, an attack like that on a girl young enough to be your granddaughter, and who was guilty of nothing but professional success, indicated a quite alarming degree of hatred. Beatrice would clearly have gone to considerable lengths to damage the girl, and anything she achieved in this line would have useful repercussions on Helen Renshaw. There was therefore a strong case for assuming that she had gone over to the studio to try to discover something damaging about Ann Cartmell, and this raised a number of questions.

In the first place, he thought, it was unbelievable that Beatrice Baynes would have gone to the length of hiding in he puppet theatre unless she knew for certain that Ann Cartmell was going to be there. Here he paused to remind himself that he had no evidence that the puppet theatre had been used for spying, only a compulsive hunch, and policemen were not allowed to build cases on hunches . . . He compromised by putting it on one side for the moment. The important thing was *how* Beatrice knew Ann would be there.

Was it possible, he wondered, that there was some job to be done in the studio which always had to be left till after Festival supper, and that Beatrice had hoped to catch Ann Cartmell out over not doing it properly, or even, conceivably, in helping herself to school stationery or something of that sort? There had been a few odd bits of clearing-up which the girls had helped with . . . Pretty thin, he decided. So thin that it seemed legitimate to concentrate on the one definite fixture in the studio that evening : the visit of Clive Torrance to select the entries for the painting competition.

Pollard lit a fourth cigarette and consulted his notes with the help of an electric torch. According to Torrance, the appointment had only been made that afternoon by means of a telephone call. Fairly early in the afternoon, presumably, if he had gone to a meeting afterwards. Was it likely that Beatrice Baynes had got to know about this call? Ann Cartmell wasn't expecting it, and therefore someone would have gone round looking for her. Afterwards, in view of her feelings about Torrance, she was probably incapable of keeping the news of his visit to herself. Why should she, after all? It seemed perfectly possible that anyone with snooping instincts as strong as Beatrice's might have got to hear about it. If he could only prove that she had, it would be almost conclusive evidence of why she went over to the studio at all.

At this moment Pollard's mind took a leap forward. If he were on the right track at last . . . if the motive for the expedition was to sit in on the meeting between Ann Cartmell and Clive Torrance, it cleared up the problem of when Beatrice went over to the School, and how she managed to do so unobserved. Her guests left her at five minutes past seven. Between this time and seven-thirty, when Festival supper began, a good many people would have been about, almost certainly strolling in the grounds as it was a fine evening . . . Pollard flicked on his torch again and hastily turned over some pages . . . Yes, Jock Eccles had only been back at the Lodge 'a wee while' before Torrance's Jaguar went streaking up the drive, say at five minutes to eight. How long was a wee while? Five minutes? Ten? Even if it were as much as a quarter of an hour, Beatrice would have had ten minutes in which to get to the studio, during which the grounds were deserted. Jock Eccles and Bert Heyward were at the Plough, Jock probably on the way home. Mrs Eccles was helping in the School kitchen, and everybody else was either serving supper or eating it.

He could visualise Beatrice waving off her friends at the gate and turning back into Applebys for the last time. She'd go across the hall to the kitchen—no! Hell! He ought to have seen the implications of the report on the autopsy. It had stated that apart from a small quantity of alcohol no food had entered her stomach for some hours. Of course that more or less ruled out the later times of going across which he had considered : she hadn't waited to have any supper. But she'd gone upstairs and changed her shoes. He remembered the smart pair by the chair in her bedroom, and the more worn pair with the lower heels which had made the tell-tale scratch marks on the studio floor. There was something pathetically human about that last change of shoes . . .

A distant vibration invaded his consciousness, increased steadily and resolved itself into the chugging of a motorcycle engine. Pollard watched an unsteady cone of light creep across the field, and the hedge on his left became sharply defined against the darkness of the sky. The rider cat-called at a supposedly necking couple as he went by, the light ebbed and vanished, and the noise gradually died down and was engulfed by the silence. Pollard's spirits which had been rising rapidly suddenly slumped again.

Was he really any further on? Take it that Beatrice had witnessed a pretty hot petting party—even, improbably, the full treatment. Why hadn't she burst out of the puppet theatre, a *dea ex machina*, denouncing Ann Cartmell and threatening to go straight to Helen Renshaw or Sir Piers Tracey? Or had she? . . . No, he was prepared to stake his reputation on Ann Cartmell's innate inability to have concealed an incident like that, still less to have been an accomplice in the murder. Well then, did Beatrice emerge as soon as they had both left the studio, to be found there by Clive Torrance returning almost at once to fetch his copy of *Artifex?* Did she proceed to abuse and threaten him?

Pollard sat staring out into the darkness. Quite apart from the entrance improbability of Torrance replying to such threats by an instant, brutal, and desperately dangerous murder, there was something which didn't ring true in this reconstruction . . . Surely Ann Cartmell was the person Beatrice had wanted to injure. Torrance would merely have been an incidental means to an end. If she had held her fire in order to deliver it more effectively later, she wouldn't have wasted it on Torrance in Ann's absence. He would have attributed her sudden appearance in the room to the fire-escape, and she would merely have given him a chilly good evening.

There were really three issues, he thought. In the first place, was it a physical possibility for Torrance to have committed the murder, concealed the body, and rejoined Ann Cartmell in the time available? This was a matter which could be established to some extent by a reconstruction after expert questioning of the secretary. He'd have to do the latter himself : for once the adaptable Toye had failed to establish sympathetic contact. Secondly, had Torrance any motive for the murder, which was clearly unpremeditated and apparently quite fortuitous? It seemed impossible that he could have known that Beatrice was there, and would never have encountered her if the magazine had not been left behind. Pollard wondered what, if anything, Chief-Superintendent Crowe's excavations into middle-class pasts had yielded . . . he'd better go back to London the next day and make a report to him . . . If Torrance killed her, there *must* have been a link between them. Even if the murder could have been carried out in the few minutes available, there quite definitely hadn't been time for a major row to build up from scratch . . .

Thirdly, if Torrance was not the murderer, who could have killed Beatrice, either before his arrival at 7.59 p.m., or in the bare ten minutes when the studio was empty while Ann

Cartmell was seeing him off? Had it, after all, been an outside job?

If it had been, he reflected, the earlier period was the more likely one. Surely no sneak-thief—or even a homicidal maniac—would have ventured into School Wing just when the kitchen helpers were dispersing, and people were almost certainly wandering about the buildings and grounds? Suppose somebody had been loitering with intent, saw Beatrice Baynes leave Applebys soon after seven-thirty, and followed her to the studio. Money or jewellery might have been demanded. She certainly wouldn't have given in meekly—more likely to have tried to raise the alarm . . . All this was far-fetched, of course, but no more so than attributing an appaently motiveless murder to a man like Clive Torrance who was so concerned with his public image. Pollard decided that he must have another talk with Superintendent Martin and Beakbane about dubious local characters and strangers in the neighbourhood. He'd have to be tactful : they'd already carried out a pretty exhaustive enquiry.

The distant chiming of a clock made him look at the luminous dial of his watch. It was a quarter-past eleven, and there was a chilliness and a smell of sea mist in the air. Aeons of time stretched between this moment and Jane in a gay house-coat pouring out his breakfast coffee soon after six o'clock . . . Pollard stretched his cramped limbs and realised how tired he was. Switching on the engine he began cautiously to back the car out into the lane.

Sixteen

'The post is non-resident, and carries no supervisory or week-end duties out of normal hours.'
   Headmistress's Letter of Appointment to Ann Cartmell

AT BREAKFAST ON the following morning Pollard gathered that Toye had, as usual, taken his relaxation in a cinema.

'I dropped off for most of the first film,' he said. 'Legs and bosoms and beds. But afterwards there was a rattling good Western. *Death Rides In Stranglers' Creek,* it was called. Took my mind right off the case.'

'I bet it soon went back to it when you came out,' said Pollard, attacking a generous plateful of sausages, bacon and tomato.

Toye admitted having settled down in his bedroom to chew over the time-table once again.

'I wondered if we were cutting out losses a bit too heavily, sir,' he said. 'It seems to me there's a gap in Miss Thornton's alibi, and Miss Cartmell's too, for that matter.'

He proceeded to point out that there was a gap of twenty-five minutes between the departure of the guests from Applebys and the beginning of Festival supper.

'Say deceased went straight over to the studio,' he said, 'and got there at seven-fifteen or even seven-twenty. We know those two were at the supper, but not when they arrived back at the School from dolling themselves up at the Staff House.'

'That's perfectly true,' Pollard replied. 'It's a point we've missed, and ought to be checked up, even it it's almost impossible to believe either of them could have bashed her head in, and then come down and eaten a meal in an apparently normal way ... It's funny how often we start thinking along the same lines, quite independently. This time it's what might have happened in the studio before Torrance turned up. Listen to what I was working out in a hayfield behind Whitesands, while you were gripping the arms of your seat at the movies ...'

Omitting his moment of illumination in the telephone kiosk, Pollard outlined his theory that Beatrice Baynes had gone over to the studio soon after the beginning of Festival supper, concealed herself in the puppet theatre and been present throughout the Cartmell-Torrance session. Toye listened intently, his eyes alert behind his owl-like born rims.

'You've got it, I think, sir.'

'It's all right as far as it goes,' agreed Pollard, 'but unfortunately that's only a very short distance unless we can establish the physical possibility of Torrance's having committed the murder. In my opinion that's closely bound up with the question of some previous connection between him and Beatrice Bayes : there simply wasn't time for a murderous row starting from scratch. I'm hoping the Yard may have got on to something, which may suggest a credible motive at the same time ... Perhaps there's a history of insanity in the Torrance family ... You notice, by the way, that I'm absolutely ruling out collusion between Torrance and Cartmell ... Let's try and get hold of that woman and have some more coffee ...'

'I suppose,' Toye said thoughtfully, when the waitress had departed, 'that assuming this small point about Cartmell and Thornton before supper clears itself up, the only alternative to Torrance is somebody we haven't got on to at all so far. Can we take it that absolutely everyone who ought to have been at the meal, either eating or helping, *was* actually there the whole time?'

'We'd better check on that too. That Western you saw seems to have made you tick, doesn't it? The bare fact is that we can't afford to neglect the smallest pointer. Let's face it. As far as it's humanly possible to see, Madge Thornton, George Baynes, Bert Heyward, and even that old turkey-cock Jock Eccles are out of it. Miss Renshaw was surrounded by Old Meldonians from suppertime onwards, to after ten o'clock, poor woman. I suppose we could tactfully vet her alibi, too, in the period before supper, but it's a pretty fantastic idea. We're left with the highly improbable Clive Torrance and A.N. Other. The sensible thing is obviously to persuade the Super to have another go at strangers in the neighbourhood and any dark horses leading outwardly respectable lives, while we go all out on Torrance.' Pollard broke off as a fresh supply of coffee was brought, and peered dubiously into the pot.

'Hot water on old grounds,' he remarked. 'Reverting to Torrance, it's occurred to me that it might be worth looking up Mr and Mrs Gavin Scorhill at Stannaford Magna, where he says he spent the rest of the weekend.'

'About twenty miles west of Trill, isn't it?'

'Yes. My idea is that you drop me at Meldon and drive over there. Time the run carefully, both ways. If Torrance took an abnormally long time, it might be suggestive. If by any chance he did commit the murder, he'd have need of a breathing-space to pull himself together and think how best to cover his tracks. Find out what you can when you get there, as accurately as possible. Then see what sort of people the Scorhills are, and how they react to your enquiries. Another thing that might be worth knowing is when the visit was fixed up . . . To be honest, I can't quite see how this is going to help until we've reconstructed Torrance's movements when he went back for the magazine, but I've got a hunch that it's better not to attempt that until I've seen what the Chief's unearthed—if anything.'

'In case it leaks out, and puts Torrance on his guard?'

'Yes. We can't do it without attracting a certain amount of attention, and it might easily get round to Ann Cartmell, and you can imagine how she'd react. Let's go, shall we? There's a chap reading *The Daily Blare* with a WHEN WILL PUPPET

THEATRE CURTAIN RISE headline . . . he's behind you, and keeps giving us looks of contempt.'

Superintendent Martin and Inspector Beakbane agreed that there was a strong case for Beatrice Baynes having gone over to the studio before the arrival of Clive Torrence, to snoop on his meeting with Ann Cartmell, and that the murder could, in theory, have been an outside job. They pointed out, however, that exhaustive house-to-house enquiries about strangers had already been made. After all, Linbridge had soon run George Baynes to earth . . .

Pollard hastened to agree, and was complimentary.

'I wasn't altogether thinking of strangers, though,' he went on. 'You must have got a few shady characters in the Meldon area, or even people who've recently come to live there, whom you don't know much about. One of them might even be a discharged mental patient . . . No one was about when we think Miss Baynes went over to the studio. She could have been followed, and perhaps threatened, or an attempt made to grab her jewellery. She was wearing some pretty natty rings . . . She was a truculent old body, and certainly wouldn't have caved in easily.'

'According to Mr Yelland who has checked with the insurance policies, all deceased's jewllry is accounted for,' said Superintendent Martin, seizing on the one indisputable fact in this sea of conjecture. 'Still,' he admitted rather grudgingly, 'something of this sort could've happened. I'll give you that. We'll check the old lags again, and Beakbane, you might have a word with Freeth about newcomers over there. But I wouldn't expect anything from it, if I were you, Inspector.'

From the Linbridge police station Pollard and Toye drove to the Staff House. Mrs Milman, who answered the door, told them that she had been over at School from six-thirty onwards last Saturday evening, helping Miss Forrest, and had no idea about anybody's coming and going. Miss Craythorne was still here, and she might possibly know . . .

They waited in the depressing atmosphere of a dismantled

common-room draped in dust-sheets, until Miss Craythorne appeared. In her middle forties, surmised Pollard. She was wearing a grey suit and black hat, and explained that she was going with Miss Renshaw to the funeral. With the feeling that his introductory remarks about routine enquiries were unlikely to be taken at their face value, he raised the question of the departures for Festival supper.

'I think I can tell you all you want to know there,' Miss Craythorne replied. 'I took Miss Thornton over in my car. We left here just on a quarter-past seven, parked, and went straight into the dining-room. I remember glancing up at the clock and seeing that it was a minute or so after twenty past. The room was pretty full, and I got caught up at once, but I saw Miss Cartmell there. She left here a few minutes before I did. I know the sound of her car starting up.'

Pollard asked if anyone had been late for the meal.

'Oh dear, no,' replied Miss Craythorne. 'Miss Renshaw isn't a martinet, by any means, but punctuality is one of her "things" : it's well known. She had already arrived when I got there, and was beginning to edge the High Table party towards their places.'

He thanked her, and made a conventionally sympathetic remark.

'Time seems to have ceased to mean anything,' she said. 'It feels like a hundred years since last Monday. Miss Renshaw feels she can't possibly go away until his awful business has been cleared up—or put into permanent cold storage, I suppose.'

'I hope not,' said Pollard. 'Cold storage, I mean. It's a far from straightforward case, but I assure you that quite a lot of ground has been covered already.'

'What is going to happen about that unfortunate child Ann Cartmell's trip to America?' she asked as she escorted them to the front-door. There's a sobstuff paragraph about it in *The Daily Blare* this morning.'

'I shall be discussing it again with my superiors at Scotland

Yard later today,' he told her. 'There's just one more small point I'd like to check with you. About what time did you drive past Applebys on your way home last Saturday night?'

Miss Craythorne wrinkled her brow.

'I came away from Miss Renshaw's flat soon after nine,' she said, 'and did one or two tidying-up jobs in the Staff Room. I suppose I left the car park about a quarter-past or a bit later. Say twenty to twenty-five past . . . This is all very mysterious . . .'

'Just check and counter-check,' he told her.

'Blast the Press,' he remarked to Toye as they drove off. 'I bet Torrance put *The Daily Blare* up to it. Not even murder's going to interfere with his plans for his protégée . . . Looks as though your bright idea about the presupper period's a wash-out, I'm afraid.'

According to the arrangements made over breakfast, Pollard was dropped at Meldon and Toye set off on his mission to Stannaford Magna. After a careful study of a road map, he had decided to make a détour and use main roads rather than to cut across country through a maze of lanes. Even if Torrance were a frequent visitor to Flete House, he would normally go straight there from London on the more direct route. He seemed to have been a scorcher, according to Jock Eccles. Toye had no intention of hazarding the police car, and decided on a cruising speed of fifty, allowing for faster driving by Torrance.

There was a fair amount of traffic, but he made good going, and ran into Stannaford Magna in exactly twenty-six minutes from leaving Meldon. An enquiry at the post-office sent him on through the village to the drive gates on its outskirts. He turned in through a well-tended and prolific garden, and a few moments later drew up on a gravel sweep outside the house itself.

Flete House was what estate agents describe as a period-style, architect-designed luxury residence, with every adjunct for gracious living. Toye sat for a moment taking in the expensive garden furniture on the terrace, and the big french doors which stood open, revealing a handsome room within. Then he got out of the car and rang the front-door bell. After a fairly lengthy interval he heard footsteps, and the door was opened by an obviously foreign girl of South European appearance. An au pair, he thought ... Italian or Spanish. In reply to his request for Mr Scorhill she told him that he had gone to London. Mrs Scorhill? Yes, she was in ze 'ouse. On hearing that Toye represented the police she clasped a hand to her mouth and fled with a stifled cry.

'Meeses Scorreal! Meeses Scorreal!' he heard her call, and waited in some amusement. Finally a door at the back of the hall opened and a woman came towards him.

'Do come in—er—?'

'Detective-Sergeant Toye of New Scotland Yard, madam.'

She stopped abruptly, opening her grey eyes widely under their immensely long and patently artificial black lashes. About forty, he thought . . . mutton dressed as lamb. Mrs Scorhill was beautifully made up and her vivid red hair youthfully dressed. She wore a yellow little-girl shift frock and elegant pin-heel sandals.

'Sergeant,' she gasped, clasping her hands. 'Not my *husband*? Not an accident?'

He recognised a probably unconscious act, and took his cue quickly.

'Oh no, madam. I am very sorry indeed if I startled you. I have simply come to make a few routine enquiries if you can spare a few minutes, as I understand that Mr Scorhill is not available.

She relaxed with a faint smile.

'Dear me, you must think me very foolish, Sergeant, but really with these terrible road casualties. . . Do please come into the lounge.'

He followed her into the enormous room with the french doors and reflected that unlike the late Miss Baynes, the Scorhills splashed their lolly around. He had never seen a larger television set or a more comprehensive bar in a private house. The chairs and settees were luxuriously upholstered. There was a great heap of glossies on a side table, but not a book to be seen, he noticed, and nothing you'd really call a picture ... Mrs Scorhill indicated a sumptuous armchair in front of the open windows, and sank into its twin and gazed at him.

'My husband commutes to his London office ever day,' she said. 'It's a dreadful anxiety for me, and tiring for him, too, but we both felt it was worth it, just to breathe air that really *is* air, if you understand me, Sergeant. Do you live in London? Ah, well, you will understand ... The stifling petrol fumes and the terrible noise ...'

A silly gusher, thought Toye with satisfaction. He assured Mrs Scorhill that he understood perfectly. It was always a let-up to work on a case out of London ... Yes, he was carrying on the routine enquiries in the Baynes case, and was very sorry to trouble her, but under regulations the movements of everyone who had been on the scene of the crime had to be checked. Mr Clive Torrance had therefore been obliged to give Mr Scorhill's name and address, as he had spent the weekend at Flete House.

'Dear Clive,' she said, a rapt expression in her eyes. 'How appalling for a real artist like him to have got mixed up in this *dreadful* business. He's *such* a remarkable person, Sergeant, you know. So *utterly* absorbed in his work and so *interesting*, and yet not a bit patronising to ignoramuses like my husband and myself. Was it you who interviewed him? He rang us up.'

'That would have been one of my superior officers, madam. Does he often visit you here?' Toye enquired with interest.

'We hope he will in future, Sergeant, now that he has taken the plunge, although a man like that must be simply *inundated* with invitations, mustn't he? Last weekend was his very first visit to us, and we were *so* delighted. We first met him last autumn at one of those huge, noisy cocktail parties one has to go to in London, and got talking about this part of the country, and when he said how attractive he thought it was, we *begged* him to run down if *ever* he found himself with a free weekend. I never imagined we'd hear any more about it, and it was *such* a thrill when he wrote a most charming letter a few weeks ago, asking if we'd really meant it. Imagine it!'

'I expect a gentleman as high up in the world of art as Mr Torrance works a lot harder then people think,' suggested Toye.

Mrs Scorhill, reclining langorously with an arm behind her head, and showing an appreciable amount of thigh, expatiated at length on this subject. Presently he succeeded in bringing the talk round to the previous Saturday evening.

Yes, she told him, poor Mr Torrance hadn't arrived until after a quarter-past nine : she couldn't remember to a minute. He'd warned them that he might be late, but *really* she'd begun to get worried . . . the Sergeant would begin to think she'd got a thing about road accidents, wouldn't he? No, they never minded people not turning up on the dot . . . it wasn't tiresome, really, with a simmering oven, and the sort of meals that were *elastic,* if the Sergeant knew what she meant . . . Mr Torrance? Yes, he'd looked simply *exhausted* when he did turn up. He'd had such a day : busy in the Gallery all the morning, and then one of those tiresome meetings that go on for ever, in all that terrific heat, too. And on top of it all he'd stopped off on the way down to do something for that *wretched* School, and just because of that had got himself involved in this *miserable* case.

Toye commiserated, and said that he expected a couple of nights in such a lovely place had soon put Mr Torrance right.

Mrs Scorhill's shoulders registered despairing frustration . . . It had been only *one* night, as things had turned out. Mr Torrance had been *so* apologetic, but there'd been some unexpected crisis over a picture, and he felt he simply *must* be on the spot the very first thing on Monday morning. They'd offered him breakfast at *dawn*, and he'd been so appreciative, but said he'd have to get in touch with the other directors, and it was all a bit confidential for the phone. 'We were *heartbroken* : we'd asked quite a few people in to meet him on Sunday evening.'

'A big job never really lets you off the lead,' Toye agreed. 'All that worry must have quite spoilt even the very short time Mr Torrance was able to spend at Flete House.'

Well, Mrs Scorhill didn't know if she'd go quite as far as that. He'd soon zipped up after a few drinks, and been so witty and amusing . . . they'd roared with laughter at the things he'd said . . . He'd been a really *delightful* guest . . .

Toye came to the conclusion that there was probably little more of interest to be extracted from Mrs Scorhill, and began to disengage himself by asking if she recommended the main road or the cross-country return route to Meldon. Here she was most emphatic. They often ran down to Whitesands, out of the tripper season, of course, and *always* by the main road as far as the Trill turning. The lanes were *hopeless* : one met *endless* tiresome farm tractors and things, and did nothing but back. Finally, after the usual arguments abut accepting refreshment when on duty, Toye took his leave, carefully noting the exact time of his departure.

After Toye had driven off to Stannaford Magna, Pollard went into the hall of Old House with no very clear-cut plan of action, beyond the intention of talking to Helen Renshaw before she left for the funeral. The place seemed very quiet and deserted. The door of the secretary's office was open, and there were papers on the desk, but no sign of Joyce Kitson. He thought he could hear distant voices, and tracked them down to the headmistress's office. Acting on impulse he went to the door and knocked. Invited to enter, he opened it to find Helen Renshaw dictating to Joyce Kitson. They looked up at him in surprise, and he thought he detected disapproval in the latter's face. He apologised for disturbing them.

'I saw Mrs Kitson was not in her office,' he said, 'so I

ventured to try here. Is it a very inconvenient moment to have a few words with you, Miss Renshaw?'

'Of course not,' Helen replied. 'Come and sit down.'

Joyce Kitson had gathered up her pad and some letters, and was making to leave them when Pollard interposed.

'As a matter of fact, I rather wanted to see Mrs Kitson too. Could we have a sort of talk *à trois,* do you think? It's often very helpful to have a discussion.'

'By all means. Draw up that other chair, Inspector.'

This is a bit of luck, he thought, as he complied. Kitson looks as sticky as they come, but she can hardly be obstructive in front of her boss . . . He opened his notebook on his knee, and smiled pleasantly at the two women.

'One of the puzzling things about this case, as you know,' he told them, 'is why Miss Baynes went to the studio at all last Saturday evening. She was elderly, and no doubt tired after a long day, and she had already visited the art exhibition. The police are satisfied that she was murdered there, and it is virtually impossible that she was taken there by force, so she must have gone on her own free will. Up to now we have been unable to find anyone who saw her on her way there. There is some evidence that she went across between half-past seven and a quarter to eight, when there was no one at the Lodge, and the whole community as far as we know was occupied with supper.'

Helen Renshaw nodded appreciatively.

'It has been suggested,' he went on, 'that her motive in going was to be present during Mr Torrance's visit to Miss Cartmell, and that to do this without their being aware of her presence she concealed herself in the puppet theatre.'

Pollard watched the two faces in front of him. He saw Helen Renshaw's registered distaste which quickly gave way to anxiety. Joyce Kitson reacted more slowly. She looked baffled and incredulous, and then frowned as if trying to work out some problem.

'The difficulty here,' he went on, 'is how Miss Baynes could have known that Mr Torrance was coming. He has assured me that he had never given a firm undertaking to advise on the selection of paintings for the competition, and that in fact the whole matter had gone out of his head until he was packing his bag for a weekend visit to friends at Stannaford Magna after lunch last Saturday. He then suddenly remembered about it, and realising that Meldon wouldn't be far out of his way, rang up Miss Cartmell to ask if the paintings had already been sent off. I realise what a busy afternoon it must have been, but I wonder if by chance anything is known about this telephone call? Was Miss Cartmell summoned to take it over a loud speaker, for instance?'

Helen Renshaw looked amused.

'We aren't quite as streamlined and up-to-date as that,' she remarked. 'The call would have come through the secretary's office in the usual way.' She glanced interrogatively at Joyce Kitson, who nodded.

'Yes, I took it myself. It was a personal call from London for Miss Cartmell.'

'Can you remember the time it came through?'

'Well, not exactly. People were in and out all the time. It was not like taking a message, when I should have noted down the time as a matter of course. Between two-thirty and three, I should think.'

'Was Miss Cartmell expecting a call?'

'I've no idea,' replied Joyce Kitson rather tartly. 'She hadn't said anything to me about it.'

'The non-resident staff aren't encouraged to have incoming calls over here unless it's something urgent,' Helen Renshaw explained. 'Mrs Kitson can't waste her time running round the School looking for people. If anyone knows an important call is coming for her she is asked to be on hand, or let Mrs Kitson know where to find her. In this case I'm quite sure Miss Cartmell wasn't expecting one from the way she spoke to me about it later in the afternoon.'

'I see,' said Pollard. 'Was it difficult to track her down in the crowd?'

'Not in the least,' replied Joyce Kitson. 'I knew that she

would be up in the studio showing O.M.s round the art exhibition, and I asked one of the Sixth Form to go and fetch her.'

'In the case of a personal call the operator doesn't give the name of the caller, so presumably anyone who overheard the message being delivered wouldn't have been any the wiser. Did Miss Cartmell come down to your office to take it?'

'Yes.' There was a worried look on Joyce Kitson's pale face as she pressed her rather thin lips together. 'I told her to take it in what we call the inner office. It's really a part of the room partitioned off, and there's a telephone extension in there . . .' She broke off uncertainly.

'Have you any reason to believe that Beatrice Baynes could have overheard the conversation?' asked Helen Renshaw.

'Well, yes, I think she might. Just as Ann Cartmell dashed into the inner office I saw old Mrs Findhorn looking helpless in the hall, and went out to see if I could do anything for her. I was away for a few minutes, and when I got back Ann had gone, and Miss Baynes and Mrs Elkinshaw were standing at my desk.'

'And the receiver of your telephone had been left off and was lying on it, of course?'

'Yes,' said Joyce Kitson unhappily. 'Just by where Miss Baynes was standing. I suppose I oughtn't to have left the office until the call was over.'

'My dear Joyce,' Helen Renshaw said kindly, but firmly, 'I never heard anything so absurd. This isn't the British Embassy in Moscow, is it, Inspector?'

'I don't think anyone could conceivably feel that Mrs Kitson was negligent,' Pollard replied. 'I hope you'll dismiss the idea from your mind at once,' he said kindly, turning to her. 'In any case, there's no proof that Miss Baynes overheard the conversation, although obviously the incident could have been the source of her information.'

'I feel very disquieted,' Helen Renshaw bluntly said, when Joyce Kitson had left them. 'I'm afraid this may make you suspect that Ann Cartmell was involved in the murder, perhaps in collusion with Mr Torrance.'

'I won't insult your intelligence by pretending the idea hadn't occurred to me,' Pollard replied, 'but I've rejected it on several grounds. In the first place there is the psychology of both of them. Then it was an unpremeditated murder, and so far as I can discover there appears to be a total absence of motive. What do you think,' he went on 'Miss Baynes could have hoped to gain from this particular piece of snooping, assuming for the moment that it actually took place?'

'I doubt if she would have had a very clear idea herself,' said Helen Renshaw thoughtfully. 'I think she was quite beside herself with anger after the events of the Annual General Meeting, and would have seized any opportunity of damaging Ann Cartmell — and indirectly myself. She had a thing about the sex life of the younger staff — arising from her own repressions, presumably — and I can very well imagine how she would have reacted to the chance information that Ann Cartmell was going to be in the studio with a man. And it probably sounds absolute drivel to you, but the studio was an emotive place to her : where the old order hung on longest, with her friend Miss Leeke. It seems to me perfectly in character for her to have gone up there in the hopes of seeing some improper behaviour."

'And what do you think she actually saw?' asked Pollard.

'I think any idea that she saw Ann and Mr Torrance having sexual intercourse and threatened to report them to me and the Governors is simply ludicrous, Inspector. Ann Cartmell is free to spend almost any weekend of term and all the holidays with him if she likes. It's fantastic to suggest that anything of the sort happened in what was virtually a public place. You've met Mr Torrance, I take it? Can you imagine for a single moment that he'd risk his reputation like that?'

'Not for a single moment, as you say,' Pollard replied. 'All the same, I want to talk to you about Ann Cartmell. I don't suspect her either of murdering Miss Baynes or of being an accessory. But I've got a feeling—very ill-defined—at the back of my mond, that she is some how relevant to the murder. Unknown to herself, I mean.'

Helen Renshaw looked interested.

'I see what you mean. Theoretically, that is.'

'We did touch on the relationship between her and Mr Torrance before. Do you think you can possibly add anything to what you told me then?'

'Isn't the implication of all this that you suspect Mr Torrance as distinct from Ann? You know, I think it's quite incredible, quite apart from the practical difficulties.'

'You mustn't question a police officer, Miss Renshaw,' Pollard replied gravely.

She laughed.

'Touché, Inspector. All right, I'll talk, if I can only think of something to tell you.' She rested her head on her hand and stared at the roses on her desk. 'I'm sure in my own mind that they haven't been living together,' she said at last. 'Ann would have been compliance itself if he'd wanted her, but she isn't his type, and he's much too experienced to get himself inconveniently entangeld.'

'You know, this interests me,' Pollard told her. 'It struck me that in spite of Miss Cartmell's obvious inexperience, there was a kind of complacency about her when she spoke of Mr Torrance. Something of the air of having landed her man, so to speak. Also, she was extremely remote : almost incredibly unconcerned with the murder, considering that it had happened in her own workshop, and that she had been on the spot at various times during the evening.'

Helen Renshaw looked doubtful.

'Well, if we're both right, it suggests that there was some development in their relationship last Saturday, doesn't it? But you know, I don't think it need have added up to much. In her present emotional attitude to Mr Torrance, a mere friendly farewell kiss would probably be taken to mean something much more significant. She was very excited about the

oil colour-box he had sent to her from Brocatti & Simpson's
... As to her remoteness, she is still childishly self-absorbed
in some ways, although so excellent at her job. She's a lob-
sided and late developer : I only hope she eventually meets
the kind of man she ought to marry.' She glanced at her
watch.

'I mustn't keep you,' Pollard said. 'Miss Craythorne told
me you and she were going to the funeral. But this discussion
has been very helpful. Just one more question—about Mrs
Kitson? We're finding her a bit—well, difficult to talk to.'

'That doesn't mean anything. She's absolutely sound, but
terribly on the defensive. She made one of those hasty war
marriages which broke up afterwards, and her little boy died
of polio. One has to try all the time to restore her confidence,
and make her feel valued. She's a first-class secretary, incidentally.'

'Thank you for telling me that. And I want to thank you
for all the questions you haven't asked, Miss Renshaw, and to
tell you quite irregularly and in confidence, that I don't think
you need worry about Miss Thornton, or Bert Heyward.'

'I can only say in all sincerity,' Helen Renshaw replied,
'that I'm thankful that you personally are carrying on this
investigation.'

Seventeen

'Please check the draft time-table for next year and report any discrepancies.'

H. RENSHAW
Headmistress's Notice on Staff Room Notice Board

TOYE HAD NOT returned from Stannaford Magna, and Pollard went into the Library after leaving Helen Renshaw. Sitting down at the table in the now familiar bay, he began to work on an up-to-the-minute edition of the time-table, and was soon completely absorbed. Half-an-hour later he sat back and began to meditate on the result of his labours.

SATURDAY EVENING		CONFIRMATION
approx.		
6.30	Jock Eccles leaves for Plough.	Landlord (arrival)
6.50	Bert Heyward leaves for Plough.	Landlord (arrival)
7.05	Beatrice Baynes sees off friends.	Mrs Steadman and Miss Watman
7.18	Ann Cartmell arrives in dining-room	Departure from Staff House noted by Miss Craythorne

approx.		
7.30	Festival supper begins.	
	? B.B. goes over to Studio?	Saw Torrance arrive about 7.55
7.45	J.E. returns from Plough.	
7.59	Torrance reaches School Wing.	A.C.
8.01	A.C. reaches Studio.	C.T.
8.20	B. Heyward passes Applebys.	M.T. and J.E.
8.22	M.T. crosses over to Park.	J.E.
8.29	A.C. and C.T. leave Studio	
8.31	C.T. returns to Studio for *Artifex*	A.C.
8.32	A.C. reaches Secretary's office.	Joyce Kitson

approx.		
8.36	C.T. reaches Secretary's office.	J.K. and A.C.
8.38	C.T. drives off.	J.K., A.C. and J.E.
8.41	A.C. and two girls return to Studio.	
8.58	George Baynes reaches Applebys.	Fits in with time Aggett met him on road
8.59	A.C. and girls leave Studio	Sister Felicity and Mrs Fleming
9.02	Sister F. and Mrs Fleming reach Studio and settle down on fire-escape.	
	A.C. offers M.T. lift in drive.	M.T.
9.03	George Baynes in Applebys porch.	A.C.

approx.		
9.05	M.T. reaches Applebys.	G.B.
9.10	M.T. leaves Applebys. Goes to spy-hole.	G.B.
	A.C. reaches Staff House.	Several witnesses
9.20	M.T. sees Miss Craythorne drive past.	Craythorne supports this
9.35	G.B. leaves Applebys and enters park.	M.T.
9.40	B. Heyward leaves for locking-up round.	Mrs Heyward and Mrs Hinks
9.50	Sister F. and Mrs Fleming found by B.H. who locks up Studio.	All three
9.53	Locking-up of School Wing continues,	Sister F. and Mrs F.
10.12	M.T. returns to Staff House.	Mrs Milman
10.15	B.H. returns home from locking up.	Mrs Heyward

The minutes slipped past. He scrutinised and tried to assess the significance of it all, item by item. It was like looking through a telescope, he thought, at the soundless but significant activities of a distant group of people combining in an evolving pattern of which he had not yet detected the underlying motif . . . Jock Eccles pedalling slowly down the road . . . elderly ladies getting decorously into a car and waving good-bye . . . a small figure in a navy-blue coat hurrying up the deserted drive, desperately intent . . . a Jaguar scorching down the London road . . . a young man in a green shirt striding over Clintridge and exchanging a brief greeting with

the rustic Aggett, homeward bound from the Plough ...
Then, quite suddenly, Pollard experienced a kind of mental
electric shock ... Good Lord! To think he hadn't picked on
that unsupported statement before, when such a lot hung on
it. Seizing his pen he began a series of scribbled calculations.

The sound of a car drawing up outside distracted him. A
couple of minutes later Toye came in, impassive of counten-
ance as ever, but Pollard who knew him well detected a
latent excitement.

'You've been the hell of a time,' he said. 'Anything in the
bag?'

Toye came and sat down facing him.

'To my mind, sir,' he replied, 'this visit of Mr Torrance's
stinks.'

Pollard put down his pen and listened.

'It's not the sort of thing you can base a case on,' he said
thoughtfully, when Toye had finished, 'but it could be
damned useful supporting evidence. You had luck, of course,
with that woman being such a fool, but you've done a rattling
good job. Now, if only they've unearthed something about
Torrance at the Yard ... We'll run up presently, but first of
all, I want you to take a look at this. It's wide open at one
point.'

A few minutes later Toye put his finger on the blank in the
third column opposite 8.29 p.m., and looked up interrogatively.

'Yes, that's it. We've been a couple of clots. This timing
rests on Torrance's statement only. Ann Cartmell said quite
definitely that she didn't notice the exact time when they
came down, and I can quite believe it. She was still in a
seventh heaven from the petting party, unless I'm very much
mistaken. She only said "it must have been about half-past
eight." Torrance, on the other hand, was quite specific.' Pollard referred to his notes. 'He said it was jsut on half-past
eight, and that his watch was reliable. You couldn't get anything definite from Mrs Kitson, so it's quite on the cards that

there's a margin of several minutes here. It might make all the difference. Suppose they came down at eight-twenty-five, and Torrance still didn't arrive in the Secretary's office until eight-thirty-six. That would give him nine minutes from the time he got back to fetch his *Artifex*.'

'What about the other end?' asked Toye.

'I don't think eight-thirty-eight is far out. Ann Cartmell didn't hesitate at all over saying that it was just on twenty to nine when he drove off, and she seems to have had her eye on the time because of finishing the clearing-up in the studio before nine, when Bert Hayward should have started his locking-up. And this seems to fit in with what the two girls and Mrs Kitson thought the time was, and Jock Eccles too.'

'Isn't it possible that *someone* might have seen both of them coming down, or Torrance on his own? The kitchen squad when they were dispersing, for instance. Shall I nose round a bit?'

Pollard considered.

'On the whole,' he said, 'I think we'll hold our hand down here until we've been up to the Yard. Some information on Torrance may have come in which alters the whole situation. If he did commit murder, he's one of the coolest and slickest customers I've struck as yet, and the last thing we want to do is to put the wind up him. We're still in a hopelessly weak position, even if we can demonstrate that he could have done the job in the time.'

'On the question of motive, you mean?'

'Yes. Still, the immediate job is concerned with practical possibilities. Great Scott, look at the time! Let's go and get a belated snack and start for Town. We'll call in at the Linbridge station just on chance.'

The report session with Chief Superintendent Crowe later that day began inauspiciously. He indicated a scatter of evening papers with a jerk of his head.

'They're in full cry,' he remarked. 'How many of your suspects have you cleared out of the way? Sit down.'

Pollard sat down.

'George Baynes, Madge Thornton, and Bert Heyward, sir,' he replied. 'Also Ann Cartmell acting independently of Torrance.'

'A pretty comprehensive clean sweep. Let's hear your grounds for making it.' Crowe leant back in his chair, his bright, birdlike stare trained on his subordinate, prepared to miss nothing. As Sister Felicity emerged in the curse of the narrative he gave a shout of laughter.

'My God, you had some luck there, Pollard. First time I've heard of a case with a holy nun parked on the scene of the crime like a sitting hen.'

Pollard grinned.

'I'm dashed grateful to her,' he said. 'In the long term, that is. In the short, she's cut out all the likely suspects and left a situation in which it seems to be either Torrance on a ridiculously tight schedule and with no motive, or a roving maniac. Has anything come in on Torrance, sir?'

'Don't jump the gun. Go on with your report in an orderly manner.'

Pollard went on. He set out his case for Beatrice Baynes having gone over to the studio soon after seven-thirty, with the object of sitting in on the Cartmell-Torrance appointment, and passed over a copy of the time-table. Crowe put up a hand for silence, and studied it for a full two minutes.

'Go on now,' he said.

'As you see, sir, the case against Clive Torrance rests on the short period round eight-thirty. At first sight it looks like being a sheer physical impossibility that he could have committed the murder in the time, but we only have his unsupported statement that they came down at eight-twenty-nine approximately. Miss Cartmell said she hadn't noticed the exact time. It seems to me that it could quite well have been earlier — say, four or five minutes earlier.'

'Have you tried to get corroboration of this statement? Surely there must have been people about?'

'Yes, I expect there probably were, sir, but I don't think it's at all likely that they'd have been time-conscious within just a minute or two, which is what we're after. It was a sort of holiday occasion, and all the official fixtures were over. They'd just have been wandering about nattering, without anything very definite in mind.'

'Fair enough. Why haven't you had a trial run over the ground, though, to get some idea of the time the job would have taken?'

Pollard explained his reasons for not having drawn attention to Clive Torrance. 'And I thought the enquiry might have brought in something relevant,' he said in conclusion.

'Unfortunately nothing much has turned up about any of 'em,' replied Crowe, pulling some type-written sheets towards him . . .

Clive Torrance, born in 1917, came from a comfortable middle-class London hime, his father having been an architect. He had been educated at one of the smaller public schools, going on to the Slade and afterward studying art in Paris. At first he had exhibited with some success and achieved a reputation as a teacher, gravitating later to work in connection with national schemes for art education in which he had become a well-known figure. After his father's death he had bought a share in the syndicate which owned the Domani Gallery, of which he was now managing director. The Gallery appeared to be doing well, and there was no suggestion that its activities were other than impeccable.

From enquiries in the mews where he garaged his Jaguar, it transpired that he kept somewhat erratic hours, and was known to transport a lady passenger apt to leave such things as odd gloves, lipsticks, and wafts of classy perfume behind her. The woman who cleaned his rooms reported fairly frequent overnight absences, allegedly on business, but the general opinion was that he was a decent sort, open-handed and always with a pleasant word for you. The attitude of his own circle was less favourable, at any rate as far as its male element was concerned. While his work was generally respected, he was thought to be a conceited bounder in some quarters, and one who did himself damned well. This latter achievement was put down to his flair for picking up pictures and backing promising young artists, and to his brilliance as a bridge player. He did not appear to drink or bet heavily, or ever to have suffered from mental illness. As far as could be discovered, no connection had ever existed between the Torrance and Baynes families, or between Clive and Beatrice as individuals.

'So there you are,' commented Crowe. 'Nothing to suggest a motive there, on the face of it. He seems a bit warmer than you'd expect in his position, but look what pictures fetch these days.'

'All the same, sir,' said Pollard, with the pleasing sensation of being about to produce a trump card. 'Toye thinks that visit to the Scorhills at Stanaford Magna stinks. I sent him along this morning, to see if he could pick up anything.'

Crowe paid the tribute of a single blink.

'Why does it? Toye's a damn sound chap. Not quite enough drive, but no flies on him.'

'Several things struck him as odd, sir. It was Mrs Scorhill he interviewed—Mr Scorhill was up here at his office. Toye says she's as dumb as they come. Not literally : she drivelled for the best part of an hour, but too silly to try to put anything across you. He particularly noticed that there were no books in the living-room, and no decent pictures. Unless Mr Scorhill's a very different type, it seems peculiar that a man like Torrance with his circle of friends should cultivate people like that unless he had some ulterior motive. Toye says the place simply reeks of money and looks like a luxury hotel. Whatever sort of chap Torrance is, he's intelligent and cultured, and his surroundings show it.'

'Then,' Pollard went on, 'he seems to have invited himself down there. According to Mrs Scorhill they met quite by chance at some cocktail paty last autumn up here, and got talking about Upshire. Torrance remarked that he thought it an attractive part of the world, and they seem to have frozen on to him and urged him to come down and stay with them. Mrs Scorhill said rather naïvely that they never expected to hear any more of him, and were delighted to get a letter a few weeks ago proposing himself for last weekend. He suggested coming down latish on Saturday evening and staying over until Monday morning. In the end he didn't show up until after a quarter past nine. Mrs Scorhill wasn't more exact than that.'

Crowe grunted, indicating keen interest.

'Toye timed himself carefully on the run from Meldon. He took twenty-six minutes on the outward journey, and twenty-eight coming back. There's evidence that Torrance is a fast driver, and there wouldn't have been much commercial traffic about on a Saturday night. But if Torrance left Meldon at just on twenty to nine and didn't get to Scorhill's place till after quarter-past, he was at least thirty-five minutes on the road.'

'If he had committed the murder, are you suggesting that he stopped to get rid of the weapon?'

'Yes. We haven't been able to find it anywhere. And if, as you say, Torrance was the murderer, surely he'd have wanted a few minutes to pull himself together as soon as he was clear of the School? Both Ann Cartmell and the secretary mentioned how he had gone tearing off. According to Mrs Scorhill, he arrived looking utterly exhausted, but bucked up after a few drinks and became the life and soul of the party.'

There was a fairly lengthy pause.

'If it was rigged, it's certainly suggestive,' said Crowe thoughtfully. 'It ties up with what we've been able to pick up about the Scorhills.' He pushed another type-written report towards Pollard. It stated briefly that Mr Scorhill was a self-made man and a very prosperous director of several companies producing a variety of consumer goods, and that nothing was known to the police against either him or his wife. They had a circle of friends with similar business interests, and appeared to have no connection with the world of artists and other intelligentsia.

'We've nothing on the Cartmell girl either.' Crowe produced a third report. 'Normal middle-class home and school, and art career. Flopped in her first job because she couldn't manage East End teenage toughs. No evidence that she's living with Torrance. I see you completely exclude collusion between her and Torrance.

'Well, yes, sir. As you said, one simply can't see Torrance committing murder in front of a wittness.'

Crowe, who appreciated being hoist with his own petard by a subordinate, gave Pollard a mock salute.

'What about Ann Cartmell, sir? Are we to let her go? Did you see that paragraph in this morning's *Daily Blare*? I wonder if Torrance put them up to it.'

'If he did, he's bloody keen for her to go, isn't he? To answer your question, I think it depends on whether it was possible for Torrance to have done the job in the time. You'd better go down first thing tomorrow and set about some sort of reconstruction. Establish to your complete satisfaction what is the minimum time he could have taken, and whether that time was available or not. If it was, I think there's a case for packing her off on a plane on Monday. We'll have to put it up to the A.C., of course. You've done quite well so far, and I think you were quite right not to show much interest in Torrance's movements up to now, but as things have turned out it's the only line you've got to follow up at the moment. What's biting you?'

'This business of motives, sir. If there was no previous link of any sort between him and Beatrice Baynes, and he isn't bonkers, what reason *could* he have had for killing her more or less on sight?'

'That's up to you to work out, my boy,' replied Crowe, stretching to indicate that the interview was coming to an end, 'always providing that the job was a practical possibility. If it wasn't, you'll have to make a fresh start on the whole business. I'll expect you back here latish tomorrow.'

Jane Pollard possessed the rare art of being unobtrusively self-effacing when her husband's cases were approaching crisis level. She neither indulged in bright chatter, aimed at distracting him, nor took refuge in obviously tactful silence. She provided appetising food and occupied herself whole-heartedly in some unfidgety ploy. Tom Pollard watched her absently from the depths of an armchair as she plied a tapestry needle.

'How on earth can you get a rather tight-lipped woman whose whole life has come unstuck, and who's got a chip on the shoulder to be co-operative?' he asked suddenly.

'Which one is this?'

'The School secretary. A Mrs Kitson.' He repeated the tragic history given to him by Helen Renshaw.

'How utterly ghastly,' said Jane with feeling. 'I don't wonder she's tight-lipped. She must have tremendous guts to have taken on a demanding job like that. What do you want her to be co-operative about?'

'The length of time Ann Cartmell was in the office doing up those pictures. A sort of acted reconstruction is the only way of getting at it, I think, and I just can't see her doing it.'

Jane put down her tapestry and considered.

'She probably finds some compensation in priding herself on coping with the toughness of life. I'd stress the rotten side of having to hunt people down, even if they are criminals, and imply that you take her for the kind of person who'll be prepared to lend a hand.'

'Clever girl, aren't you?'

'Students' technique for the handling of difficult,' she said. 'Have you recovered sufficiently to tell me if Ann Cartmell's being allowed to go? I'm consumed with curiosity.'

He told her of Crowe's decision.

'You know,' she said, 'I still feel that girl's up to the neck in this business, even though she obviously isn't a murderess, and I can't believe she's Clive Torrance's mistress. You've no further information on that score, I suppose?'

'No, none. Miss Renshaw absolutely scorns the idea too. The only thing I've discovered is that he gave her an oil colour-box as a kind of reward for getting this scholarship.'

'Quite an expensive present,' remarked Jane. 'Was it a good one?'

'I expect so. It was sent from Brocatti & Simpson's. Not exactly an emotive present, though.'

'No,' she agreed. 'There's nothing emotive about being given the tools of your trade as a present.'

'I'll bear that in mind,' he promised her.

'Good. Only two months to my birthday.'

Silence descended once more Tom Pollard lay back and smoked, eyes half-closed. Presently Jane folded up her tapestry.

'Bed for me,' she said. 'If you want a drink, there's plenty of milk in the fridge, and some made black coffee. And beer, of course.'

'Sorry to be so lacking in entertainment value,' he said. 'I'll try not to disturb you.'

He tried to concentrate on the reconstruction, but the problem of motive kept fretting at the back of his mind. What made people kill more or less on sight? Not thugs, but educated, civilised people . . . There was self-defence, of course, but in what conceivable way could the elderly and undersized Beatrice Baynes have threatened a hefty chap like Torrance, if it was really their first meeting? Or anyway, their first meeting of any significance . . . He visualised the encounter in the studio over and over again, until the scene became quite jerky with repetition, like a real puppet show.

This won't do, he thought, raising himself, and forced his thoughts back to tomorrow's programme. He'd to see Helen Renshaw first, of course, and explain what they were going to do. Perhaps she'd be able to think of some means of keeping people out of the way . . .

Eighteen

'Time travels in divers paces with divers persons.'
Context questions in Upper Fourth examination paper in
Meldon

IT HAD RAINED during the night, and the next morning was
cool and fresh, with big post-depression cumulus clouds sailing across the sky. Pollard picked up Toye at the Yard soon
after eight. The worst traffic was incoming, and they made
good time in getting out on to the now familiar road to Linbridge.

'I can't make up my mind,' he said, sniffing the rain-
freshened air, 'if having a case in an area puts you off it for
good, or not. It's an attractive part of the world down there,
but at the moment I feel as though I never want to set eyes on
it again.'

Toye thought it wore off in time. Look at that chap Inspector French. First thing he always did in the tales was to make
up his mind to come back to the scene of the crime for his
next holiday. Personally, he didn't feel all that struck on Upshire. A bit tame, he thought. Now, a case in Devon or
Cornwall at some nice place on the coast would suit him
down to the ground . . .

After discussing their plan of action for a time, they agreed
that a third man would be useful, and that the Super should
be asked for the loan of Constable Freeth or anyone available. There were really two distinct jobs ahead of them. The
first was to work out the basic minimum of time that Torrance would have needed to carry through the murder. The
second, and much trickier, was to establish much more accu-

rately the length of time Ann Cartmell had spent in the Secretary's office before being rejoined by Torrance.

'I'll have a bash at Mrs Kitson myself this time,' said Pollard, 'while you're writing up the reconstruction. I don't know when we shall be through, but I must get back as quickly as I can, especially if we get what you might call a positive result.'

On arriving at Linbridge they went straight to the police station, and Pollard put his request for a helper to Superintendent Martin.

'You'd better take Beakbane along,' Marti said. 'Acting's right up his street. He's a leading light in the Linbridge Dramatic.'

Pollard would have much preferred a humbler colleague of lower rank, but Beakbane's pleasure at the prospect of taking part was so evident that he hadn't the heart to demur.

'I suggest that you stand in for Miss Baynes,' he said, thinking quickly. 'It'll be a great help if Toye and I can give our whole minds to getting over the ground at the right sort of speed.'

'Good thing he hasn't got to be jammed into the puppet theatre,' remarked the Super. 'Chap of his girth would've bust it.'

After further badinage the three men left for Meldon in convoy, Beakbane driving Pollard in a Linbridge police car in order to be brought up-to-date in the case.

'You two had better go and read a nice book,' Pollard said as they got out of the cars. 'I'm going to spend a bit of time preparing the ground.'

Remarking that he didn't think he'd opened one since he left school, Beakbane led the way to the library . . .

Helen Renshaw was upstairs in her flat, and received Pollard in her sitting-room. She looked at him shrewdly as he outlined the reconstruction he proposed to attempt.

'As far as attracting attention goes, you've hit on a rather good moment,' she said. 'It's the last cleaning day, and the women have worked round to New Wing which doesn't overlook the Quad. We haven't touched the studio yet, of course. As soon as you give the all-clear, I'm having the decorators in.'

'I hope we really shall be able to hand it over early next week,' he told her, and went on to explain what he wanted from Joyce Kitson.

'I'm perfectly sure she could remember very accurately indeed what happened when Ann Cartmell was there. She's got an almost photographic memory.' Helen Renshaw hesitated. 'I was going to suggest having a word with her myself about co-operating, but on the whole I think not. It suggests at once that we've discussed her attitude. Better for me just to warn her that you'll be about the place doing a reconstruction. Your talk with her will follow on naturally from that.'

School Wing smelt of disinfectant and floor polish. It had been closed for the holidays, and it was a relief to throw open some of the studio windows and let the air in. Standing in the middle of the untouched disorder and accumulated dust, Pollard briefed Beakbane and Toye.

'We'll assume that the puppet theatre is in the old place,' he said, 'and that Beatrice Baynes is hiding inside it. That's you, Inspector. I'll play Torrance to Toye's Ann Cartmell. We two go down, quite briskly, because I realise I'm going to be very late getting to the Scorhills. As soon as you hear us going downstairs, come out and go over to the table. What else you ought to be doing, I'm afraid I haven't a clue at the moment. As soon as we get out into the Quad, Toye asks me if I remembered to pick up my copy of *Artifex*. I haven't, and brush aside his offer to come back for it, telling him to run on ahead to the office and get the parcel ready, while I go back myself. I turn back into the building and hurry up the two flights of stairs. Not hell for leather, for I'm in my forties and carrying quite a bit of weight, but I don't hang about. Then I shove open the swing doors and am in this room before I see you' — he turned to Beakbane — 'standing here, by the table. I'm afraid at this stage. I'm still not clear about what you're doing, or exactly what happens next. I rather think you challenge me, making some really serious accusation or threat. I probably deny it flatly, see that nothing's going to stop you taking action, snatch up this stone,' Pollard extracted one of the remaining large flat pebbles from the box and put it out on the table, 'and smash down on your skull with it. You collapse in a heap on the floor. I look round, probably with some idea of carrying you into the next room and hiding you there, and catch sight of the puppet theatre. I think I have to go over and take a look at it, in case it's full of gear. It isn't, so I carry you across the room, stuff you into it, and shove the whole contraption up against the wall. Then I hurry back to the table, pick up the stone, and cram it into my pocket, missing the spot of blood it's left on the table. I take a look round to see you haven't left a handbag or gloves or anything lying about, and I'm just starting for the door when I remember the copy of *Artifex* which I came for. I find it under the discarded paintings on the table, and dash down the stairs and out into the Quad, slowing down a bit in case my speed attracts attention. Arriving at the office, I make my lateness an excuse for rushing out to the car rather unceremoniously. That's the general idea, I think. All right?'

'Would you have done anything about your prints?' asked Beakbane.

'I don't think so, except possibly putting a handkerchief over my hand before touching the puppet theatre. I'm pretty fly, and realise rough hessian probably won't take them. If they're found on the table and door and so on, that's fine. I've been up here for half-an-hour on perfectly legitimate business.'

After a further short discussion, the three men went into action. Beakbane went across the room and took up a position in his corner, his back to the wall where the puppet theatre had stood. Pollard arranged a heap of books to represent *Artifex* and the paintings, and took a stop-watch out of his pocket.

'Right,' he said, pressing the release catch. 'Let's push off, Toye.'

They went smartly to the door, which Pollard held open for Toye to pass through. As they went rather quickly down the stairs, it closed behind them with the little thud which Sister Felicity had commented on. The door into the Quad stood open. After they had taken a few steps, Toye suddenly stopped short.

'Have you got your *Artifex*?' he asked.

'Damn! I've left it upstairs.'

'I'll dash back for it, shall I?'

'No. I'll go. You run on and get that form filled in. I'll join you in the office.'

Turning back, Pollard hurried into the building again. It was extraordinary, he thought, how much detail you noticed when you were doing something self-consciously which was normally automatic, like going upstairs. The half-landings were quite big as you swung round . . . the banisters of hard polished wood a decided help to anyone in a hurry. He reached the top, and plunged through the doors which thudded noisily behind him.

Beakbane had emerged and was standing by the table on the far side of the room. He swung round sharply. Pollard was quite startled at the aggressive vindictiveness which he managed to convey. The man certainly could act . . .

'Yes, I was here all the time,' he said with an unpleasant note of triumph in his voice. 'I heard every word. And I'm going straight to Miss Renshaw and then to the police.'

'I don't know who you are or what you're talking about.' Pollard had come up to the table and stood only a few feet away.

'You needn't try that nonsense on me. I heard every word

you said. I'm going now.' Beakbane made a move towards the door.

In a flash Pollard grabbed the stone and tapped Beakbane's head with it. The latter collapsed on to his knees. Remembering to pause and look round, Pollard dashed across the room, snatching his handkerchief out of his pocket, and mimed the dragging out of the puppet theatre from the wall. Back again, he assisted Beakbane to his feet.

'As you're about seven stone heavier than Beatrice Baynes, you'll have to walk,' he said. 'Not too fast . . . that's about it. I let you down again here while I pull the thing out further. Now then, you've got to be packed in . . . not all that easy . . . it's narrow . . . there, that would have done it, I think. Now I shove the whole contraption back, as close to the wall as I can . . . there, about like that . . .'

He ran across the room, snatched up the stone and stuffed it with some difficulty into his trousers pocket. Then, on the point of turning to rush away, he checked himself and scrabbled at the pile of books to extract the one at the bottom. The next second he was through the doors and running downstairs at full speed.

Slowing down to cross the Quad at a normally hurried pace, he entered Old House, came into the entrance hall, and arrived outside the door of the secretary's office where Toye awaited him, his fingers closing on the catch of the stopwatch at the exact moment of his arrival.

'Eight minutes,' he said. 'Say it was three minutes from the time he arrived here to his actually driving off at eight-thirty-eight . . . I expect Cartmell stood gazing after him. Say eight-thirty-five . . . That means they must have come down at eight-twenty-seven at latest . . .'

Beakbane gave it as his opinion that more time should be allowed for the stowing away of the body, arguing that it would have been quite a difficult job in the restricted space of the puppet theatre.

'I reckon she was wedged up against the wall,' he said.

They re-staged the whole business, letting him determine the length of the stowing away. This time they took nine and a half minutes, pushing back the descent from the studio to 8.25½ p.m.

'It's perfectly possible, as far as that goes,' Pollard said as they conferred once more in the studio. 'The only thing I'm not sure about is what he did with the stone. I had a devil of a job getting this one into my pocket. The next thing is to find out if Ann Cartmell could have taken all that time to do up the paintings, in spite of the fact that both she and Mrs Kitson declare that Torrance arrived so quickly—'

He broke off as footsteps sounded on the stairs, and there was a knock on the door. Toye opened it, to reveal Jean Forrest, white-overalled and imperturbable as ever.

'I don't want to disturb you,' she said, 'but Miss Renshaw thought you might like some coffee?'

'That's most kind,' Pollard replied, 'if it isn't giving you too much trouble . . . I wonder if you could spare us just a moment? Do come in and sit down. It's this endless business of checking up on times, I'm afraid. I suppose there was a good deal of clearing up to do after supper on Saturday. Have you any idea of when it was finished?'

'Wait a minute,' she said, 'just let me think. Actually it didn't take long. There were only about sixty people . . . a much smaller affair than lunch, and we washed up as we went along. I mean, there were only two courses and biscuits and cheese, and each lot of plates and cutlery was dealt with as it came out . . . Yes, the women went off at about twenty-past eight. They'd had a hard day, and I said we wouldn't do more than bare essentials, as cleaning was due to start on Monday, anyway. I was pretty whacked myself, and just saw them out, and came through to Old House and up to my room, and put my feet up. I didn't see any signs of life over here, as I told your sergeant.'

Pollard thanked her and she went away, saying that the coffee would be put in the library.

'I suppose we could try all the Old Meldonians and Sixth Formers again, asking specifically about Torrance,' he said. 'What about those two girls you interviewed, Toye, who were hanging around and offered to help Ann Cartmell?'

Toye consulted his note-book.

'They weren't hanging around on this side. They were dodging about in the front, to see if he kissed her goodbye, they said. When he didn't, they nipped round to the Quad again.'

Inspector Beakbane remarked that posh schools or secondary moderns alike, girls had only one idea in their heads as far as he could see.

'How did they know he was here?' asked Pollard.

'They saw him arrive, from the dining-room, just as the supper ended. They had quite a giggle about it, they said.'

'I don't see how you can hope for confirmation of the time within such narrow limits,' said Beakbane, 'especially as the daily women had all cleared off. The thing that sticks out a mile is the chap's apparent lack of motive. He could have done it—just, but why the flipping hell should he?'

'I only wish I knew,' said Pollard. Let's go down and have that coffee . . .'

After Inspector Beakbane had left for Linbridge, Pollard went across to the secretary's office and knocked politely. On being told to come in he opened the door and found Joyce Kitson standing at a filing cabinet with her back to him. She glanced over her shoulder.

'Do you want Miss Renshaw again?' she asked rather curtly.

'No thank you. This time I want some help from you, if you can spare me a few minutes.'

Without answering Joyce Kitson returned to her desk and

sat down with an air of resignation, indicating another chair as she did so.

'Thank you,' said Pollard, moving it slightly in order to get the light from the window full on her face. She looked tired, he thought, and generally under the weather, with dark shadows under her eyes.

'The enquiry,' he said, 'has reached a critical stage. A stage at which the investigation has to take calculated risks. As you are a person accustomed to dealing with confidential business, I realise that I can afford to put my cards on the table, and save quite a bit of valuable time.'

'I know nothing beyond what I've already told your sergeant,' she said, sitting primly with her hands clasped on her blotting-pad.

'We've made a good deal of progress since he interviewed you,' Pollard told her. 'I'm now interested in a different aspect of the case. I want, with your help—and no one but you can do this—to carry out a carefully-timed reconstruction of everything that happened during Ann Cartmell's visit to this office last Saturday night, down to the minutest detail.'

He watched first astonishment and then startled comprehension come into her face. She made an involuntary gesture of pushing something away from her.

'I loathe all this hunting down of human beings like animals,' she said vehemently, 'whatever they've done. It's—it's degrading, somehow.'

'Unfortunately there are certain degrading jobs which have to be done if society is to survive. Admittedly they call for guts—I know that.'

'What exactly do you want me to do?' she asked in an expressionless voice, after a brief pause.

'I want you to relax, first of all, and then imagine that you are back in Saturday evening. You've had a very busy and tiring day, which must have held up your normal end-of-term work. After supper when things have calmed down, you decide to put in a spell at your desk on the arrears. Am I right so far?'

'Quite right,' she replied, looking at him with some surprise.

'Hold it then, as they say on the film set. All right? Now then, you hear someone come running across the hall outside, and Miss Cartmell bursts in. Can you go on? Your first reaction is annoyance, surely?'

'Well, yes. I'd hoped for a little peace and quiet to get on with things. She—she almost fell into the room, looking very flushed and excited. And young and attractive,' Joyce Kitson added, wtih a slight tinge of envy in her voice.

'Can you remember what she said?'

'Not to swear to the exact words. Something like "Can I have that entrance form for the art competition? Miss Renshaw said she'd given it to you. Mr Torrance is here and he says he'll take the paintings back, and he's in a frightful hurry." As she spoke she came right in and up to the desk, and stood there in front of me.'

'This is exactly the sort of thing I want, Mrs Kitson. You made the next move?'

To Pollard's surprise Joyce Kitson looked embarrassed.

'I don't know why I'm telling you this,' she said without looking at him, 'but I just sat for a moment or two. I couldn't remember where I'd put the wretched form. I just panicked.'

'In case it was mislaid?'

'Yes. I know it's idiotic, but I often do if there's a hitch.'

'Why? You surely can't be afraid of losing your job?'

'Yes, I am. It's not just a job. I've managed to get a sort of foothold here—the rest of my life has just gone to bits. However, this is quite beside the point. I remembered quite quickly that I'd put the form in a drawer—this one. I opened the drawer and found it almost at once under one or two other papers, and gave it to her, and said it would save trouble—Mr Torrance taking the paintings, I mean.'

'What did Miss Cartmell do with it?'

'She looked round rather wildly for somewhere to write, so I cleared a few things off this end of the desk to make a space for her. She'd forgotten to bring anything to write with, and asked me to lend her something, so I produced a biro. She had a piece of paper in her hand, and started copying the names and ages of the girls whose paintings were being sent in onto the entrance form.'

'Try to visualise her doing it, if you can. Did she take long?'

'She made a mistake — put a name in the wrong column, I think — and exclaimed about it. I said it wouldn't matter if she crossed it out neatly. Then she steadied down and did the job quite quickly, and asked me for a clip to fasten the form to the top sheet of cardboard : she'd got the paintings sandwiched between two bits. I gave her one out of this bowl of oddments I keep handy. Then she began to do up the parcel with the brown paper and string she'd brought along — very badly.'

'Badly? I should have expected her to be good with her hands.'

'Yes, you'd think anyone who draws so well would be, but she's ham-fisted over everyday practical jobs. I watched her making a hash of it and then offered her a roll of that gummed brown paper strip, and held the parcel steady for her. It was still a botched-up affair, but would hold together, I think.'

'And at this point Mr Torrance came in?'

She paushed again.

'No, not quite. She said something about writing on the outside, and I saw her print "Entries from Meldon School, Upshire," in block capitals, and just as she was finishing, Mr Torrance appeared at the door — which she'd left half-open, incidentally.'

'All this has been extraordinarily clear and helpful,' Pollard said. 'Now this is a distasteful job, but I want to act it all out, standing in for Miss Cartmell myself. As we go along, tell me if I take too long or not long enough over anything. I'm going to time us with this stop-watch . . . Could you fix me up with something like the form and the parcel?'

Things were going better than he had expected, he thought, as Joyce Kitson assembled brown paper, cardboard and string . . . He found her an intelligent cooperator, cutting short the time required for filling in the entry from, but halting him during the pause while she tracked it down and while the recalcitrant parcel was done up.

'Mr Torrance now arrives in the doorway,' he said finally, cutting out the stop-watch. To his surprise six and a half minutes had elapsed since he had burst into the room in the role of Ann Cartmell.

Thanking Joyce Kitson, he asked her rather apologetically to go through the sequence of events once again, as a check. The result differed by only a couple of seconds. When he told her that Ann Cartmell had been in the office for approximately six and a half minutes, she looked astonished and confused.

'I can hardly believe it,' she said. 'I didn't mean to be misleading . . . Sometimes when you're very tired, time doesn't seem — well, to run on in the usual way, if that's clear.'

'Yes,' replied Pollard. 'One's power of assessing it gets out of gear, doesn't it? Anyway, we've now got all this satisfactorily cleared up, thanks to your help. Tell me, did Mr Torrance come into the office?'

She shut her eyes once more, and frowned slightly in concentration.

'Not really. He stood in the doorway there and said "good evening," and that he was in a great hurry. He obviously didn't want to dally at all. Ann Cartmell grabbed the parcel and went towards him. Then he gave me a brief acknowledgment-of-existence bow—sorry, but I can't stand the man—and they disappeared in the direction of the front door.'

'Was he carrying anything?' asked Pollard, turning towards the door and trying to visualise the scene.

'He had a big glossy under his arm. It looked like one of the art periodicals. Oh, yes, and he was carrying his brief-case.'

'His brief-case?' Pollard struggled to cut any inflexion of surprise out of his voice.

'Yes, I remember it from before, when he came down to lecture.'

'Perhaps he brought it down to put the paintings in?'

'Oh, it wouldn't have been nearly big enough for that. I expect he had papers and things in it. Anyway, I think men like carrying round a brief-case—it's a sort of executive status symbol.'

Pollard laughed.

'I think you've got something there,' he said.

After chatting for a few minutes, he renewed his thanks for her help and left the office for the library . . .

'You know how it is,' Pollard said to Toye, as they faced each other across the table in the bay. 'You blunderbuss about and land yourself in umpteen dead ends, and then quite suddenly stumble on what you *know* is significant, as you did at Stannaford Magna. This brief-case. Torrance isn't an office executive who tags a brief-case round with him automati-cally. Even if he's brought down work to do on Sunday, it's astonishing that he lugged it up to the studio—unless he wanted it up there.'

'To bring something in, or take it away?'

'Yes . . .' Pollard made a sudden convulsive movement, and brought his fist down on to the table with a crash. 'God! What mugs we've been! *That's* why he came! *That's* why he's raising such a hell of a stink about Ann Cartmell going to America! Why he wangled this scholarship for her . . . He's using her to get something out . . . dope, or—Good Lord, can he be in the spy racket?'

Toye whistled.

'I'll hand it to you, sir. Does she know, do you think?'

'Possibly. It's not like being a party to murder. Smuggling's illegal, but very few people feel it's really wrong. They think it's a way of getting your own back on the Government for taxes, and so on . . . But I think she's too naíve for him to have risked letting her know about it, let alone the blackmail side of it . . . Remember, she was going to be met by pals of his. It would have been simple enough for them to get at her luggage.'

'If she isn't mixed up in it,' said Toye, looking at the time-tabe, 'Torrance must have put whatever it was into something he knew she was taking with her, mustn't he?'

'But when? That's the devil of it! All right, I'm coming down to earth flat on my face, as one always does after a brainwave. But this is the goods. I'm positive it is.'

'Must've been when he first arrived,' said Toye, looking puzzled. 'In a bare two minutes, though? Couldn't have been when he went back for the book, though . . . time's tight enough for the murder, let alone—'

'Murder, violence and sudden death!' She must have seen him doing it and let him know that she had.'

Nineteen

'Persistent hammering at the weak spots in the defence led to the break-through which brought the Cup back to Meldon.
Report on match played by the First Lacrosse Twelve

IT WAS ONLY a matter of minutes before the single-mindedness of a man on the brink of a major undertaking took possession of Pollard. This new theory about the murder had got to be taken to pieces and examined from every conceivable point of view. It was still only a theory, but it suggested ramifications of the most far-reaching type, ramifications which would ultimately take the case to a higher level of authority altogether. He saw that his return to London was a matter of urgency, and set off with Toye for a hasty meal at Linbridge and a parting call at the police station. Rather to his relief both Superintendent Martin and Inspector Beakbane were out. No progress had been made in the search for strangers and other possible suspects, and making sure that any reports of these would be telephoned to them immediately at the Yard, the two C.I.D. men started for London.

The run gave Pollard an opportunity for some hard thinking. The fact that he was unable as yet to prove his theory stuck out a mile, but he decided not to let this worry him for the moment. He wanted to think round the situation and absorb its implications.

The reconstructions had established that it was a practical possibility for Clive Torrance to have committed the murder. That in itself was an important step forward. The suggestion—he didn't dare call it an inspiration at this stage—that Beatrice Baynes had been killed in order to silence her, seemed to him to transfer the whole business from the realm of the fantastic to that of credibility . . . Of course, he ought to have realised long ago that the key to the case was this carefully engineered visit to Meldon. In one sense the murder he was investigating was simply an irrelevance, the chance result of a periodical being overlooked. And if the theory were sound it disposed of the small lingering doubt about whether, if Ann Cartmell hadn't remembered, Clive Torrance would have done so himself, having spotted Beatrice Baynes and realised that he *had* to go back . . . Pollard came down finally on the side of the forgetfulness having been perfectly genuine, and the murder its fortuitous outcome.

Toye was a good driver, taking every opportunity but no risks. Pollard looked at his watch, saw that they were making good time and relapsed into thought once more. It was extraordinary, he reflected, what an important part pure chance seemed to have played in the case, confusing the issue and leading to lamentable waste of time. Suppose Mrs Thornton had lived another week . . . that George Baynes had backed a winner on the afternoon of the murder, and, more especially, that Beatrice hadn't turned up in the office at the precise moment when Torrance was telephoning to Ann Cartmell and Joyce Kitson had gone off to cope with some decrepit O.M. in the hall . . .

Thrusting these speculations aside, he returned to the subject of the engineered weekend. It struck him that if Torrance had planned to use Ann Cartmell for some illicit purpose, the scheme looked like a long-established one. He wondered when the idea of her applying for the American scholarship had first been mooted. If he knew anything about such matters, applications would have had to be in early in the year, if not before Christmas. Had he had his eye on the girl from the time he got her the job at Meldon? If so, this would explain the surprising amount of attention he seemed to have given to the school's art department . . . On the other hand, Helen Renshaw had found his vanity a convincing enough explanation of this. Then, how essential had the Scorhills been to the plan? Torance's meeting with them last autumn was surely the purest chance? But if they hadn't materialised, a man in his position would have had little difficulty in wangling an offer of hospitality somewhere in that part of the world, even if not quite as handy for Meldon. Or he could have thought up some perfectly good reason for staying at an hotel . . . No, the Scorhills seemed to have been a bit of sheer good luck for him.

There was something curiously impassive about Toye's profile, Pollard thought, glancing round at his companion.

'Had any great thoughts?' he asked him.

'I've been thinking that if you're right about the smuggling idea, sir, Torrance must have had contacts, mustn't he? And you'd think Special Branch would've got wind of it if he's been moving in circles known to be in touch with the likely embassies.'

'They've been known to miss things, haven't they? Then there are all these cultural exchanges nowadays, providing jolly useful cover. If he's done anything in that line it might be a pointer. There's the American end to consider, too. I wonder about these Vanderplanks that Ann Cartmell was going to stay with in New York . . .'

'Do you think it's more likely to be drug-running?' asked Toye.

Pollard was silent for half a mile or more as Toye threaded his way skilfully through increasingly dense traffic.

'On the whole, no,' he said at last. 'If Torrance is in the drug racket on a big scale, I think he's more likely to be part of a highly efficient organisation. This long-term cultivation of Ann Cartmell just for one single trip would hardly be worth it. I agree that secret documents and so on are cloak and dagger stuff, but that sort of thing does go with a long, leisurely build-up. The top people in espionage don't work in terms of quick results.'

On arriving at the Yard Pollard asked for an immediate interview with Chief Superintendent Crowe, and within ten minutes was summoned to the latter's room. Crowe looked at him interrogatively without speaking.

'I've established that Torrance could have murdered Beatrice Baynes, sir,' Pollard told him. 'My theory — unsupported by evidence as yet — is that his motive was to silence her.'

'Let's have a detailed report, and your justification for this theory, then.'

Pollard embarked on an account of the two reconstructions which he had carried out. When he had finished Crowe nodded briefly.

'That appears to be quite sound,' he said. 'Now about this silencing idea of yours.'

'I'd like to go back a bit, sir, if I may. All along I've had the feeling that the whole business somehow centres on this girl Ann Cartmell, although I've been convinced from the start that she wasn't involved in the murder. When it began to look as though Torrance's visit to the Scorhills had been contrived, it suggested that he wanted to be able to call in at Meldon last Saturday evening without making too much of a thing of it. Going down specially from London just to choose those paintings really would have stuck out, but dropping in on the way to stay with friends was another matter. He told me that he had rung up the school earlier in the day to find out if Ann Cartmell was still there. I think he knew very well that she was. He had arranged for friends of his to meet her and put her up when she arrived in New York, and must have discussed with her when she would be able to leave, and heard about this Old Girls' affair which would keep her at Meldon until the Sunday morning.'

'I'll accept all that provisionally,' said Crowe. 'What are you suggesting was the big idea?'

'Using her to get something across to America, almost certainly without her knowledge. I can't imagine anyone planning an important coup taking Ann Cartmell into his confidence, and using her as an accomplice. I suggest that Torrance hid whatever it was in the painting gear he knew she was taking with her, and that it was to be removed by these friends of his when she got there. The trouble is that I can't see how he had time to do it.'

'Never mind about that for the moment,' replied Crowe unexpectedly. 'It's the murder you're supposed to be investigating. I take it you're suggesting that Beatrice Baynes spotted him doing this conjuring trick, taxed him about it when he went back to fetch the magazine, and that he slugged her rather than risk it getting out?'

'Yes. Exactly that.'

'And what do you think this contraband was that he was trying to get across in this complicated way?'

'I think it's possible that he's working for the Communists. Or, much less probably, that he runs drugs over when he can.'

The gleam which came into Crowe's eye did not escape Pollard, who felt a flicker of amusement. The Chief's views on the Special Branch were well known to his subordinates. The chance of one of his own men being a beat ahead would have a strong appeal . . .

'Have you got the name and address of these people the girl was going to stay with?'

Pollard handed over a type-written slip. Crowe glanced at it and pressed a bell-push on his desk. Pollard had the sensation which never failed to thrill him, of a vast, intricate machine going smoothly and inexorably into action.

When an enquiry about the Vanderplanks had been composed for despatch to the F.B.I. in New York, Crowe hesitated for a moment, his hand hovering over the telephone receiver.

'The A.C. suggested a conference this morning. He's up-to-date with the case apart from this report you've just made. Before we go along is there anything more you want to discuss? Mind you, Pollard, I don't say I accept this theory of yours, but there's just the chance the whole business is going to break big, and steps may be needed which mean authorisation from the top.'

Pollard was little given to day-dreaming, but on occasions he had pictured himself conducting an enquiry which not only hit the headlines but brought him into direct contact with top-level C.I.D. circles, and even with the Government. He shifted his position and took a firm grip on himself.

'I'd like to stress Torrance's obvious anxiety to get Ann Cartmell off to America,' he said. 'It might be worth finding out who put the *Blare* on to her being held up. Of course I realise I've no explanation so far about how Torrance knew for certain what gear she was taking with her, or how he could have planted it without her noticing at the time, or discovering whatever it was afterwards. He'd either have to have done the job while she was routing about for paper and string to do up the parcel, or in the bare two minutes before she arrived in the studio just after eight.'

'There is an alternative, don't forget.' Crowe looked at him quizzically. 'She may have led you up the garden path, and be in it up to the neck. Collusion over smuggling's a very different proposition from collusion over murder. Easy for him to ask her to take along a nice box of expensive British cigarettes, and just keep quiet about it, for instance. Not too easy for her to refuse, either, come to think about it.'

'Of course I admit that possibility, sir. But I still maintain that no one in his senses with a really big job on hand would risk letting Ann Cartmell have anything to do with it . . . I can't see how he stowed the stuff away, but I haven't really worked on that yet.'

'You'd better work on it like hell, my boy. Well, we'll put the whole idea up to the A.C., and if he asks you what course of action you suggest, I assume you've something to put forward. No point in delaying any longer.' He picked up the receiver and asked for the Assistant Commissioner's office.

It was definitely off-putting, Pollard thought, to report to a man who sat slumped back in his comfortable desk chair gazing at the ceiling, apparently unconscious of your presence. But as he rightly surmised, apparently was the operative word. Finishing what he had to say, he waited in respectful silence.

'How do you propose that this rather melodramatic theory of yours is put to the test, Pollard?' enquired the well known, slightly lazy drawl.

He drew a deep breath and stepped forward into zero hour.

'If some object was transferred to Ann Cartmell last Saturday evening, with or without her knowledge, sir, I think the odds are that it's still in her possession. Torrance has no reason to suppose that we're interested in anything but the actual murder. I suggest that we give her the all-clear for flying over to New York on Monday. This ought to allay any suspicions or idea of calling the job off. We undertake to meet her at Paddington and drive her to the airport, on the grounds that there may be some difficulty about the seat at such short notice. We ensure that she gets up here in good time, and our chaps then take her luggage to pieces. We can take along a policewoman to search her if necessary, and put up some story about a special request from Interpol in connection with a jewel robbery.'

'What happens if we find nothing?' enquired the voice.

'I'd let her go all the same, sir, and have the F.B.I. alerted to weigh in again on the other side. Meanwhile we ask them to get cracking on these friends of Torrance, the Vanderplanks.'

'Can't see them finding something we've missed,' asserted Crowe stoutly.

'We could give them the chance, perhaps . . . The important thing is whether Pollard can find out by Monday morning how the microphotographs of our secret defences or latest radar device were actually planted. Assuming the whole thing isn't a mare's nest, of course.'

'I'll do my best, sir,' Pollard replied, aware of a sinking feeling in the pit of his stomach.

'No man can do more,' the A.C. remarked, assuming an upright position. He flicked a switch and summoned his secretary. 'Now I suppose we bring in the Special Branch and the Drugs Squad, although I think your reasoning against this being a case of drug-running is quite sound, Pollard.'

Further sections of the machine purred into action . . .

As the evening went on, Pollard, caught up in ever-widening official activity, wondered despairingly when he would be able to concentrate on his own particular problem. After a brief discussion with Crowe there were several matters to be put in hand. Arrangements were made to keep both Torrance and Ann Cartmell under observation. There followed an urgent request for a seat on the Monday afternoon plane to New York, and an investigation into the times of trains from Bath to Paddington. Pollard took advantage of a lull to ring up his wife.

'I've arrived,' he told her, 'but don't expect me until pretty late, possibly with the milk. Don't wait up, will you? Very heavy traffic tonight.'

This was their code for rapid developments in a case.

'Right,' Jane replied. 'I'll expect you when I see you—if I'm awake, that is. There'll be soup in a thermos, and sandwiches as usual. Good hunting.'

The Special Branch's initial reaction had been one of complete scepticism, changing to guarded interest when it was established that Torrance had visited Moscow three years earlier to discuss a possible exhibition of British paintings there. Further enquiries disclosed that he had attended several social functions at the Soviet Embassy. Pollard restrained his impatience while lengthy discussions took place, largely unintelligible to him. From time to time he was asked a question.

Released at last, he prepared to ring up Ann Cartmell, only to be held up once more, this time by the Drug Squad. Unlike their colleagues in the Special Branch, its officers had pounced on the chance of a fresh lead with enthusiasm, and interrogated him with the greatest thoroughness . . .

'You're through to Bath,' the switchboard operator told him, and a few seconds later Pollard heard Ann Cartmell announce herself at the other end of the line, unmistakable pent-up excitement in her voice.

'Inspector Pollard of New Scotland Yard speaking, Miss Cartmell,' he said. 'I'm contacting you to say that my superiors feel justified in letting you leave for New York on Monday. I take it you can be ready?'

'Oh!' she gasped, 'how absolutely marvellous! Of course I can — I've been sitting all ready and hoping for days . . . I just can't believe it after all this ghastly worry . . . But what about a seat on the plane? Can I get one as late as this, do you think?'

'We're fixing it for you,' he told her, and went on to explain that she would be met at the station and driven direct to the airport.

'Oh!' she said again. 'It seems too good to be true. I can hardly take it in.'

'Before you go we shall want you to read over the various statements you have made to me, and sign them if you agree with them.'

'Of course,' she said, obviously uninterested. 'Anything I can do to help, Inspector. You've been so kind : I'm so very grateful to you. Oh, does Mr Torrance know I can go after all?'

'I'm just going to ring him up and tell him, so that he can contact Mr and Mrs Vanderplank about meeting you at the other end. I expect he'll ring you as soon as he's heard from me.'

'Perhaps he will!' she exclaimed, with a catch in her voice.

'Well, Miss Cartmell, I think that's all quite clear, isn't it?

You know where to find me if you should want to enquire about anything else. And I expect I shall be seeing you at the airport. Good-bye.'

Pollard rang off, and sat for a few moments assessing his reactions. No change, he decided . . . Just as self-engrossed and as emotional about Torrance as ever. It suddenly struck him that Ann Cartmell might very well be in for one of the worst jolts imaginable, poor kid. Lifting the receiver again, he asked for Clive Torrance's private number. The call got through almost at once.

'Torrence here.'

'Inspector Pollard of New Scotland Yard, Mr Torrance.'

Was he imagining it, or was the ensuing pause fractionally too long?'

'Good evening, Inspector. I've been hoping to hear from you. Can it be that you're letting poor little Cartmell go?'

'That's what I'm ringing you about, Mr Torrance. My superiors have authorised her departure, and we've fixed her up on the three-thirty plane on Monday afternoon. Perhaps you'd like to take down the times, as you'll be wanting to get into touch with your friends over there, I expect.'

'Yes. Just a sec. while I get something to write with . . . Go ahead.'

Pollard gave him the flight number and the aircraft's scheduled time of arrival.

'We're anxious to help Miss Cartmell in every way we can,' he told Torrance, 'so we've arranged with her to meet her train at Paddington and run her down to Heathrow. Someone will see her on board in case there should be any hitch over the last-minute booking.'

'That's very handsome of the police, Inspector. I'd no idea they were so human. I might turn up myself to wave her off after all the hurroosh there's been. How about the fare? I'll foot the bill if she has to pay more, as I told you.'

Pollard assured him that this would not be necessary, and made to ring off.

'How's your case going, by the way? Or mustn't one ask?'

'That's a question one mustn't answer, I'm afraid, sir,' he replied pleasantly. 'Good night.'

Once again he sat on after replacing the receiver. A vivid picture of the man he had been talking to rose in his mind. With quite astonishing clarity he could see Torrance in his sitting-room over the Domani. He was not his usual impeccably-groomed and turned-out self, but was wearing an unbuttoned shirt, slacks and slippers. He hadn't even shaved, and there were little beads of sweat on his face. An incongruous figure in his elegant surroundings . . . The smell of good cigarettes came back to Pollard and he visualised the windows open at the bottom on this close evening, the beautiful curtains moving very gently to and fro, and the muted roar of the traffic in Regent Street forming a background.

I can't believe, Pollard thought, that he's the kind of chap to sell his country down the river for an ideology . . . he's not big enough. His world begins and ends with himself. But I believe he'd do it for money. He needs quite a bit of money to maintain the Clive Torrance image . . . the rich, successful director of the Domani . . . the acknowledged authority . . . the man with a cultural mission and the patron of young artists . . . the Jaguar . . . the lady with the expensive perfume . . . the little trips abroad . . .

Aware that his thoughts were trailing off, Pollard pulled himself up with a jerk. It could be drugs, of course . . . A dangerous man, Torrance, with that cool, calculating mind, so well camouflaged, by his obvious weaknesses of vanity and self-indulgence. The sort of mind capable of the patience needed in long-term planning, and at the same time able to meet a sudden appalling emergency with ruthless efficiency. It was to be hoped that the chap detailed to shadow him was on top of his job . . .

Abruptly remembering that he had yet to produce proof that Torrance was involved in either attempted smuggling or murder, Pollard emerged from his meditations under a cold douche of realism, and looked at his desk. Even at the end of a fifteen-hour day there were still papers marked VERY UR-GENT and dealing with other cases which he hadn't touched. He'd better clear them off before he went home and really got to grips with this bloody Baynes business.

The accumulation was considerable, and took much longer to deal with than he had expected. Midnight struck, and one . . . The church clocks round about were chiming the dead hour of two when he slipped his latchkey into the lock and went softly up the stairs to his flat, realising that he was too tired to think to any purpose that night.

Twenty

'Choose your equipment carefully, especially your paints.'
Lecture by Clive Torrance at Meldon on Oil Painting for
Beginners

'I HAVEN'T A a clue about today,' Pollard told his wife at breakfast on the following morning, setting down his empty coffee cup. 'The hell of a lot of hanging about, of course, waiting for New York's report on the Vanderplanks, and anything that Special Branch or Drugs have managed to dig up. You go ahead with whatever you've planned to do. I don't expect to go out of Town, but I'll ring you if I have to.'

'O.K. by me,' Jane replied. 'I think I'll go along to the shops right away before the Saturday crowds pile up. Then I'll be in. The place must have a good clean — I've hardly touched it this week. Then I've got my stuff on the refresher course to finish.'

Tom Pollard pushed back his chair and went to collect his hat and brief-case, returning to kiss Jane rather abstractedly before starting off. She stood listening to his footsteps as he ran downstairs, and then went over to the window and watched him cross the street and vanish round the corner in the direction of the bus stop. He had forgotten to look up and wave to her . . . This stage in a case was particularly tricky for the detective's wife, she reflected. One could so easily put a foot wrong by over-solicitude or an excessive display of interest.

Jane Pollard was not, however, cast by Nature for the role of passive onlooker. Frowning, she extracted a cigarette from a box, lit it, and sat down by the window, oblivious of the uncleared breakfast table and the dust . . .

After the high-pressure activity of the night before, Pollard found the atmosphere of the Yard static, and was absurdly irritated by the preoccupation of his colleagues with their own cases. Becoming aware of this reaction, he was amused at himself, and hurried hopefully to his room. Disappointingly, the only reports awaiting him were those on Ann Cartmell and Torrance, neither of whom had shown any signs of leaving home during the night.

'What the devil are those New York chaps doing?' he asked Toye rhetorically. 'Let's finish making the arrangements for Monday morning, anyway.'

After discussion it was settled that Toye should meet Ann Cartmell's train and drive her to the airport. This would ensure that she was quickly recognised, and Toye, as an officer engaged on the case, would be in a position to act authoritatively if Torrance himself turned up with his car.

'The one thing that mustn't happen is giving him a chance to abstract anything he may have planted on her,' Pollard said. 'Quite apart from espionage and drugs, it would kibosh the motive for the murder—unless I'm absolutely wrong about the whole business, that is.'

'Suppose he runs down to her home today or tomorrow, and gets the stuff back by putting up some cock and bull story?' suggested Toye. 'What's to stop him?'

'Nothing. But there's a police car behind the block where he garages his Jaguar, and we've got the chaps at Bath lined up. If he tries it on, the Chief agrees that we'll have to take the risk of intercepting him as he leaves the Cartmells. It's a hundred to one that the stuff would be on him, or in the car ... We'd better get on to the airport police next ...'

Careful arrangements were made for the interception of Ann Cartmell's luggage, and its examination by experts.

'And I only hope to God we find whatever it is,' Pollard said with feeling. 'I don't mind admitting I'm getting bloody cold feet.'

Toye was solidly reasuring.

'The A.C. and the Chief wouldn't have O.K.'d the scheme,

sir, if it hadn't looked pretty good to them. Neither of 'em spotted a hole in it, or could put up a better one. And there's not a cheep from Linbridge about some complete outsider turning up.'

As there was now nothing to do but wait, Pollard decided on reading through all the case notes directly or indirectly connected with Torrance. They settled down to the job, and silence descended, broken only by the turning of pages, and the occasional striking of a match. Cigarette smoke wreathed itself out of the open window.

The break was as sudden as it was unexpected. Toye looked up as Pollard gave vent to a lurid comment on his own intelligence.

'Look at this,' he concluded, pushing Toye's own report on his first interview with Jock Eccles across the desk. 'The old so-and-so says he shook his fist at the backside of the Jaguar because it scorched up the drive as though a madman was driving it. Why the hell did Torrance run it so fine? Surely he must have meant to allow himself reasonable time if he planned to plant something? As it was, he barely missed finding Cartmell up in the studio when he got there. If we can prove he was delayed for some reason, it's another pointer.'

Remarking that he himself was a bigger fool than he'd ever thought, Toye suggested engine trouble or a puncture, involving a delayed start or a call at a garage on the way.

'Let's get on to the motoring organisations,' said Pollard. 'They'd know if there were any fixtures or a smash on the road causing a hefty traffic jam. Or if one of their patrols stopped to help Torrance. Failing that, it will mean garages— a much longer job.'

When Toye had gone off to make these enquiries he went back to the notes, but his mind kept straying off and worrying away at just what Torrance could have done . . . Something that was obviously suspicious and capable of being spotted by Beatrice Baynes through a chink in the curtains of the puppet theatre, and at the same time simple enough to have been carried out in the bare two minutes before Ann Cartmell arrived. Or else by sleight-of-hand while she was ferreting about for wrapping materials for the paintings ... There certainly wouldn't have been any time for niggling and fiddling operations, like unscrewing things, for instance. And how could he have been absolutely certain about what she was taking with her? The oil colour-box that he'd given her was a virtual certainty, but suppose she had already packed it at the Staff House? Perhaps he'd told her he'd like to have another look at it, as it had been sent straight from Brocatti & Simpson's. On the other hand, if he'd planned to use the box, why not bring the present along with him, having done the job of concealment at leisure? Or was having it sent direct a precaution, so that if something were discovered he could prove that it had never been in his possession?

Pollard scowled and resettled himself in his chair. Microfilms were small, of course, and could be hidden in a dummy tube of oil paint. Could Torrance have substituted one for a genuine tube, either when buying the colour-box, or on the Saturday evening? Risky ... suppose Ann Cartmell had decided to try out some of the paints? Not very likely, but it couldn't be entirely discounted. And it wasn't a substitution you could do in a split second, either. You'd have to extract the corresponding genuine tube, labelled in the same way ...

His reflections were interrupted by the return of Toye, radiating success.

'We've got it in one, sir,' announced the latter triumphantly. 'The A.A. say there was a bad smash and a big pile-up two miles this side of the Medlingstone by-pass, just after six on Saturday evening. It was an hour before they got even single-line traffic going again, and meanwhile there was a diversion round minor roads and lanes. I asked what it would have added on to a London-Linbridge run, and they said quite a quarter of an hour.'

It was while they were digesting the implications of this discovery that the long-awaited report on the Vanderplanks came through. Pollard read it with a tremendous sense of relief.

RE R.V. [it ran] WEALTHY COMPANY PROMOTER STOP NO POLICE RECORD BUT SUSPECTED BEHIND GOLDEN ACRES FRAUD STOP PROSECUTION DROPPED IN DEFAULT OF EVIDENCE STOP WIFE WELL-KNOWN AMATEUR PAINTER STOP BOTH FREQUENT VISITORS TO EUROPE STOP NO KNOWN COMMUNIST OR DRUG MARKET AFFILIATIONS STOP.

A period of intense activity set in. Chief Superintendent Crowe expressed guarded satisfaction. The A.C. in the briefest of interviews approved Pollard's plan to enlist the help of the F.B.I. in the event of nothing being found on Ann Cartmell at London Airport, and to urge them to make further enquiries into the activities of the Vanderplanks. Pollard, unused to making transatlantic telephone calls, experienced alternating excitement and apprehension about his own future. Ultimately he surfaced to find that it was three o'clock and that neither he nor Toye had had any lunch.

After a hasty meal they returned to the notes of the case with renewed enthusiasm, but the morning's run of luck had petered out. Neither intensive concentration nor discussion *ad nauseam* yielded the vestige of a fresh idea. Soon after seven Pollard stretched, and rubbed his tired eyes with the backs of his hands.

'Let's pack up, Toye,' he said. 'We're getting nowhere. I—'

The desk telephone rang. He snatched up the receiver.

'Mrs Pollard, sir,' the switchboard operator told him. 'Shall I put her through?'

'Yes.' Pollard spoke curtly ... Jane ... The case dropped away from him.

'Tom?'

'Here,' he said.

'Come home. It's something vital—the case.' The telephone in the flat was in their bedroom, but she was speaking quietly. 'Come in quite casually.'

'Are you all right?' he demanded, with a sudden disturbing vision of Clive Torrance.

'Absolutely.'

'Coming right away.'

The receiver clattered down as he grabbed at papers, stuffing them into his brief-case.

'My wife's got on to something.' he told the astonished Toye. 'I may be ringing you.'

'Oh, jolly good,' Jane Pollard exclaimed as her husband walked in. 'I was hoping you'd turn up. This is Tom, Diane. Diane Moss, Tom. She's from my home town and is working at Brocatti & Simpson. It's so exciting! When I dropped in there for a sketching block this morning she told me she actually sold Clive Torrance Ann Cartmell's colour-box.'

'Nice to meet you, Diane.' Pollard sank bewildered into a chair, and contemplated a round-faced blonde, patently naïve under attempts at a with-it appearance. 'Is he a boy-friend of yours?'

Diane bridled with pleasure, casting up big blue eyes with immense false lashes.

'Do tell Tom what he said to you,' encouraged Jane.

She took a deep breath and prepared to hold her audience.

'Well, Mr Legge—he's the Sales Manager—usually serves the posh customers, but we'd a rush on that morning,' she confided. 'I saw Mr Torrance come in at the door. He took a look round, and then he—y'know—made straight for me ... Moppet, he said, you're on commission, aren't you? Your number's come up. I want a Wynne 1A oil colour-box ... That's the priciest one we stock,' she explained turning to Pollard.

'Lucky Ann Cartmell,' commented Jane.

'Then I suppose he asked you to get it packed up and sent off?' prompted Pollard, feeling his way but completely befogged.

'That's right. I made out the docket for Dispatch, for it to go the same day, without fail. But that wasn't the lot.' Diane paused dramatically. 'He said he wanted another 1A, fitted up exactly the same! Biggest commission I've ever had!'

In the ensuing silence Pollard realised that his mouth had gone dry.

'Where did you have to send the second one?' he asked her.

'Oh, that one didn't have to be posted off. I just — y'know — wrapped it, and Mr Torrance took it away.'

Twenty-One

'Veritas Praevalebit.'

Motto of Meldon School

MR JONATHAN RISLEY, Manager of Brocatti & Simpson's, created a flutter by arrving at the shop at eight-thirty on Monday morning. He went straight to his room and immediately summoned Mr Legge, the Sales Manager. After an interval of ten minutes or so, the latter emerged looking portentous, and vanished into Accounts, where he remained closeted for a considerable time. In the shop speculation flourished, and the morning's first customers received service much below the normal standard. The Accounts typist sent down to make an enquiry whispered to a crony that all sales dockets for the week before last were being vetted. The news was rapidly disseminated and conjecture became rife. Was it a customer or something inside?

Mr Legge's appearance was the signal for a feverish concentration on customers and their requirements. He did not, however, return to his normal stance, but made for the store. He was soon out again, a large, flat object wrapped in brown paper under his arm, and, almost beyond belief, left the premises wearing his hat and still carrying the parcel. He was seen to hail a passing taxi.

A bright spark suggested having a look at the withdrawal book . . .

The station platform slid slowly out of Ann Cartmell's sight, bearing away her parents. She returned to her compartment,

243

grateful at having secured a corner seat in a crowded train. Her mind was a confusion of relief, excitement and nervous apprehension. The Avon valley glided past unnoticed as she stared unseeingly out of the window : meadow, river and canal ... bright patterns of boats moored in clusters and awaiting hirers ... old grey appropriate houses and harsh new discordant ones ...

He'd said he'd come to the airport if he possibly could. Ann thrust to the back of her mind that seeing her off wasn't a priority. If he really cared ... And she'd been able to dissuade her parents from postponing the start of their own holiday and coming to see her off. Her thoughts rested on them for a brief moment ...

It was marvellous to feel a sense of leisure. She hadn't for ages, really, not since the end-of-term rush started. For the first time she found herself giving the murder of Beatrice Baynes her full attention. Honestly, it was the most extraordinary thing she'd ever heard of ... in the studio, of all places. It was difficult to believe that it could possibly be true ... But it was. Next term ... Would one keep thinking about it? And the girls? What would be the best line to take, she wondered? Rennie would say something at the staff meeting before term ... talk to the School ...

The train journey ahead of her seemed to stretch to eternity. She looked at her watch. It must have stopped. With some annoyance she intercepted an amused glance from a man on the opposite side as she held it to her ear. It hadn't stopped. She opened a book resolutely and tried to concentrate ...

As the train ran through the outer suburbs of London she restrained herself from assembling her belongings too quickly. Sudden panic seized her. Would a *uniformed* policeman be meeting her? She hadn't thought of that. If not, how would they know each other? Surely Inspector Pollard wouldn't come himself? She hoped not : he was kind, but something about him frightened her. Not that he could be much good really ... a whole week and they still hadn't found the murderer.

Detective-Segeant Toye had made so little impression on her preoccupied mind that she did not recognise him at once when he came towards her as she got out of the train at Paddington ...

'That isn't locked,' she said anxiously on arrival at London Airport, as her canvas hold-all was labelled and swept away with the rest of her luggage. 'It's my painting things.'

Toye reassured her. 'No need to carry it round, Miss Cartmell. You can pick it up again after the Customs. I'll be along to fetch you for that. You've plenty of time to go and have some lunch now.'

He escorted her to the restaurant, and indicated the departure lounge before leaving her.

Almost too tense and excited to eat, Ann ordered an omelette and some coffee. As she ate, she wondered what was the earliest moment at which she could reasonably hope to see Clive Torrance. Her plane left at three-thirty, and you'd have to board it soon after three surely? Say half-past two, or perhaps a minute or two later ... Another whole hour to spin out ... She dallied over her coffee, looking about her and sometimes forgetting her anxieties in the interest of the kaleidoscopic movement of people around her. All the same, she thought, there was something eerie about an airport. Not quite earth and not quite air. A sort of limbo, with hollow voices from nowhere issuing summonses which set up sudden surges of travellers on the first lap towards improbable destinations. And the sinister background music of revving-up engines, going straight through nerve and flesh to your very bones.

She had moved to the departure lounge, and settled herself in as conspicuous a seat as she could find when the incredible happened. One of the hollow voices called her name. 'Attention, please. A message for Miss Ann Cartmell. Miss Ann Cartmell,' it repeated, with the un-human blend of emphasis

245

and unconcern. 'Will Miss Ann Cartmell, passenger to New York, go to the Enquiries desk, please.'

There was an audible click, and silence. She scrambled to her feet, clumsily scattering her gloves and stooping impatiently to snatch them up. He wasn't coming . . . but he'd sent a message . . . a message, anyway . . .

Then the anticlimax. A man in an official uniform, saying she was wanted in the Customs.

'But I'm expecting a friend to see me off,' she protested frantically.

'Leave a message with us, madam,' an Enquiries clerk suggested helpfully.

She left Clive Torrance's name, giving it with a kind of pride, and turned to follow.

To her surprise they did not go into the Customs Hall, but through a door marked Private, and on to another. Her escort knocked, and opened it for her to pass through. It was a small room and seemed rather full of people. Inspector Pollard who was standing at a table turned as she came in.

'Oh,' she said. 'You wanted me to sign some papers, didn't you, Inspector?'

There was an odd little pause, during which she noticed Toye in the background, and it struck her that Pollard looked expressionless.

'Good afternoon, Miss Cartmell,' he said. 'No, we won't worry about your statements for the moment. Unless you'd like to make one about this.'

He moved aside. Neatly stacked on the table were the contents of the hold-all in which she had packed her painting gear. The paint-box lay apart, and Pollard indicated it and looked at her interrogatively.

'About my paint-box?' she exclaimed. 'I don't understand. There's nothing dutiable in it, if that's what you mean.'

'Are you prepared to swear that, Miss Cartmell?' he asked her gravely.

246

'Of course I am,' she said impatiently. 'What on earth is all this fuss about?'

Pollard nodded curtly at another man, who stepped forward and picked up the box. He opened it, produced some small and delicate tools from his pocket, and began to work on the inside of the lid.

'You've no right to damage my property,' Ann burst out angrily. 'It's a brand-new colour-box — an expensive one. A present. And why have you taken the paints out?'

She turned indignantly to Pollard, to find his eyes fixed on her.

'Any damage we do will, of course, be made good,' he replied. 'The paints are quite safe.'

The man at the table skilfully removed several screws of miscroscopic dimensions and took up a thin blade.

'Oh, please be careful!' Almost in tears, Ann took a step forward. There was an inperceptible closing-in of the other spectators. The wafer-like blade working round the inner side of the lid appeared to be loosening a thin panel of wood. With infinite care it was prised up and removed, revealing a blueness showing through a sheet of something semi-transparent. Ann uttered an incoherent exclamation.

'Get that up too, Rogers,' Pollard ordered. 'You can't be too careful. Put the lid flat.'

The paper was lifted out with a pair of tweezers . . . a small patrician face looked up at them, radiant with childhood's glow, charmingly conscious of the sky-blue bonnet crowning the flaxen hair.

There was an almost tangible silence, finally broken by Ann Cartmell.

'But it's Raeborough's Blue Bonnet,' she gasped, 'the one that was stolen from the Wrexham Collection.' Looking round in bewilderment her eye lighted on Pollard. 'It must have been put in at Brocatti & Simpson's. The box was sent from there.'

'No, Miss Cartmell, it wasn't, he told her. 'You see that isn't the box which you received from Brocatti & Simpson.'

'But it *is*,' she insisted, her face a study in sheer incomprehension. 'It came to Meldon — I've had it ever since. It *must* be the same.'

'It was only the same until the evening of last Saturday week, when this box on the table was substituted for yours by Mr Clive Torrance.'

Her faced flamed with anger.

'How dare you,' she stormed, 'I never heard of anything so preposterous! Anyway, he's coming to see me off . . .'

Something in Pollard's expression made her break off.

'He isn't coming, Miss Cartmell,' Pollard said. He glanced round at the others with a movement of his head. The next moment they had left the room.

'Shall we sit down?' he suggested.

Speechless and trembling Ann subsided on to a chair.

'I think you know my wife,' Pollard went on. 'She was Jane Holloway before she married me. You were both on an art course at Wendlebury Manor two years ago. Do you remember her?

Ann nodded dumbly, realised that she was gripping the edge of the table, and released her hold.

'I've some bad news for you, Miss Cartmell. I think when you've heard it you may want to postpone your journey for another day or two. Jane asks me to say that if you don't feel like going back to Bath tonight, she'll be very happy to put you up.'

'Is it about — Mr Torrance?' she whispered.

'Yes. He wrote me a letter this morning, telling me how he stole the Blue Bonnet over three years ago. I needn't explain why you were to take it to America, need I? In his letter he made it absolutely clear that you knew nothing whatever about it.' He paused, seeing the colour draining out of her face.

248

'You haven't told me everything.' The words were barely audible.

'Miss Baynes who was spying on you — hiding in the puppet theatre — saw Mr Torrance change over the boxes before you arrived in the studio from supper that evening. When he went back to fetch the copy of *Artifex* she charged him with it. He couldn't face the risk of exposure, either then or this morning, when he found out that I had discovered it too . . .'

He caught Ann as she slipped from her chair to the floor.

Jane Pollard looked up as her husband came into the sitting-room.

'Jordan passed,' she said.

'She got off all right, then?' he enquired, coming over to the window and sitting down.

'Yes. Her father picked us up here in a taxi, and we found Miss Renshaw waiting at the airport, so she had a good send-off from the three of us. The stiff upper lip was a bit in evidence, but she had herself well in hand and was very composed and sensible with the Press. She's got guts, all right. I hope everything goes smoothly at the other end.'

'It should do. Being met by a plain clothes man ought to get her through the formalities at the double, and then he'll see her on to the right train for the place where the summer school is.'

'What intrigues me,' Jane said, 'is the line the Vanderplanks are going to take.'

'Horrified incredulity, and attempts to shower hospitality on Ann is my guess.'

'She says nothing will induce her ever to meet them. I suppose there isn't a hope of bringing a case against them?'

'Not a hope. There isn't a shred of evidence as far as I can see. But you'll be interested to hear that during the week they were in London, staying at the Washington, Brocatti & Simpson sold an identical oil colour-box to an American lady

249

for cash . . . No, not the unbelievable Diane this time. A more senior assistant, who remembered the sale quite clearly. I take it that a second substitution would have taken place when Ann arrived at the Vanderplanks. Neat?'

'One of the neatest things I've ever heard of. Of course there are endless questions I'm dying to ask you, but shall we get off ourselves now? The car's all packed up and there's a picnic supper on board.'

'God, yes,' said Pollard. 'I've never wanted a week's leave more.'

The Pollards' refuge for short holidays was a farmhouse in a fold of the Wiltshire Downs, remote from traffic and crowds. During the days they walked the ancient trackways, two moving specks in the vast, rolling landscape under immense skies. They ate their sandwiches reclining against the grassy ramparts and burial mounds of a vanished world, and afterwards sprawled happily in the sun listening to cascades of larksong overhead.

'By the way,' Jane said one day, 'I never asked you if the Old Man said anything.'

'He threw out a casual statement about going down to Devon to look at a bungalow for his retirement, but of course it mayn't mean a thing.'

'Sez you,' she commented.

Stretched out on the turf side by side they looked at each other . . .

'How do you feel about it all in retrospect?' Jane asked presently.

'It's been an absolutely fantastic case,' Pollard replied after a pause. 'The murder itself was pure Grand Guignol, to start with . . . A fascinating case, too. Personalities have counted for so much. Poor old warped B.B., for instance, and Torrance himself, absolutely obsessed with his own image : a sort of fleshy middle-aged Narcissus. And Ann—an extraordinary mixture of ability and immaturity. Then there's the unfortunate Madge Thornton and the skeleton in the Baynes cupboard, like a Victorian novel.'

'You've made them all so real. George Baynes seems to have been one of the most attractive. I should like to meet George.'

'Just try, that's all! Young scoundrel! I admit his charm, though. As a matter of fact I think all this may have sobered him down. Yelland—the solicitor—rang me up about one or two points, and said Madge is having Applebys as part of her share, and is making a home for George whenever he wants one. She proposes to retire and spend her time gardening. Helen Renshaw will be overjoyed.'

'Reverting to Torrance, was the Blue Bonnet the coup of a lifetime, or has he done this sort of thing before, do you think?'

'I very much doubt it. He'd never have been able to resist bragging about it in that incredible letter he wrote me before he shot himself. The first part of it was sheer unadulterated gloat at having pulled off the theft and fooled the Yard.'

'It was at Christmas, wasn't it?'

'Yes, three and a half years ago, on the afternoon of Christmas Eve. Several of the staff had been let off early : there was a stink about it afterwards, if you remember. Torrance went in not long before the Wrexham closed, disguised of course, and with the replica he'd painted under a duffle coat, and when the room was empty switched them over. Then he oozed out into the Christmas crowds. They closed soon afterwards, and the substitution wasn't discovered until they re-opened after Boxing Day. As neat as the colour-box scheme for getting it out of the country.'

'And of course there was absolutely nothing to connect it with Torrance?'

'Nothing in the world. And it was a big job, and he could afford to wait. Extraordinary that a small painting like that can have a market value of about £10,000.'

251

'What I think is so amazing,' said Jane, 'is having the patience and coolness to sit on all that for over three years.'

'I think he was determined to make it the perfect, untraceable crime. His colossal vanity came in here. Wait till the racket died down and until a perfectly normal situation developed which he could use for getting it across. After all, I can't think of a much better way than expert concealment in an art student's modest luggage, can you?'

'No,' replied Jane, 'especially if the art student looks like Ann Cartmell. But where do the Vanderplanks come in? How did he get on to them, do you suppose?'

'He went to New York on Domani business early in the year of the theft. It seems reasonable to suppose that he met Mrs Vanderplank through his contacts with the artist community, and so got in with her husband, who seems to be up to the neck in shady dealings. Who the Blue Bonnet was really destined for we shall never know, of course. I wonder what Torrance was to get?'

'What on earth did he want money for so badly?'

'His public image involved a fairly high standard of living, you know. He probably thought he'd better cushion himself against inflation.'

Jane rolled over on to her front, and absently picked at the grass.

'I see that the essence of the scheme was to have the first colour-box sent direct from B. & S. He'd never had possession of it, so if the worst happened, of course it was nothing to do with him. But surely the substitution idea was awfully risky. In the first place, how could he be sure that he'd find the B. & S. one when he arrived at Meldon?'

'Ann cleared that up. When Torrance rang her that Saturday afternoon he said he'd like to have another look at it, and she said she'd leave it out in case he got there first. He'd have had plenty of time if it hadn't been for that road smash and diversion, of course.'

'But surely he couldn't know what she hadn't used the B. &

S. box and would see the difference if the second one was intact?'

'He'd thought that out too. First of all, the B. & S. box wasn't sent off until the Tuesday. The Meldon term didn't end until the Friday. He knew quite enough about schools to realise that the chance of Ann having time for an oil painting session could virtually be ruled out. After all oils aren't water-colours, as you'd be the first to admit. Saturday morning was out because of Festival. But to make double sure he'd asked her to take the box over unused if possible, as he had shares in Wynne's and Mrs Vanderplank though some art shop she patronised might be interested.'

'Revolting brute,' said Jane with sudden vehemence. 'It makes me absolutely see red the way he played on that unfortuante girl. And to clinch it all, you know, he'd suggested that she should live with him when she came back. She broke down completely when she told me that. I told her she'd had an escape in ten million.'

'A particularly repellent type,' agreed Pollard. 'And without the excuse of a criminal background.'

A jet screamed across the sky, ripping up the silence like the tearing of cloth.

'What doesn't seem in character to me,' Jane resumed when the piercing noise had faded out, 'is the way he lost his head at the very end, after all that ice-cold calculation.'

'Lost his head? I don't believe he did for a moment. I think B.B.'s murder was the result of a quick but absolutely deliberate decision. In his letter he said she'd seen him change over the boxes and challenged him when he came back to fetch the *Artifex*. He realised he couldn't hope to keep her quite in any other way. He knew it meant a trial and long term of imprisonment, and the absolute ruin of his career. I'm quite sure he decided in a split second that killing her was a justifiable risk considering what was at stake. He knew there were a lot of people about to confuse the issue. He couldn't possibly foresee that there would be virtually no opportunity for anyone else to commit the murder, largely thanks to Sister Felicity roosting on the fire-escape with her pal. And of course if we did catch up on him there was always the final escape route . . . He damn nearly did get away with it, too.'

'You'd have got him in the end,' asserted Jane confidently.

'I wonder. Once the incriminating colour-box and its contents had vanished without trace in America, I doubt if we could ever had brought a case against him on purely circumstantial evidence, without being able to put forward a shadow of a motive. I was slow off the mark over several things. Torrance's anxiety about getting Ann off was beyond normal concern for a protégée : I ought to have paid more attention to it and thought out possible implications much earlier on. Then there was that workshop of his : obviously he was a highly skilled carpenter. That didn't make me tick either.'

'I suppose,' she said, after a pause, 'you'd have pulled him in on an attempted smuggling charge in the first place, if you'd got there in time?'

'Yes. It was a near thing. We'd decided to risk it, being sure something pretty big was involved, and had actually left with the warrant just before the Domani dialled 999. The staff had heard the shot and dashed up to Torrance's flat. If he hadn't chanced to drop in at B. & S. that morning we'd have got him. It was Diane, of course. She hailed him to tell him she'd had drinks with us, and how I'd been so interested in the two colour-boxes he'd bought. And for good measure she added the news that something funny was going on that morning about a third box . . .'

'Diane . . .' said Jane dreamily. 'She simply isn't true, is she? But what an extraordinary coincidence that he went along there that morning. Things like that seem to have popped up all through the case. The *Artifex* being forgotten, and then Ann remembering it, for instance.'

'They so often do in life, it seems to me,' replied Pollard. 'In some ways the most fantastic touch was old Beakers handing me the solution on a plate in Round One. He chipped me about the Blue Bonnet theft, you know. There's a reproduction of it in the library at Meldon.'

He turned his head and looked into his wife's face, amusement in his eyes.

'The only coincidence I haven't been able to swallow is your sudden need for a new sketching block last Saturday morning, involving that visit to Brocatti & Simpson's.'

Jane met his gaze and cocked an eyebrow.

'Honestly,' she remarked, 'you might almost be a detective.'

Other Titles in the Walker British Mystery Series